Time Without

By Veronica R. Tabares

Paperback Edition

Cover by Tara Tabares

Sun Break Publishing, Seattle, WA

Published by Sun Break Publishing, 4616 25th Ave NE #372 Seattle, WA 98105.

Library of Congress Control Number: 2017903181

ISBN: 978-1-60916-017-3

Publishers note:

This book is a work of fiction and a figment of the author's imagination. Similarities to actual characters, places, names, or events are purely coincidental.

To every woman who has ever felt invisible, and
every man who cares.

"I'M A TIME TRAVELER," a voice echoed against the cold, granite walls of the castle.

No. That was wrong. The walls weren't cold or granite, they were—

RING.

The sound broke through the protective walls of sleep and jerked Vanessa out of her dream. But Vanessa was not ready to give up her dream, so she ignored the irksome noise and snuggled deeper into her covers.

Back to the dream. She had been arguing with the owner of the castle—made of cake, not granite—about which part she could devour. She didn't remember why she was at the castle prepared to chow down, only that she was determined to eat an entire red velvet chocolate tower iced in white. The castle owner—a stingy man with a nose for negotiation—was equally determined that she would only get a single windowpane.

Vanessa was a chocoholic, asleep as well as awake, and had no intention of settling for anything but chocolate.

The man argued the red velvet chocolate tower iced in white was an integral part of the castle. Without it, the entire castle might crumble.

So Vanessa countered with a quip she could only use in her dreams. She blurted out she could travel through time and had seen the castle standing strong, in the future, without the tower.

That shut him up, temporarily at least. She took advantage of the man's open-mouthed surprise and snagged a pebble-sized piece of cake to pop into her mouth.

Umm. The cake was gloriously delicious! She took a deep breath, filling her lungs with sugary goodness. The heady aroma made her even more determined to win her prize. If she could convince that stubborn man—

RING.

Instantly, the mouthwatering, hypnotically sweet vision of the chocolate cake castle disappeared. Vanessa was sucked out of the dream faster than her daughters hid their Halloween candy when they saw that hungry look in her eye.

All that was left was a haunting echo of time travel.

She once read that dreams were the brain's way of coping with problems. She had been skeptical about the theory until four years ago when she opened the door to a janitor's closet and stepped through a time portal into the future. Stumbled right out of the present, and into the future.

The scientists of the future had wanted to *keep* her in the future, to protect the timeline from possible contamination. Until they did their research and found she was the mother of the creators of time travel.

Talk about damage to the timeline!

They cursed her with a promise and sent her back to her own time.

As much as she ached to ignore that oath of secrecy she swore to people who wouldn't be born for a millennium, she couldn't. If she shared her adventures with anyone, *anyone*, the consequences to the future of her children, and the entire world, could be devastating.

So Vanessa kept quiet in the real world, and

blabbed freely in her dreams, telling everyone she met she had traveled through time—

RING.

There was that darned phone again. Vanessa knew her best course was to answer it before it woke everyone in the household. If the kids got up, she'd lose any chance she had to return to her dreams and eat that chocolate tower iced in white.

She felt around on the bedside table until she found her cell phone. As she brought the phone to her ear, she caught sight of the clock on her bedside table.

Ten o'clock! The kids rarely slept later than eight and usually demanded immediate attention. This was the first time in years her children had let her sleep this late.

She looked around and realized that although she had been allowed to sleep, it hadn't been in solitude. The room was littered with evidence of one or more visits from her two youngest children. Zoe's favorite baby doll and Audrey's stuffed koala were on the pillow beside her, tucked neatly under the covers. Half a dozen toy cars were parked in a zigzag pattern along the headboard, and a Barbie doll on the bedside table had a couple of toy cars shoved on her feet as skates.

The most amazing thing was the bright red ball that one of the jokesters had decided to perch on her chest. How she had managed to grab the phone without dislodging it was a mystery.

Vanessa's exhaustion must have been extreme for her to sleep through the playtime represented by this plethora of toys. Too bad her one chance in a millennium to get caught up on sleep had been interrupted by the phone. Especially since it was probably one of those irritating sales calls that not only came at the most inconvenient times, but were also irrelevant.

Last week she had gotten a rare opportunity to take a nap—until her phone rang. It was someone trying to sell her a great deal on carpet cleaning, even though Vanessa tried to explain to them that she only had hardwood floors.

Then there was that time last month when she'd gotten a spare moment to finally start that book everyone had been talking about. She'd only finished the first page when her phone rang, and she found herself speaking to a salesman who wanted her to replace all the windows in her house. He didn't listen when she told him her house was owned by the university.

It was a conspiracy against parents. Vanessa was sure of it. As soon as children cut their parents the tiniest bit of slack, the rest of the world greedily stepped in and pulled the rope taut again.

RING.

Whoever was calling had no intention of giving up. She might as well answer.

"Hello," Vanessa rasped into the phone, her voice still as asleep as her brain had been a few seconds before.

"Is this Mrs. Rossi?" a man's voice asked gruffly.

Vanessa cringed as he called her by name. She wasn't awake enough to handle whatever this was. But she had answered, so she'd better power through it.

"It is," Vanessa tried to put a smile in her voice. "Who is this?"

"Dr. Brown. At Madigan Hospital."

Madigan was an Army hospital. Why would a military hospital have her name?

"I was wondering why you weren't here yet," Dr. Brown, at Madigan Hospital, continued curtly.

"What?" Vanessa was now even more confused. This doctor thought she was supposed to be at

Madigan. He probably thought she was a volunteer at his hospital who had forgotten about her shift. He was angry his volunteer hadn't shown and had dialed the wrong number.

"Doctor," Vanessa began, "I'm afraid you have the wrong—"

"Mrs. Rossi," Dr. Brown interrupted sternly, "your husband needs you. How can you sit at home when your husband has been in a car crash? Why are you not here?"

Vanessa blinked at his words. Blinking was all she could do as her brain struggled to sweep away the fog of sleep so she could process what she had just heard. The man on the phone, this man who claimed to be a doctor at Madigan Hospital, thought her husband had been in some kind of traffic accident.

Vanessa panicked for a split second, until she realized that there was no way Tony could have been in a car accident. He had left for work at 5:30 in the morning and would have gotten to work by 6:30. He was part of a flight crew, and since the plane could not take off without its entire crew, someone would have called to check on him if he had not arrived on time.

She looked at the clock, which read 10:12. Almost four hours. By this time, Tony had been at work for almost four hours. The plane was in the air by now.

Vanessa closed her eyes and sighed in relief. Yes, there was no doubt about it. Tony was safe. It was all a mix-up. The doctor had simply been given the wrong information and had called the wrong person.

"He was hit by an eighteen wheeler," the doctor stated bluntly, "around six o'clock this morning."

"What!" Vanessa yelled as the words 'six o'clock' shocked her system into action. She sat up so fast anyone watching would have thought she had been scalded by a bucket of boiling water. The harmless red ball perched on her chest became a missile as her body catapulted it across the room like a rocket. After it thudded against the wall, it bounced harmlessly out the door.

But it wasn't boiling water that had shocked Vanessa, but the realization that at six this morning, Tony would have been driving on I-5, only halfway to work.

Vanessa's head spun as she realized the doctor hadn't called the wrong person. The timing matched too well. Tony, *her* Tony, had been in an accident.

Vanessa was unaware of the sob that escaped her, but the doctor heard it and gasped as he realized what that sob probably meant. He stayed silent for several moments as he replayed the conversation with Vanessa in his head, and when he finally broke the silence, he made sure to use a much gentler tone of voice.

"Now don't worry," Dr. Brown continued. "He's going to be okay. He was brought in to Madigan around 6:30 this morning."

"But how—?"

"Excuse me, ma'am," Dr. Brown interrupted, not willing to continue further until he got to the bottom of this mystery, "but did you get a phone call letting you know about your husband's accident? Maybe someone from the hospital called you earlier?"

"No! How could you think—?"

"How about from his work? His commanding officer maybe?"

"No one has called. Please tell me—"

"Those lazy, good-for-nothing, sorry excuses for—," Dr. Brown muttered loudly. Vanessa pulled the phone away from her ear to avoid the string of expletives that began to pour from her phone.

Then she heard the doctor's tone change and she realized that he was again speaking to her. She put the phone to her ear in time to hear him saying in a loud but kindly voice, "Your husband is extremely lucky. He's conscious—"

"Conscious?" Vanessa broke in, happy for a spark of hope. "That's good, right? If he's conscious—"

"Still, we want to watch him for a while, to make sure he doesn't have any internal injuries we can't see. You should come right away."

"Internal injuries? That sounds bad. Do you think—?"

"Just a precaution. We'll keep him here a few days while we check him out. There's a hotel just off base so you can stay close while you wait for him to be released."

"I'll be there right away…but, why Madigan? Wasn't the accident closer to Harborview?"

"Protocol. He was in uniform."

"Protocol! But—"

"Ma'am, I have patients. Just come soon."

"Right. Thank you."

As Vanessa hung up the phone, she could hear the sound of her children playing quietly in the other room. The sound should have comforted her, but instead it made her shiver uncontrollably.

Tony, her wonderful husband, the father of those four beautiful girls playing so innocently in the other room, had been in an accident. Her husband, the man she planned to grow old with, was in the hospital. Her Tony, her strong, dependable, fearless husband, was hurt and injured, in a hospital bed, over an hour away.

The image of a huge truck barreling down the road popped into her head, and before she could stop it, her imagination made it crash into the car Tony always drove to work—a cute little red Honda. A car that looked like a child's toy next the colossal bulk of one of those huge trucks.

Fear gripped her heart and wrung it like a two-year-old squeezes play dough. That doctor had gone on and on about how she needed to get to the hospital fast. What if Tony was hurt worse than the doctor had let on? What if he did have internal bleeding? Tony might—

"Mommy," a voice interrupted her thoughts,

"who was on the phone?"

Until that moment, Vanessa hadn't realized that anyone had come into the room. It was Becca, her twelve-year-old daughter. Vanessa wondered how long she'd been there. What had she overheard? What should Vanessa tell her? What was the right thing for a mother to do?

"Mom?"

"It was Madigan, the army hospital," Vanessa stated baldly, deciding the absolute truth was her only true option. "Your father was in an accident—he's going to be fine, so don't worry—but we need to go visit him."

"Daddy?"

The sheer terror in her daughter's voice nearly broke Vanessa's heart. It also reminded her that Becca was still just a child, with a child's fears. The biggest being the loss of a parent.

Chapter 2

THE VIOLENT SLAM OF a door shook the room, knocking pictures from the wall and marring the peaceful calmness of the lobby. Philip, embarrassed, glanced at the other applicants in the room. The other applicants, also embarrassed, quickly looked at their fingernails, out the window — anywhere but at Philip.

"You can't do this to me," Philip Jensen whispered at the closed door. "I'm just as qualified as any of these other applicants. More qualified than most."

Philip stood facing the closed door for a few more seconds, but since he knew that of all the technology that had been invented over the years, a door that gave a vocal response when slammed, kicked, or otherwise abused was not one of them. Not in the year 3027, at least. So Philip turned away from the evidence of his shame and continued toward the exit.

Philip had nearly made his escape when he heard a faint noise behind him. Without thinking, he looked back into the lobby right into the intense gaze of a middle-aged man with bright red hair. Philip hung his head in embarrassment and hurried out. Having a door slammed in your face, particularly in front of a room full of your peers, was not an experience likely to improve a person's self-esteem.

There was no doubt about it, the job interview had not gone as planned. Not even close. Instead of being appointed as the chief scientist of the DTA lab—the job he had been working toward his entire career—he would have to go home and lick his wounds. Again.

Philip, an unlucky soul who looked more like a Greek statue than the brilliant scientist he was, had been unemployed for over two years now. The stress of not being able to get a job in his field was beginning to get to him.

He refused to believe that he was being turned down for jobs because of his Adonis-like looks. After all, he had proven himself in the scientific community. He had won awards, gotten accolades, been touted as the preeminent expert in his field of time travel—all through hard work. Surely professionals could overlook what he had once overheard being termed as "disgustingly perfect male beauty."

It was a burden he'd had to bear his entire life, this tendency for some to judge him for his looks rather than his mind. So to counteract the prejudices, he had played every sport, worked harder than most of the other students in college, and had successfully managed to make a name as an expert in the scientific world.

Even after all that, many scientists met him for the first time, took one look at his pretty face and muscular physique, and immediately discounted his brain. As if they believed that brains and beauty were incompatible and could not coexist in a single body.

The scientific world needed to grow up and move away from such twenty-first century thinking. They needed to lose the antiquated view that made them judge inner worth by outer appearance.

If only he could break through whatever barrier was keeping him from getting a job, from living up to his potential.

Chapter 3

PHILIP WAS SEATED ON the couch reading a book when Annabel, singing quietly as she often did, breezed into the small loft apartment. His wife, whose cherubic face and softly curling brown hair hid a razor sharp intelligence, tossed her work bag on the table and raced to plop herself down beside Philip.

"So," Annabel asked, biting her lip to contain her excitement, "how did it go?"

She leaned toward him and a mischievous smile lit up her elfin face. The sparkle in her eyes coupled with her shoulder wiggles and dancing eyebrows made it obvious that she thought Philip had gotten the job.

Usually just being in the room with his sunny-natured wife put Philip in a good mood. She was one of those people whose smile was contagious, who exuded happiness and good will.

But not this time, because Philip feared that even Annabel's good humor was no match for his streak of ill fortune. He was tired of feeling like he had let her down, like she made a bad deal by tying her life together with his.

She looked so happy, so pleased about life, that Philip could barely look at her. The last thing he wanted to do was disappoint her.

"Come on, spill!" she coaxed, nudging him with her elbow.

Philip took a quick look at his wife and realized he wasn't ready to dampen her happy glow. Instead, he shrugged his shoulders and enveloped her in a big hug.

But Annabel knew her husband too well not to be able to read the signs that something was wrong. She wiggled out of his arms and looked at him suspiciously.

Philip tried to look anywhere but at Annabel as he pasted the fakest smile Annabel had ever seen on his face. But Annabel grabbed his jaw and turned his head so he had no choice but to meet her eyes.

"I didn't get it," Philip admitted, his shoulders slumping.

"Of course you did," Annabel replied with a tilt of her head and a scrunch of her forehead. "I heard about it at work."

Philip sighed and shook his head.

"But I heard they made their choice."

"I'm sure they did. But it wasn't me."

"I don't understand," Annabel said as she jumped up from the couch and paced like a caged tiger. "You were a shoe-in." She turned to face Philip. "You were by far the most qualified applicant."

Philip shrugged and grimaced.

"No. There's a mistake somewhere. You must have gotten the job. I saw the CVs. No one else had even half your experience."

"That might be true, but I didn't get the job."

Annabel paced a bit more before she turned to scrutinize Philip. After squinting her eyes a few times and looking at him from every angle imaginable, she sighed.

"Well, I don't get it. What's wrong with people? You're nice, smart, and good-looking. What's not to like?"

Philip smiled, but it was a defeated smile. Annabel's heart melted faster than butter in a microwave. She plopped down next to her husband and grabbed his hands.

"Tell me exactly what happened."

"Just let it go," Philip said as he blinked several times and shook his head.

"Come on."

"It's too embarrassing."

Annabel grabbed Philip's ears and pulled his head close so she could kiss him enthusiastically.

"Philip Jensen, I love you, and I'll always love you. When we got married, we said there would be no secrets between us. So share."

Philip paused for only a split second before he gave a definitive nod.

"Okay. But you're not going to like it."

"I'm listening."

"So I met Dr. Morgan."

"Dr. Morgan, I know her. She's known for being tough, but fair."

"Tough maybe, but hardly fair."

"Why do you say that? What did she do?"

"It's not so much what she did as what she *didn't* do," Philip said through gritted teeth. "As soon as I walked in the door I could tell she didn't like me. She wouldn't even shake my hand."

"What?" Annabel looked truly surprised.

"And as soon as she opened her mouth, I knew I didn't have a chance. She only asked me two questions."

"Okay. And they were…?"

"What gym do I use, and could I give her advice on face cream."

"No!"

"She rushed me out of there so fast that I don't think the whole interview lasted even two minutes. She didn't ask a single question about my qualifications."

"No!"

"And to make matters worse, she slammed the door in my face. In front of a room full of people. "

"That was you? I heard about that."

"I'm sure everyone heard. I was mortified!"

"Hmm. So she kept the interview super short and slammed the door, did she?" Annabel looked suddenly thoughtful as she tapped her fingers on the arm of the couch.

"Right in my face."

"Do you remember a man there," Annabel asked with another bird-like tilt of her head, "with bright red hair? In his, I'd say, late forties?"

Philip nodded.

"Oh, that's not right! Not right at all."

"What?"

"I know why she did it."

Philip raised his brows.

"There have been rumors. But I didn't really think she'd stoop to cronyism."

"Cronyism? You think she hired a friend?" Philip asked with a grimace.

Annabel gently turned Philip's face until their eyes again met.

"Not a friend," she said with a kind smile, "her husband. I'm pretty sure that red-haired man was her husband. They've been having problems with their marriage and I saw his name on the list of candidates. I can guarantee she gave him the job."

"Any word?"

Philip was waiting at the door for Annabel when she came home from work, just as he had been every day for the past week.

"It's official," Annabel said as she reached up and gently kissed Philip on the cheek. "Dr. Morgan made the announcement today. She said that after a rigorous search, she was surprised but pleased to find that her own husband was the best qualified for the job. He'll take over as department head next week."

"He doesn't even have a degree in time travel!" Philip said through gritted teeth.

"Maybe not," Annabel countered calmly, "but he does have the job and there's nothing we can do about it. Dr. Morgan is in charge, and she has the authority to hire whoever she wants."

"Even if he's not qualified?"

"Qualified or not, starting next week he's going to be my boss."

As Philip opened his mouth to say more, Annabel covered it with her hand.

"Philip, I know you're upset. But I'm really, really tired. Do you think we could just eat dinner, and talk about this some other time?"

Philip scrunched his eyes closed as he realized that his wife was still standing in the doorway with her workbag on her shoulder. He grinned contritely.

"Sorry. Let me take that." Philip pulled the heavy bag from Annabel's shoulder. "Dinner will be ready in a few minutes."

Instead of letting go of the bag, Annabel held on until Philip turned. Then Annabel took a step toward him and wrapped her arms around his neck.

"Philip Jensen, you are my kind of man."

"What, the kind who will carry your bag and cook your dinner?"

"No," Annabel said with a grin, "the kind who will give me a piggyback ride to the couch so my achy feet can get some rest."

Philip laughed, scooped up Annabel, and twirled her around a few times as he carried her the short distance to the couch.

Chapter 4

THAT NIGHT, PHILIP'S SLEEP was disturbed by a series of dreams in which Dr. Morgan slapped his face in front of a room full of his peers, which caused those peers to chortle at his discomfort. Each time those chortles turned into full-blown laughter, and he awoke in a sweat, thrashing about, the mocking roar of disparaging laughter still ringing in his ears.

Halfway through the night—after the seventh or eighth time his flailing arms had slapped her awake—Annabel gave up, kissed Philip gently on the forehead, and made a bed for herself on the couch. She said it was because she needed her sleep, but Philip suspected she just wanted to be out of reach of his flapping arms.

Philip couldn't understand why he was having so much trouble with the loss of this job. He was usually a very self-controlled person. So self-controlled, in fact, that of his many friends and family, only Annabel knew how much being unemployed for an extended length of time had disturbed him.

Philip suffered through several more disturbing dreams, until finally he decided that he had had enough. He would break the rules and use Annabel's professional grade sleep machine.

Sleep machines had been around for a millennium, ever since doctors discovered that brain patterns changed during sleep. But most sleep machines did little more than flash a series of lights and provide subliminal messages, like "You are well rested," and "Every day is a beautiful day."

The sleep machine assigned to Annabel by the DTA was different, much different. It was a powerful and efficient device that did more than just manipulate brainwaves, it created them. It utilized an advanced technology not available to the common population and saturated the brain with waves almost identical to the ones produced naturally by the brain. Except, of course, they were the very waves desired by the sleeper to fulfill a specific purpose. The result was almost magical.

The brainwave technology had been developed shortly after the DTA was formed and the first group of time adapters suffered catastrophic mental breakdowns. That's when it was discovered that moving through time portals wreaked havoc on the human brain. Everyone thought time travel would prove to be too costly in terms of human lives.

Time travel was halted, until one scientist received a sleep machine as a present and realized that since the brain reset itself during sleep, that natural process could be used to help the brains of time adapters recover.

It took ten years of dedicated work, but the scientists and engineers of the DTA succeeded in creating a machine that allowed their time travelers to jump about the timeline without losing their minds.

Then, about a generation later, it was discovered that certain people, fewer than one in a million, had no real need for the machine at all. They had a rare gene that gave them the ability to travel through time without any adverse effects.

Someone had the bright idea to call them time monkeys, since they could freely swing through time like monkeys swing through the trees, and it stuck. Annabel had inherited the gene from her mother's side of the family. She was a true time monkey.

So even though a sleep machine had been assigned to her, she never used it. Which made Philip's decision to use the machine even easier.

After all, there was nothing sadder than great technology going to waste.

The machine did its job and the next morning Philip awoke with an answer to his problem.

Annabel opened her eyes to find Philip beside the couch, gazing down at her with a quizzical look on his face. It was so unlike Philip to wake her this way that she sat up quickly and they almost butted heads.

"What's wrong?" Annabel asked. Annabel usually needed several minutes to fully wake in the morning, so she had to blink to make her eyes work properly.

"You believe in me, don't you?" Philip asked as he sat on the couch beside Annabel. "You believe

I'm the best person to lead the DTA, don't you?"

"Of course I do!" Annabel replied with a crinkle of her nose. She raised a hand and gently stroked Philip's cheek. "You have to know I believe in you."

Philip sighed in relief. Then he looked nervously at Annabel before he reached over and grabbed both of her hands.

"I've thought it out," Philip said as he worriedly searched Annabel's face. "I know how I can get the job."

"What!" In Annabel's excitement, she neglected to notice Philip's uneasiness. She grabbed her husband, pulled him into her arms, and squeezed him tight. "What are you going to do? Write a letter—"

"Annabel, wait." Philip gently pushed Annabel away and stood to pace. "You might not be so happy when you hear my plan."

Annabel took a good, hard look at her husband. He was nervous, sweaty, and somehow reminded her of a puppy she'd had that couldn't resist chewing her best shoes.

Guilt was not something Philip did often—or well.

Philip shot Annabel a series of sideways glances as she waited patiently for him to continue. After several false starts, in which Philip opened his mouth but no words came out, he finally stopped pacing and sat down on the couch.

"It involves," Philip paused, gulped, then squeezed out the word, "you."

"*Me*?" Annabel was taken aback. She loved her husband and would help him if she could, but she had tried for two years to come up with a way to support him, and had always drawn a blank.

"How can I help?" Annabel tilted her head as she searched her brain for ways she could help. "I don't have connections in high places. At least none that I associate with. You know my family are—"

"You can go—"

"I can't go," Annabel said with a firm shake of her head. "I'd be disowned."

Annabel rolled her eyes at the confused look on Philip's face. She had told him the story before they were even married. He should understand.

"You know my family history," Annabel reminded him. "My father and his brother haven't spoken in years. So even though my uncle *could* use his pull to help you get a job, he probably wouldn't want to. Besides, it wouldn't be worth it. It would break my father's heart. He and his—"

"Annabel, you don't understand," Philip interrupted. But his words dried up when Annabel's eyes hardened with suspicion.

"You don't care what my father thinks, do you? You want me to do it anyway, don't you? You want me to go groveling to my uncle, begging him for a favor."

Philip shook his head. "No—"

"You want me to dump my mother's side of the family like a bag of trash and align with my father's family. The *powerful* side of my family." Annabel's glare had become so sharp it hurt Philip to look at her.

Annabel was an even-tempered person who rarely got angry, on the outside at least.

Most people whine, yell, or complain to relieve the tension created by day-to-day irritations. But Annabel was the type of person who wanted to spread smiles, so instead of blowing off steam like most people, she shoved the irritations into a dark corner of her mind and pasted a smile on her face. She believed that if she made herself forget those nasty little irritations, they'd disappear in a *poof* of smoke, never to be seen again.

Unfortunately, the human brain didn't work that way. Instead of the irritations dissipating, they joined forces and fermented. So when Annabel uncorked and let her anger show, it tended to be fierce. Like a bottle of champagne, or maybe even a volcano.

No one liked to see a normally happy person angry, so Philip became very interested in the state of his fingernails. It was the wrong thing to do. Annabel took it as a sign of guilt.

"I knew it!" Annabel said as she slammed her fist on the arm of the couch. "You don't like my mother's family, do you? You never have!"

"Of course I like your mother's family, Annabel," Philip assured her as he dug imaginary dirt from under his pristine nails.

"Sure you do," Annabel sniffed. "That's why we never spend time with them."

Confused by this unexpected accusation, Philip forgot about his fingernails and searched his wife's face, only to realize that sometime in the last few moments, her anger had morphed into sorrow. The only thing Philip dreaded more than Annabel angry was Annabel sad.

"Last week. My mom's parents invited
us to dinner. You *said* you had to prepare for an
interview."

"I *did* have to prepare for an interview. The one
at the DTA," Philip responded. Then he shrugged.
"Or at least I thought I did."

"And a month ago," Annabel continued as if
Philip hadn't spoken, "Uncle Joe, my mom's
brother, invited us to a restaurant, your favorite
restaurant, and you said we were busy. And a few
months earlier, my cousin had a birthday party, and
I had to go by myself because you said you were too
busy."

A lone tear broke free from the corner of
Annabel's eyes and rolled down her cheek.
Annabel was so caught up in anguish that she
seemed not to notice.

"No, Annabel, no!" Philip exclaimed,
heartbroken that he had caused his wife
unnecessary pain. "You've got it all wrong."

Annabel sniffed, unconvinced. Philip sighed.

"I'm ashamed, Annabel," Philip admitted, "that
I can't get a job."

"Ashamed?"

"Of course I'm ashamed! I want your family to

be proud of me." Philip's eyes asked Annabel to understand. "Like they're proud of you."

Annabel blinked several times as she processed this new information.

"So let me get this straight." Annabel used her sleeve to wipe away the tears that had been pushed out when she blinked her eyes. "You *don't* want me to crawl on my hands and knees to my uncle? You don't want him to help you get a job?"

"As much as I want a job," Philip said with a shake of his head, "I like your dad too much. I'd never purposely hurt him."

Annabel leaned back against the cushions of the couch with a sigh of relief. She closed her eyes for a mere millisecond before they popped back open.

"Philip," Annabel said suspiciously, "what is it that you want me to do that you think I won't want to do?"

Philip's fingernails suddenly became intensely fascinating again. He couldn't seem to pull his eyes away from a tiny chip out of his pinky nail that he was sure hadn't been there a few minutes earlier.

"Philip, look at me," Annabel commanded.

Philip reluctantly dragged his eyes away from

his nails to look in her direction. Annabel squinted her eyes as she studied the entirety of her husband's face. After a few moments she nodded her head, satisfied by what she saw.

"Do you promise that it doesn't include groveling to my uncle?"

Philip shook his head.

"Because you do understand, don't you, that groveling would be the absolute worst thing you could ask me to do?"

Philip nodded. "I understand."

Annabel cocked an eyebrow as she continued to study her husband's face. "So if it's not betraying my family, what is it?"

"You won't like it any better," warned Philip.

Annabel looked at Philip's worried face and caved.

"Tell me. You know I'll do anything I can to help you."

Philip opened his mouth to speak, but before he could get any words out, Annabel continued.

"Short of hurting my dad. That I will not do. Period."

Philip jumped up from the couch and prowled around the room. He turned several times toward

Annabel as if about to speak, but never
did. Then he spotted a statuette on a bookshelf and
picked it up.

The statuette was about four inches high and
triangular in shape, with a working door embedded
in the center. After studying it for several moments,
he turned to face Annabel.

"I was so proud of you when you won this,"
Philip said. "Do you know you're the first time
adapter to ever win it?"

"Of course I know," Annabel responded,
disturbed by Philip's change of subject.

Philip used a single finger to open and close the
door several more times. He seemed to have
forgotten everything but the tiny door.

"Philip, why are you playing with my time
adapter trophy?" Annabel spoke softly, as if unsure
if she should break into her husband's thoughts.
"What are you thinking about?"

"I'm thinking that I'm the luckiest man alive,"
Philip replied with a mischievous grin. Then his
eyes glazed over and he looked to be about a
million miles away.

"Philip?" Annabel raised a questioning eyebrow
at her husband, but he took no notice as he

continued to mindlessly open and close
the tiny door of the trophy. Annabel reached out a
hand to him, but he was so lost in thought that even
the touch of her hand on his arm failed to pull him
out of his trance.

"*Philip*," Annabel prodded, shaking his arm like
it was a piggy bank and she was checking it for
money. But Philip continued to open and close the
tiny door of the trophy and stare off into the
distance. Her efforts to get his attention were no
more productive than that of an ant trying to move
a full-grown sequoia tree.

Frustrated, Annabel decided to change tactics. If
nice didn't work, she'd have to ramp it up a bit. She
climbed on the couch, used Philip's shoulder to
keep her balance, leaned over, and yelled "Philip!"
at the top of her lungs, right in his ear.

That got his attention. Unfortunately it also
made him jump like a scalded cat, and when the
shoulder Annabel was using as support suddenly
disappeared, she lost her balance and tumbled
sideways.

Philip caught her about halfway to the floor and
set her on her feet.

"Sorry," he said. He put the trophy back on the

shelf and turned a guilty face to his wife. "I was lost in thought."

"About what?"

"Things."

"What things?"

"That you're probably the only person who could successfully adjust Dr. Morgan's timeline without anyone finding out."

"What?" Annabel asked, confused momentarily. Then she yelled, "Philip, no!"

Annabel was no longer confused but as panicked as a college freshman realizing she had not even begun the research paper that was due the next day.

"Annabel, please," Philip begged. He put an arm across her shoulders. "I've thought this through. She *needs* to be somewhere else. If you would just go back to her childhood—"

"No!" Annabel shoved Philip's arm away and turned to pierce Philip with a look that demanded he pay full attention to her words. "Messing with the timeline is dangerous."

"Please, Annabel?" The pleading in Philip's eyes matched that of his words, but Annabel simply shook her head.

"You know how dangerous that would be!" she said firmly.

"Of course I know," Philip said with a shrug. He was frustrated that Annabel hadn't immediately accepted his plan, but he had no intention of giving up that easily. "I am the top time travel theorist in the field, after all."

"That's what I don't understand. In your paper on adapting—"

"I know," Philip huffed.

"You pointed out the dangers of the tweaks we do—"

"I know!" Philip said more loudly in an attempt to interrupt Annabel's lecture.

"—Clearer than anyone ever had—"

"Annabel, stop! I know what I wrote." Philip slammed his fist into the palm of his hand. "But that paper didn't get me the job. Dr. Morgan blocked me."

Annabel's mouth snapped shut as she looked, really looked, at Philip's dejected face. What she saw there made her heart melt.

"Don't you get it, Annabel?" Philip asked gloomily, "She didn't give me a fighting chance. And she never will. She's prejudiced against me.

Just because of the way I look."

Annabel took a step back and examined her husband from head to toe. When love began to cloud her eyes she shook her head and shoulders several times, assumed an arrogant stance with hands on hips and chin held high, and looked again. Her intention was to put herself into Dr. Morgan's shoes so she could see Philip through her eyes. After a few moments of this, she managed to see him as if for the first time, the way Dr. Morgan saw him, and she nodded her head thoughtfully.

"Does that mean...?" Philip began, but stopped short as the fragile bud of hope sprouting in his heart was drowned by a wave of gloom.

Annabel was studying her husband's face and did not miss the wave of gloom that extinguished the flicker of hope so quickly and thoroughly. It pained her to see her husband like this, depressed and vulnerable.

Maybe she could help him, just this once. She'd made hundreds, maybe thousands of trips through time for the greater good. Philip was a good man. Wouldn't helping him also be serving the greater good?

Annabel studied her husband's face for a

moment or two longer before she spoke. "I might," she conceded warily, "be able to make a few careful adjustments."

"That's all it would take." Philip's quick jump from despair to optimism made Annabel smile. "Just a few careful adjustments here and there. Nothing much at all."

"I'm scheduled to jump this week," Annabel confessed, "back forty years, to help clear up that chlorine mess that was created then."

"That will be perfect!" Philip could barely contain his excitement so he grabbed Annabel and gave her a kiss. "I've got it all figured out. All we have to do is encourage Dr. Morgan to go into a different field."

"A different field?" Annabel asked, pulling away from Philip slightly.

"I'm the most qualified for the job. If Dr. Morgan's not in charge of the DTA where she can block me—"

"I don't know," Annabel interrupted with a shake of her head. "Usually an entire panel of scientists study the repercussions of each modification before we make it. What if we do something that hurts Dr. Morgan, or the timeline?"

"We won't. We'll be careful," Philip promised. "And remember, you've done this type of thing hundreds of times."

"True," Annabel admitted. "But not while—"

Annabel's eyes suddenly widened and she turned white as the snow-topped crest of Mt. Rainier. She stayed that way for a split second before her hand flew to her mouth, she gulped loudly, and her eyes snapped shut.

"What's the matter?" Philip was worried. He'd never seen Annabel's face that particular shade. "Are you sick?"

"I'm fine."

"You don't look fine. You look like you're about to—"

Annabel opened her eyes and gave Philip a look that silenced him immediately. He sat back, surprised by this unusual display of temper.

"Look Philip, we can't do this," Annabel said firmly. Then some of the firmness was lost as she paused to take a quick breath and swallow loudly. "Not now. What if I did something that harmed—?"

"No one will be harmed, Annabel, I promise," Philip began soothingly, but excitement crept into his voice as he warmed to the subject. "I know you. You're the best adapter they've got. You can do this. You're an expert."

Annabel was far from convinced. She took several deep breaths, which helped to return the roses to her cheeks, which of course emboldened Philip further. He took both her hands in his.

"This is your life's work," Philip pleaded. "You're better than an expert, you're *the* expert."

Annabel rolled her eyes at the sweet talk.

"Look, Philip," she said with a shake of her head, "an expert, or even *the* expert can slip up. If I make the wrong adapt, it might—"

"Annabel, get over it, I'm not asking you to change anything important." Philip's sudden switch from flattery to frustration surprised her a bit, but only a bit. She knew how important the job was to Philip.

"Get over it?" As Annabel said this, she raised one brow toward the ceiling and sent the other plummeting toward the floor. The result was comical, but seemed to have no effect on Philip, until she sent the up brow down and the down brow up.

This made Philip blink several times, but his

shoulders remained tense and stiff. So Annabel ratcheted it up a notch and seesawed her eyebrows up and down until Philip smiled and shook his head, all tension gone.

"Sorry, monkey face," Philip apologized. "You're right, that was uncalled for. It's just…I'm not asking for you to change anything important—"

"No, just a woman's life's work."

"She can find a different life's work. I'm sure she's good at more things than ruining lives."

Annabel raised an eyebrow at Philip.

"Don't start that again, please. I can't take it."

"Then don't talk nonsense."

"It's not nonsense. She's ruined my life, and who knows how many other times she's allowed her prejudices to make decisions for her."

Annabel bit her lip as she thought.

"You know it's true."

"I don't know, Philip," Annabel said with a shake of her head. "It seems selfish to—"

"It's not selfish! Besides," Philip argued, "in the big scheme of things, one woman's choice of career isn't very important."

"Who's to say," Annabel returned heatedly, "what's important and what's not? You know as well as I do that even the smallest—"

"A change of careers, Annabel. That's it." Philip's voice softened as he realized that the conversation had gotten entirely too heated. "All you have to do is point Dr. Morgan toward a different field and our lives will be better."

"It's too dangerous."

"Please, Annabel." Philip reached over and gently pulled Annabel toward him and positioned her so her back rested against his chest. He wrapped his arms around her and gave her a gentle squeeze. "I want to start a family. We'll never be able to afford to get out of this small apartment unless I'm working. I need this job. We need this job."

Annabel shifted slightly so she could better look at her husband. "Philip?" she asked in a gentle voice.

"I'm sorry, Annabel. I was wrong to try to convince you to do something you don't think is right. Let's just forget it."

"But Philip," Annabel began again, twisting so she could face her husband as she snuggled closer.

"Let's not argue," Philip said with a gentle smile. He kissed his wife on the lips.

"I agree, we shouldn't argue," Annabel said. "But that's not what I was going to say."

"Oh? And just what were you going to say?"

"There is something I need to tell you."

"If it's about applying to other types of jobs"—Annabel felt Philip's shoulders stiffen as he huffed out the words—"I've done it already. I—"

"Wait," Annabel raised a hand to stop Philip's words. Then she wrapped both arms around Philip's neck and reached up to kiss him gently on the cheek. "It's not about that."

"So, what then?" Philip asked suspiciously.

"It's about starting a family."

"I want to, too. We just have to wait until—"

"No, Philip listen for a minute," Annabel insisted. She pushed out of Philip's arms and sat up straight, facing him. "I'm trying to tell you that I'm pregnant."

"What?" Philip asked. He grabbed Annabel by the shoulders and looked at her stomach. "You don't look pregnant. How far along—"

"About a month. Oh Philip, we're going to have a baby!"

"How long have you known?"

"Not long. I wanted to wait until after your

interview so you wouldn't feel more stressed. But now…"

Philip smiled and pulled his wife close.

"Annabel, this is great news. We're going to have a baby!"

"You know, Philip…" Annabel paused to bite her upper lip before she pushed away so she could study her husband's face. Then she gave a definitive nod and straightened her shoulders. "I happen to know that Dr. Morgan almost became a geologist. I guess I could plant some interesting rocks in her childhood home."

"You would do that?"

When Annabel saw hope bloom on Philip's face, she could no more deny him her help than she could give up breathing. But he had to know where she drew the line.

"It'll take several trips, you know. It's never good to rush these things. Small changes are much safer than sudden ones."

"Oh, Annabel! I'll have a chance."

"And I won't do anything that might cause her harm. It wouldn't be right."

"Of course not. I wouldn't expect you to."

"You'll have to be patient. It could take a while."

Philip smiled as he gently pulled Annabel back into his arms.

"I love everything about you, Annabel. Even your hardcore ethics."

"You're right. A bigger place would be nice," Annabel said as she snuggled into Philip's arms.

"For our growing family," Philip added with a nod toward Annabel's midsection.

Annabel placed a hand on her abdomen and smiled happily. The time travel gene ran strong in her family, so there was a good chance that this child would be a time monkey, like her. She couldn't wait until she could—

Annabel bolted out of Philip's arms and turned to face him, eyes sparkling with excitement. Now that she knew she and Philip agreed what should be done, she was eager to start the project.

"I'll run a few scenarios tomorrow at work and come up with a plan."

"I love you, Annabel," Philip said as he smiled up at the love of his life. "I don't know what I would do without you."

∞

"Philip! Have you heard the news?" Annabel called as she slammed the front door. She spotted her husband and rushed to him. "Everybody's talking about it! Dr. Morgan's husband was just offered a prestigious job at Harvard. He's leaving!"

Philip had dozed off on the couch and was dreaming he was being interviewed to become head of the DTA. Just as he accepted the job, Dr. Morgan popped her head through the door to say that they didn't need his brand of beauty cream.

Annabel's voice woke him. As her words sunk in, his face lit up and he sprang off the couch.

"He's not taking the job?" Philip asked, that spark of hope that Annabel loved so much again evident. Annabel nodded happily.

"You'll get another chance!"

Philip grabbed Annabel, picked her up, and twirled her around. Annabel smiled, even though Philip's tight squeeze robbed her of the ability to breathe.

"They're calling everyone who made the short list, which includes you, next week," Annabel continued as soon as she was able to gasp a full lungful of air.

Without warning Philip dropped Annabel and sat down dejectedly. Annabel had to scramble to catch her balance.

"What does it matter?" Philip moped as he dropped his chin onto a fist, hope dissolving faster than a microwave melts butter. "Dr. Morgan still won't hire me."

"But we're making changes to the timeline," Annabel reminded him as she maneuvered her way around the couch to sit beside her husband. "She's going to choose a different career."

Philip just shook his head.

Annabel leaned closer to Philip and whispered in his ear. "Have faith in me, Philip. I can do this."

A smile crept onto Philip's face as he snaked an arm around Annabel and pulled her close. She snuggled even closer.

"Faith I have. What I don't have is time."

Annabel looked up at him with a question on her face.

"You said it would take months to complete the adapts. I don't have months. This chance isn't likely to come around again for a long time."

Annabel looked at the face that most saw as perfect, but that she saw simply as the façade behind which her wonderful but vulnerable husband hid. She loved him for who he was on the inside—the outer trappings were just frosting. She would do anything for him, anything. Even…

Annabel pushed out of her husband's arms and sat up, her face completely blank. Philip had never seen this particular expression, or rather lack of, on his wife's face before and was unsure if he should be concerned.

"Annabel?" he whispered. He tried to recall if this was one of the symptoms for regular time travelers. "Are you okay?"

Annabel was so deep in her thoughts that the sound of Philip's voice could not penetrate. She sat stiff and motionless as her mind sped through a series of scenarios and calculations quicker than most would think humanly possible. Just as Philip was about to grab her shoulders and give her a little shake, a ghost of a smile flitted across her face. Philip breathed a sigh of relief.

"It'll be okay, Philip." Annabel's eyes came into focus as she spoke. "I know what to do."

"Whatever you do, don't ever do that again! You scared me half out of my wits!"

"I was only doing a little deep thinking."

"Well, give me a warning next time. So I won't think you're comatose and in need of medical attention."

Annabel scoffed. "If we're going to work together, you might as well get used to my thinking face. You'll be seeing it often."

Philip saluted Annabel. "Aye, aye, captain."

Annabel rolled her eyes. "Anyway, I'm pretty sure I can speed up the process without causing any damage."

"How sure?"

Annabel raised an eyebrow.

Philip blinked several times. "Was that what that heavy duty thinking was about?"

"Of course it was. But I'd still like to run the scenarios on the computer. To double-check my calculations."

"How often are you wrong?"

"Not often."

"What's the rate? Twenty percent? Thirty?"

Annabel shook her head.

"Come on. You can tell me."

"Fine. I've never been wrong."

"Wait," Philip said, respect glowing from his eyes. "You're telling me you can do the calculations necessary for time travel, the actual calculations, in this cute little head?" He grabbed each side of Annabel's head. "Without a computer?"

"That's how I've always done them," Annabel said as she swatted at his hands with irritation. Philip ignored the swats and kept his grip on her head.

"I'd heard there was someone in the department who could do that, but I thought they were making it up," he studied Annabel's head as if it contained some strange curiosity.

"Snap out of it, Philip," Annabel commanded as she wrenched his hands away from her head. "I'm the same me I was two minutes ago, the same me you married."

Philip ignored her words and continued to scrutinize her as if she were a rare specimen.

"*Philip!*"

"One minute, Annabel. I want to compare the shape of your head to—"

"*Philip!*"

Startled by the pain in Annabel's voice, Philip

stopped studying her head and looked into her eyes. What he saw there made him immediately drop his hands.

"Annabel?" Philip was confused by the pool of tears in his wife's eyes. "What's wrong? Why are you upset?"

Annabel shook her head and turned her face away.

"But Annabel, you should be happy! Those calculations...to be able to do them in your head! Why did you never tell me?"

Annabel shook her head and stubbornly kept her face turned away. Philip watched in horror as a giant teardrop followed the curve of her cheek and plopped onto Annabel's shoulder.

"Annabel, please. Talk to me. Why—?"

"Because," Annabel's voice was so soft Philip had to lean in to hear her, "I didn't want you to look at me like...like—"

"Like what?"

"Like you're doing right now," Annabel said gruffly.

She turned to face Philip, pain and anger mingling on her face.

"Like I'm an alien, a weirdo, an oddity. The way

every teacher I've ever had has looked at me. The way—" Annabel stopped and brushed away tears.

"But being able to do those calculations is a gift. I would have thought—"

"A gift. Like your perfect looks?"

Philip pulled back as if he'd been slapped.

Annabel noticed and continued more gently. "You complain that people judge you by your outside. That your perfect looks intimidate them and so they don't take the time to get to know the real you."

Philip nodded, but Annabel noticed that he was looking at her like she was a favorite puppy who had just nipped his hand. Guilt made her bite her lip, then she took a deep breath and continued.

"I'm perfectly fine with people judging me by my outsides. I know I don't look the least bit intimidating or scary."

"Annabel—" Philip's words halted when Annabel raised a hand.

"Let me finish. My problem happens when they *do* get to know me. Or I guess I should say, when I trust people enough to let them know me. The real me."

As Annabel hung her head, a fat tear
lost the battle with gravity and plummeted to the
floor. "Can you blame me for not telling you? I love
you so much. I don't want to lose you too."

She hung her head even lower, and the next
words came out in a whisper. "Every time I let
someone really know me, it turns out bad. I let them
in, they run for the hills."

"Annabel!" That single word held a world of
sympathy, but Annabel refused to look his way. So
Philip gently took her chin and raised her face.
Annabel, tears now falling freely, kept her eyes
stubbornly pointed downward.

"Annabel, look at me!"

"I can't," Annabel cried as she shook her head.
"I would die if you looked at me like that. Like I'm
a freak."

Philip stared at the top of Annabel's head for
several seconds before he grinned. "If you look at
me, I'll make a deal with you."

Annabel sniffed, but still refused to look up.

"You promise to keep judging me by my inside,"
Philip said with a mock stern voice, "and I'll
continue to judge you by your outside."

Annabel tried to keep her eyes pointed down,

but something in his voice drew her eyes
to his face like bears to honey.

"It's a deal?"

There was no mistaking the love shining from Philip's eyes, so Annabel threw her arms around him and gave him a huge squeeze. As soon as she released him, he grabbed her and gave her a kiss.

"You are my Annabel, and I'll always love you," Philip said. "Are we good now?"

When Annabel nodded happily, Philip gave her another quick kiss and headed downstairs. When he got to the bottom of the steps he paused to yell back up, "While you're double-checking the calculations, I'll cook dinner."

"What's it going to be?" Annabel called back in response, glad that they were back on familiar footing.

"My specialty, of course. Peanut butter soup."

"Yum!" Annabel yelled. Then she shook her head in disgust as she turned to enter her study at the top of the stairs. "Five years of marriage and he still doesn't know that I hate peanut butter. One of these days, I'll have to tell him."

As she crossed the study threshold, her eyes were drawn to the picture of Philip receiving his

doctorate that she had displayed on her
desk. He looked so proud and full of hope.

"But not today," she said softly as tears formed
in her eyes. She gently touched the smiling face in
the frame. "First I need to get that smile back, for
good."

∞

An hour later Annabel looked up from the
complicated chart she had created, her face
beaming. Everything was going to be perfect now
that she knew exactly what she needed to do to
encourage Dr. Morgan to choose a different career
path.

"Philip, Philip, Philip dear," she sang as she
jumped up and ran to the top of the stairs.

Philip rocketed out of the kitchen and waited
expectantly at the bottom of the staircase. Annabel
only sang when she was very happy.

"Philip, I did it!" she continued to sing. "The
change will be easy, easy, easy."

She stopped singing and finished excitedly, "As
long as it's made before they begin the next set of
interviews, there shouldn't be any problems."

"Really? You're sure?"

"Absolutely. It actually will be much easier than I first thought. After I laid out the chart I realized that some of the adapts I had planned weren't necessary. Not if I went right to the source."

Annabel smiled and her eyes glazed over as she became lost in thought. "The key is the source," she said dreamily. And then she said no more.

Philip waited patiently approximately five seconds before he couldn't take the silence any longer.

"Annabel, please!" Philip prompted.

Annabel jerked as Philip's voice penetrated her thoughts, which showed how much she loved him. She was quite capable of going so deep into her own thoughts that nothing and no one could reach her.

"What?" she asked, still so dazed that she was still unaware that she'd only given Philip part of the story.

"Sweetie, what source?" Philip was using every ounce of self-control to remain patient. He even resorted to holding his hands behind his back in an effort to hide his building frustration.

"Portland."

Philip blinked several times as he tried to put the

pieces together on his own, but he gave up
a moment later. "I don't get it," he admitted with a
sigh.

"You don't?" Annabel's confusion might have
seemed funny to Philip, on another day. But today
his sense of humor seemed to be on vacation.

"Annabel," Philip said as gently as he could
manage, "I know you have it all worked out in your
head, but I don't have it in mine. I don't think
you've told me as much as you think you have. I'm
going to need a little more information. Such as,
why Portland?"

"Didn't I tell you that? She grew up in Portland,"
Annabel explained with a smile.

"She?" Philip asked. "You mean Dr. Morgan?"

"Yes, only she was Alicia Thibidoux then."

"Alicia Thibidoux, I would have never guessed,"
Philip mused to himself. Then to Annabel, "Okay.
Dr. Morgan began life as Alicia Thibidoux. The
name sounds somehow too flowery for Dr.
Morgan."

Annabel nodded. "Back then she had dreams of
becoming a ballerina. Only at the ripe old age of
seven—years before the Dr. Morgan we both know
and love came into being—little Alicia had an

epiphany."

"An epiphany about—?"

"What she wanted to do with her life, of course."

"Of course. And what caused this epiphany?"

"Well," Annabel said with relish, "it seems that little Alicia found an old comic book about time travel. It sparked her imagination and pretty much defined who she would become."

"Wait! You're telling me that a comic book made her give up her lifelong dream of becoming a dancer?"

"Lifelong?" Annabel scoffed. "She was seven, Philip. Seven."

"Still, what seven-year-old decides to become a time monkey?"

Annabel instantly pulled her shoulders back and held her head high.

"She's not a time monkey. You have to be born that way, like me. And I'll have you know that being a time monkey is a noble profession. Generations of my family—"

"Annabel," Philip coaxed, "it's okay. I'm only teasing. You know that I know that time traveling is the noblest of professions. And that you're the best of the best."

Philip ran up the stairs and wrapped his arms around his wife. Annabel continued to look offended for a split second before she melted happily and laid her head on his chest.

"How do you know this, anyway?" Philip asked.

"It was in her employee file. She talked about it at her job interview."

"Well that's convenient. I think. Except I don't quite understand how knowing about a comic book she found when she was seven will help us."

"It's all we need!"

Annabel was so excited that when she pushed out of Philip's arms, he had to grab the rail to keep from tumbling down the stairs. "I'll switch the comic book. It's in a time capsule in her yard. If I take out the time travel comic and replace it with another, she'll never become fascinated with time travel."

"Is it as simple as that? According to theory—"

"You theorists are all alike," Annabel grumbled as she held up her hand to stop Philip's words. "You always try to complicate the issue. Trust me, I've made hundreds of adjusts. This will do it."

"Brilliant!" Philip's face lit up with a smile and he grabbed his wife for another hug. "When can you get started?"

"The sooner the better. I'll do it first thing tomorrow morning. I'm scheduled for a trip anyway, I'll just make a slight detour."

"Annabel," Philip said as he squeezed her for all he was worth, "not only are you the love of my life, but you're the best wife a man could ever have."

"I love you too, Philip."

"Now, let's eat. The soup's ready."

"Philip?"

"Yes, my sweet, brilliant, beautiful wife."

"Do you feel better now?" Annabel asked, the dimples of her cheeks highlighting her mischievous grin. "I mean, really better?"

"A thousand percent," Philip answered. He recognized Annabel's grin for what it was. She had something to tell him, but was unsure how he would take it.

"Great," Annabel continued. Then maybe" —she paused to bite her lip—"maybe now would be a good time to tell you."

"Tell me what?" Philip asked, concerned.

Annabel sighed. "I hate peanut butter," she admitted, glad to finally get the dark secret out into the open.

"What?" Philip asked as he pushed Annabel out to arm's length to look deep into her eyes.

Annabel hung her head in shame. "I can't lie anymore. I hate peanut butter, and I think peanut butter soup is absolutely disgusting."

A smile split Philip's face and he broke into laughter.

"You, my darling Annabel, are the best wife, ever!"

"Your feelings aren't hurt?" Annabel asked, as she searched his face.

"Not a bit. I hated that soup, too. I only made it because I thought you liked it."

"Really?"

"Yep, really. Let's go out to dinner."

Annabel smiled in relief.

"I can deal with that! Give me five minutes and I'll be ready."

"Great," Philip said as he raced down the stairs, "I'll get rid of the soup."

Annabel rushed to her closet and quickly changed into a nice pair of slacks. Looking at the clock on her bedside table, she decided she had just enough time to run a brush through her hair and put on a little lipstick. The she smiled at herself in the mirror and headed to the stairs.

She had only taken two steps down the stairs before she realized she had left her phone on the dresser. She twirled around to head back to her bedroom, lost her balance, and tumbled noisily down the stairs.

The sound of the crash shook the tiny apartment and Philip rushed to see what had caused the noise. Horrified by the sight on his wife's inert body lying crumpled at the bottom of the staircase, he ran to her and gently brushed a finger across her forehead.

"Annabel, are you hurt?"

Philip could have slapped himself for asking such a ridiculous question, because it was painfully obvious she was hurt. Then he took a closer look and panicked when he realized that she was not breathing. He reached down and grabbed her shoulders, lifting her slightly off the floor.

"Annabel," he yelled, shaking her slightly in the hope that he could reach her. "Annabel, do you hear me?"

Whether it was the shaking, the yelling, or just good luck, Annabel gave a cough, a groan, and began to breathe again. This would have reassured him had her breathing not been raspy and painful to hear. He pulled her close and hugged her tight. Her eyes remained closed, but when he looked at her face, he noticed that a tear had broken free of her left eyelid and rolled down her cheek.

"Annabel, darling. Hang in there, I'll get help."

Philip gently lowered Annabel to the ground and tried to look around, but the panic he felt was so strong that he was nearly blinded. It was a full minute before he could make his eyes function properly so he could find his phone. As he reached for it, he noticed that one of Annabel's hands was reaching for him. Carefully, now conscious that his movements might hurt her, he gently took her hand. The relief he felt when she gave a gentle squeeze was almost more than he could bear.

"I'll take care of you Annabel," he whispered softly. "I'll never let anything happen to you. I love you too much."

Chapter 5

THE SMELL OF CHOCOLATE was intoxicating.

Vanessa was soaking in a bathtub of it while hummingbirds of every color flittered about, catering to her every whim. A bright yellow hummingbird adjusted the gossamer curtains, dimming the bright sunlight until it was muted and soothing. Another hummingbird, this one the brightest orange ever imagined, pulled a rolling table to within easy arm's reach, allowing easy access to a glass of iced tea. Two bright blue hummingbirds flew into the room carrying what to them must have been a gargantuan tray of strawberries.

Vanessa thanked the hummingbirds as they placed the tray beside the iced tea and smiled as she reached for a strawberry. Chocolate covered strawberries were one of her favorite treats—

Ring.

Everything strawberries, chocolate, even the hummingbirds—was sucked away faster than fog in a hurricane. It had all been a dream—a lovely, wonderful, delicious dream. A dream so real Vanessa swore she could still smell chocolate—

Ring.

She sighed as the sound dispelled the last remnants of that glorious dream, along with the smell of chocolate. With no further reason to remain asleep, she grabbed that obnoxious phone that had killed her oh-so-lovely dream.

"Hello," Vanessa rasped into the phone, her voice still as asleep as her brain had been just seconds before. She looked toward the clock and noticed that it was already ten o'clock. Her children had not let her sleep this late in years.

"Is this the home of Master Sergeant Rossi?" a man's voice asked.

"Yes, I'm his wife, Mrs. Rossi. Vanessa. Who is this?"

"Dr. Brown, at Madigan Hospital. I need to talk to someone about your husband."

"What?"

"Your husband," Dr. Brown repeated slowly, using that same I-know-you-barely-understand-so-

I'll-talk-at-a-snail's-pace cadence that men often used when they talked to women. "Is there anyone I can speak to?"

"You can speak to me," Vanessa said hopefully, even though she already knew what the response would be.

"Now Vanessa, don't be silly." Dr. Brown allowed himself a snicker at this ridiculousness. "This is a serious matter and I need to speak to someone who can take charge. Do you understand?"

Vanessa nodded as she sat with the phone to her ear, resigned to the fact that she would have to wait to find out why the doctor had called.

"Vanessa," Dr. Brown snapped as the silence continued past the point the doctor thought reasonable, "I'm a busy man, so I need you to concentrate. Can you do that for me?"

"I can," Vanessa quickly replied, embarrassed that she had caused the good doctor stress.

"Good." The doctor sounded relieved. "What I want you to do is put down the phone and get the man of the house. I need to speak to him. Can you do that for me?"

"No."

"What do you mean, 'no'?" Dr. Brown asked sharply, obviously mistaking Vanessa's desire to give a simple answer for rudeness.

"The man of the house," Vanessa replied as respectfully as she could, "is my husband. And he's not home. He left for work several hours ago."

Long seconds of silence passed as the doctor thought this through.

"Doctor," Vanessa began, carefully making her voice as polite as possible, "if you need to leave a message for my husband, I can take it. I often—"

"In that case," Dr. Brown said, cutting her off not as if he were agreeing with her, but as if she hadn't said a word, "I need you to get me your husband's father's number. Can do that for me, Vanessa?"

"My husband's father died several years ago."

"How about a brother? Does your husband have a brother I can speak with?"

"My husband," Vanessa said regretfully, "has no male relatives."

"No male relatives, huh?" Dr. Brown muttered. Then he said the words Vanessa never expected to hear: "How about you?"

"Of course you can speak to me," she said as her heart soared at the thought that she could be of some help. "I'd be happy to—"

"Don't be ridiculous," Dr. Brown cut her off callously. "I meant, do you have a father or a brother I can speak with?"

"Sorry, no," Vanessa admitted as her heart lost its wings and plummeted back to earth. "My father died years ago and I only have sisters."

"I'm not sure what I should do," Dr. Brown muttered just loud enough for her to hear, "Someone should be told about the accident—"

"Accident? What accident? Has my husband—?"

"No men around, huh," Dr. Brown continued, ignoring Vanessa as if she were a frog on the other end of the phone wire. "Well, that certainly complicates things a bit."

Vanessa gulped but stayed silent. At this point all she could do was listen as the doctor muttered words she couldn't quite hear, but could guess.

"Doctor," Vanessa began, but stopped when she realized the word came out more like a squeak than human speech. She gulped and took a few breaths to calm herself. Any sign of hysterics and the doctor would hang up the phone faster than a traffic cop wrote tickets in a school zone.

"I don't like this, not at all," the doctor muttered

to himself. Then he raised his voice enough that she knew he was now addressing her. "Are you positive there are no men I can speak to, maybe a son? Think hard, this is important."

"No son, no brother, no father, no man of any kind or age." Then her voice broke as worry crept in. "Please tell me what this is about. Did something happen to my husband?"

The doctor didn't answer for quite a while. The silence dragged on so long that Vanessa worried they may have been disconnected, until she heard someone on the hospital intercom demand that additional personnel immediately report to the second floor. The official sound of that voice prompted Vanessa to take a chance and overstep the bounds of propriety.

"Please, doctor," Vanessa pleaded, "I have four daughters to take care of."

Vanessa silently prayed as she waited for the doctor's response. She knew if she pushed too hard he would simply hang up. Maybe, just maybe—

"Well, I guess there is no way around it," Dr. Brown said with a sigh. "I'll have to break protocol and hope no one hears about it. Are you sitting?"

"Yes," Vanessa answered, though in truth she

was actually lying in bed.

"Good. In that case, I regret to inform you that your husband was in a car crash this morning."

"What!" she yelled, sitting up so fast she gave herself a head rush.

"He was brought to Madigan at 6:30 this morning."

"How's he—"

"Excuse me, but I can't divulge any more information, not to a woman. You need to find a man I can speak with. See if you can get in touch with someone appropriate."

"Please! How's my husband doing? Can I come to the hospital?"

"Like I said before, the rules state that all medical information can only be given to a male relative."

"Can you at least tell me if he's conscious? Please!"

"Well, I guess I can tell you that much. He's conscious, barely. I think it would be best if one of his relatives was nearby."

"How badly is he hurt? Will he—"

"Like I said, I've already shared too much with you. Find a male relative, or even a friend, I can talk to."

"Don't you think as his wife I should be able to—?"

"I don't deal with 'shoulds.' Laws are laws. And the law states that no female will ever be placed in a position of authority or be forced to make decisions. It could cause you severe mental stress, and I would be culpable. I'm not going to risk my career just so you can satisfy your womanly curiosity."

"But—"

"Find a friend or relative I can speak to."

"Yes, doctor. I will. Right away."

As Vanessa hung up the phone, she could hear the sound of her children playing quietly in the other room. The sound should have comforted her, but instead it made her shiver uncontrollably. Tony, her wonderful husband, the father of those four beautiful girls playing so innocently just on the other side of the wall, had been in an accident. Her husband, her protector, the man she planned to grow old with, was in the hospital. Her Tony, her strong, dependable, fearless husband, was lying, hurt and injured, all alone in a hospital bed over an hour away.

And she had no way to get to him. By law she

couldn't drive a car, or even travel, without a male escort. And since Tony had just transferred to this school, they hadn't had time to get all of their resources in order.

Fear gripped her heart and wrung it like a two-year-old squeezes play dough. There was no way she was going to leave Tony all alone, in a cold hospital, under the care of an unfeeling doctor. Law or no law, she had every intention of finding a way to get to him.

"Mommy," a voice interrupted her thoughts, "who was on the phone?"

Until that moment Vanessa had not realized that anyone had come into the room. It was Becca, her twelve-year-old daughter. She was standing right by the bed and Vanessa hadn't even heard her enter the room. She wondered how long the child had been standing there. What had she overheard? What should Vanessa tell her? What was the proper thing for a mother to do?

"Mom?"

"It was Madigan, the army hospital," Vanessa stated baldly, deciding the absolute truth was her only true option. Contrary to popular belief, Vanessa knew that a woman's brain wasn't a fragile

lump of mush that would disintegrate at
the slightest sign of stress. "Your father was in an
accident—I'm sure he's going to be fine, so don't
worry—but we need to find a way to go to him."

"Daddy?"

One look at her daughter's face reminded
Vanessa that Becca was not a woman, but a child.
And she had just blurted out to this child that her
father was hurt and in a hospital.

Vanessa watched as Becca melted into a fragile
lump of mush before her very eyes. Then things got
worse.

"Daddy!" Becca wailed.

The door flew open and Becca's three younger
sisters rushed in to answer the alarm. They threw
their arms around their sister and there the four
stood, wailing and blubbering just inside the room.
Only one of them even knew what they were crying
about.

Chapter 6

PHILIP JENSEN WAS GROGGY and disoriented when he got up from the couch and stumbled into the bathroom, stubbing his toe on a table as he went by. Half blind with pain, he frantically searched his medicine cabinet for something, anything that would make the battering ram inside his head stop its assault.

He found a dissolvable tablet, placed it under his tongue, and waited for the results. Luckily, they were quick to come. The pounding began to lighten bit by bit, until finally the pain was almost bearable.

Which should have been a good thing. Except as the pain retreated, Philip's brain regained the ability to function and he realized exactly what a fool he had been. As the thick fog of pain dissolved he could see more clearly exactly how worthless his trip into the past had been. Even though the trip through time had fulfilled one of his lifelong goals, all he had to show for it was a pounding headache.

He groaned as the battering ram took a parting shot at his frontal lobe. He had heard that some newbie time adapters had the occasional twinge as their brain tried to acclimate back to their own time zone. But he'd never heard of anyone suffering pain like this.

Now that the pain had lessened to a more reasonable level, he realized that the attack on his skull was no more than what he deserved. He knew better than to ignore proper procedure and mess about in the timeline. He was married to a time monkey, and he and Annabel had often discussed how much forethought and effort was needed for each and every trip.

Who was he to think he could bypass the multitude of procedures that had been fine-tuned through years of practice? What made him think he could flounce across the time spectrum and manage a successful adapt without the proper training?

He had been the worst kind of idiot, the one who should have known better. He was the preeminent time travel theorist in the world, yet he made the rookie mistake of missing the target date by several hundred years. Several hundred!

He should have waited for Annabel to recover.

She would never have made such a blunder.

Looking back, he realized that he had acted like some sort of time tourist rather than a professional. He had been so caught up in the experience of his first travel that he overlooked a number of discrepancies that should have clued him in to his mistake. He even broke the cardinal rule and failed to double-check the date before he traveled to Dr. Morgan's childhood home in Portland, which was his target location.

He had never visited Portland in his own time, and he had been in such a hurry that he neglected to research the area. It was no wonder that he had no clear idea what to expect. So when Portland looked different, quainter, than what he thought it should, he simply thought that the town had maintained an "old town" section for tourists.

What a shock it had been when a dated poster plastered on the side of a building clued him in to his mistake. When he finally figured out that he had missed his mark by the time equivalent of a mile, he had been floored. He had botched it, miserably.

Probably the worst of it was his sudden realization that this fiasco was just one in a long

line. The habit of failure had become so
normal, so ingrained in his life, that it was almost
as if he had fallen into a crevasse of failure and had
decided that instead of trying to climb out, he had
built a little shack for himself and had snuggled
down for a long stay.

What an unpleasant thought!

Almost as unpleasant as the thought of what he
needed to do next—wake Annabel and confess to
her what he had done.

The doctors said that she was making a good
recovery. Her lung, which had been punctured by
a broken rib in the fall, was responding well to the
new treatment. She should make a full recovery in
a matter of weeks.

Which was a relief. When Annabel first took that
tumble down the stairs, Philip was petrified that he
might lose her. It brought home to him just how
important she was to him, how much he loved her
and depended on her good sense.

He would do anything to make their life
together perfect. Obviously he'd even be idiotic
enough to try to make an adapt without a trained
professional.

Not that the best-trained time monkey in the

world would appreciate that. There was a reason she was top in her field, and what Philip had done was going to make her madder than a hornet.

But Philip knew he lived in the soft spot dead center in her heart of gold. She could never stay mad at him for long, especially if he worked to make it up to her. He was confident that if he started with a sincere confession it would go a long way toward helping him obtain complete forgiveness.

The sooner he got started, the better. Time to wake his wife.

As he got up off the couch, he must have dislodged the medieval weapon in his head because it gave a few half-hearted jabs to the inside of his skull. Grabbing his temple, Philip took a detour to the kitchen to get a glass of juice. Now that the worst of the pain in his head had subsided, he could feel the strange queasiness in his stomach, which probably meant that he was hungry. After all, he hadn't eaten since…

He paused with his hand on the refrigerator door as a vivid memory flashed in his mind. He had been so disgusted with himself after he had discovered his mistake that he had disregarded every rule of time travel and wandered around Portland aimlessly.

After about thirty minutes he realized what he was doing and should have headed back to Seattle and the portal. But he was tired, hungry, and not feeling very good about himself, so he threw caution to the wind and followed a group of cheery-looking people into some sort of eatery.

He knew it was a ridiculous thing to do. He had no money from this time period so all he could do was watch. But everyone was laughing and eating, enjoying something they called a 'happy hour,' so without a second thought he took a seat at the bar.

Before he knew it he had a plate of food, a tasty beverage, and a dinner companion. It seemed the gentleman on the stool next to him was the social sort who had no problem buying a new friend a few drinks and a meal.

It was indeed an hour to be happy, with plenty of good food, drink, and conversation. The only problem was that the drink must have been significantly more potent than anything in his own time, because before he realized what was happening the room began to whirl and all he wanted to do was lie down and go to sleep.

His new friend, who introduced himself as Douglas Whitfield, kindly offered Philip his couch for the night. Since Philip could not imagine making the long trip back to the portal in an intoxicated condition, he followed Douglas the block to his apartment.

Philip's last memory before he passed out was a conversation in which he thanked Douglas, and told him that he was a credit to his time.

Philip woke in the morning with a splitting headache, a crick in his neck from sleeping on a too-short couch, and the uncomfortable feeling that he had talked more than he should have. He was concerned until Douglas walked into the room friendly, talkative, and not in the least concerned that Philip might be an alien from another time. So even in an inebriated state, he must have had enough self-control to refrain from talk about his favorite subject, time travel.

As Philip stretched the kinks out of his cramped muscles, Douglas told him that he had early morning business in Seattle and would be able to drive Philip there and drop him off on campus. Philip jumped at the chance to avoid the daunting task of finding his own transportation.

On campus, Philip asked to be let out near Denny Hall. It was still ridiculously early, and since no students had arrived yet, he was able to step into the janitor's closet that served as the portal without any concern that he might be seen.

He was even fortunate in his own time, where the late shift had left but the early shift had not yet arrived. He managed to pop through the portal and leave the lab, with no one aware he had even been there.

That gap in security would be one of the first things he would address when he was in charge. The thought of the problems that could be created if the wrong people gained access to the portal and did their own adapting was horrifying. One wrong adapt could set the entire world back to the stone age before anyone even knew there was a problem.

Still, this whole time travel business was quite an adventure! He reached into his pocket and pulled out a little metal box. He pushed a button on the side and the lid sprang open to reveal the photo of Annabel he always kept with him.

"I can see why you love your job," Philip said to the photo. "But do you love me enough to forgive me for messing this up?"

He stared at the photo for a few more moments before he nodded. "Right, I'm procrastinating. You, a flat representation of my wife, might forgive me"—he looked from the picture to the door of the bedroom where Annabel lay sleeping—"but will she?"

"Wish me luck!" Philip said as he kissed the photo, clicked the lid closed, and put it back in his pocket.

With a sigh, Philip paused at the door to smooth his hair and clothes. It was well past time for him to wake Annabel and confess his misdeeds. Ultimately, if anyone in the lab found out about his little jaunt into the past, Annabel would be the one held responsible. It was only fair that she knew and was given time to prepare for the possible consequences.

He grabbed the doorknob to the bedroom door and psyched himself up to grovel. Annabel was a wonderful and loving wife in the best of times. But now that she was pregnant with their child, the first of several he hoped, she had shown a definite tendency toward crankiness.

Not that he blamed her. Being pregnant was challenging enough, and she also had to contend with a broken rib and a punctured lung.

Not exactly pleasant when morning sickness hit.

Philip slowly opened the door and peeked around the doorjamb. He wanted to be as quiet as possible, afraid that a sudden loud noise might startle his wife out of a sound sleep and make her crabbier than normal.

But after a quick peek into the room, shock made him throw the door so wide it slammed against the wall.

Annabel was not in the bed. She wasn't even in the room. Even more disturbing was the fact that everything about her was missing. Gone were her clothes, makeup, and shoes. The room was empty of every trace of Annabel. Even her favorite antique clock, the one that ticked loudly all through the night, had vanished.

Philip's heart pounded as he tore the room apart searching for any clue to the whereabouts of his wife. When he found nothing he extended his search to the rest of the apartment.

All trace of Annabel was gone. Not a memento, not a scrap, not even a curly gold hair could Philip find as he searched the apartment. When he noticed that the deep scratch on the wall that Annabel had

made when she tried to catch herself as she
fell down the stairs was gone, Philip sunk to the
ground in despair. There was no sign that Annabel
had ever existed.

The headache Philip had held at bay began to
pound as the possibilities sank in. Yesterday he had
traveled to the past, and today his wife had been
erased from his life. Annabel, his darling, sweet,
brilliant Annabel, the mother of his unborn child,
had never lived in this apartment. That much was
obvious.

"Oh, God, what have I done?" Philip groaned.
"How will I find her? What if she married someone
else? What if—?"

Philip stood stock still as a horrible thought hit
him. He looked around for his data device but
could not find it. Finally he raced around the
apartment until he spotted a huge tome with *The
History of Time Travel* stamped in gold letters on the
side. With a shaky hand he grabbed the heavy book
and flipped through the pages, then slid into a
nearby chair in shock.

This was not the history he had been taught. The
dates were all wrong.

He sat for a full minute, stunned, until another

thought hit him. He grabbed the book from where it had fallen to the floor and slammed it onto his lap, wincing as a sharp corner stabbed his leg.

Taking a deep breath he flipped to the last chapter of the book and ran his finger down page after page as he looked for his wife's name. While researching her dissertation she had been instrumental in refining the protocols used by all time travelers and had earned a place in the history books a full two years before she earned her doctorate.

Yet there was no mention of her, or of her contribution to the field.

What had he done? How had he made such a mistake? Somehow his stumble into the wrong part of the past had changed the timeline. Drastically.

He had known the dangers, and yet he had gone. He, who had been touted as the pre-eminent expert of time travel adapting had made a monumental mistake of being that untrained person who traveled to the past. He had flubbed up and changed history.

Worst of all, based on what he had seen in the book, he may just have adapted the love of his life right out of existence.

Chapter 7

"DARLING, WOULD YOU LIKE for me to get you anything? Water, a pudding cup?" Vanessa asked the injured man in the hospital bed who strangely resembled her husband.

She knew she was going to have to get over it, since the man did not just resemble her husband, but *was* her husband. But she was having a difficult time wrapping her head around the fact that her ultra-fit, never sick husband had injuries so severe that the doctors had restricted him to at least a month of bed rest, and warned him that if he even stuck his foot out of bed, his recovery would slow to a crawl.

"How are the girls doing?"

"They're fine," Vanessa said lightly. "They're with your sister."

"Don't let them come here, I don't want them to see me like this yet."

"Okay sweetie, I won't." Vanessa took his hands and forced him to meet her eyes. She wanted him to realize how important this was to her. "But I'm telling them the truth—that your accident was a bad one."

"Fine," Tony agreed after a quick battle of wills, a battle Vanessa won. "But I don't want them to see me lying in bed like this. They'll get scared."

Instead of agreeing, like Tony expected, Vanessa bit the right side of her lower lip, something she only did when she was conflicted. As much as she wanted to make her husband comfortable, she also needed to think of her children. And—

"What is it, Vanessa, why do you look like you have something unpleasant to tell me?"

Instead of answering, she switched the bite to the left side of her lip. As if it might help her think clearer.

"Please, Vanessa?" Tony asked, his eyes big and pleading like a puppy that had just been denied a favorite bone. Vanessa held out for several seconds, which was probably a record for her.

"It's Becca," she blurted. "She's scared. Really

scared. She thinks you're paralyzed, and will never walk again. She thinks you'll be different from now on, probably weak and helpless. No longer the father she knows and loves. She's afraid—"

"Bring her." Tony said it quickly and he gave her hands a little squeeze.

"What?" Vanessa was surprised by his quick change of heart. She knew it was important to Tony to always be seen as strong. Had he suggested that she bring Becca to see him in his sick bed?

"Bring her," Tony repeated as he let go of her hands and attempted to sit up a little straighter in the bed. "I'll talk to her, let her know I'm going to be okay."

Vanessa watched him struggle for a few seconds, then grabbed a pillow from a nearby chair and arranged it behind his back. As he lay back, she placed a hand on his shoulder.

"Tony, I don't know. You'll push yourself too far. You'll want to show Becca that—"

"Just bring her."

"Are you sure? I don't want you to—"

"You might as well stop your worrying about me getting up and walking around the room to prove I can. Right now, sitting is about all I can do. I'll lie here, smile, and let her know everything will be okay. I can't stand the thought of her worrying that she's lost her dad somehow. That I won't be the same person."

"You're sure you're up to it?"

"Positive."

Vanessa retrieved her oldest daughter and as the two of them rode with the escort to the hospital, Vanessa reassured Becca that everything was going to be fine. The fear on the face of the twelve-year-old as they approached her father's room nearly broke Vanessa's heart. It was only after Becca had been able to give her dad a big hug that her little shoulders relaxed and the tenseness left her face.

As Vanessa watched the oh-so-important father/daughter bond grow, she wondered why she had an uneasy feeling that the world was awry. Something more than her husband's accident was wrong—very wrong.

That night as she lay in her own bed while Tony slept miles away in the hospital, she dreamt about a world that was a very different place. In this strange world, women attended college and had jobs, real jobs that made a difference, like the ones men had. Even stranger, they not only voted in elections, but they held public office. It was an extraordinary world, a wonderful world, a world where a woman could be valuable, clever, and able to contribute more to society than recipes and babies.

Perhaps the most amazing thing in the dream was that Vanessa was able to walk freely around Seattle without a male escort and without identity papers. There were no checkpoints, no troops, and no ten-block row of statues of the greatest US generals of World War II.

It was a crazy dream. In it, Seattle was a friendly place, a city that had not been the target of thousands of enemy bombers during the war years. Vanessa guessed that in the dream, Seattle must not have been one of the major ports that had been instrumental in finally ending that oh-so-horrible fifty-year war.

Which showed the true craziness of dreams. The

war had only been over a few decades, and everyone knew it would it take at least a hundred years for the United States to recuperate from a devastating war that had dragged on for more than half a century.

Unconscious wishful thinking, that's what it was. The trauma of Tony's accident must have triggered something in Vanessa that made her imagination conjure up an ideal world—a world where she had the ability to take care of her children, even without their father.

Sounded grand, if unrealistic. It certainly was *not* the world in which Vanessa lived.

As Vanessa sat up in bed, a tidal wave of dizziness slammed into her and sent her on a magic carpet ride around the room.

The world spun wildly out of control as pieces of furniture flew past, narrowly missing her head. Even her dresser, normally a reliable and stable piece of furniture, rushed at her like a freight train, then somehow rebounded back to where it started.

Vanessa's stomach lurched as the world whirled and swooped around her. She was so off kilter and dizzy that if she hadn't managed to grab the bedpost as it shot past her outstretched hand, she surely would have fallen to the floor in an undignified heap, much like the baked potato that had tumbled with a *splat* from the plate of her four-year-old at dinner the night before.

Several more disturbing minutes twisted by before the nauseating whirls and swirls began to slow and, one pie-shaped section of the room at a time, everything came into focus. Almost.

Vanessa couldn't point her finger at anything and say it was wrong, yet she knew that things weren't right. Somewhere, something was askew.

In fact, something was so off-kilter that as she looked around her bedroom, her stomach did flip-flops whenever her eyes rested on certain objects.

Curious about the strange gymnastics in her midsection, Vanessa methodically scanned the room. Her hairbrush caused not the slightest stir in her tummy, while a seemingly innocent wristwatch forced her insides into somersaults so rambunctious they would have been too outlandish for a circus.

Something was not right. Her insides had never started an exercise routine without her before, and this was too much to simply be the residual effect of a wonderful, yet disturbing dream.

Her eyes continued to roam until they fell on the spot where Tony would normally have been soundly sleeping. The sudden deep sense of unease that engulfed her was overwhelming. It was more than wrong that Tony wasn't here. It was beyond wrong. His absence made the universe off balance, like an elephant teetering on a one-legged stool. At any moment, everything could come crashing down around her shoulders.

Vanessa gulped a few times, wiped the tears from her eyes, and took some deep breaths. Then she reminded herself that Tony was going to be okay. Her world was not in a total upheaval, because her husband was going to be fine. In a few weeks, he would be back home where he belonged and the balance of her world would be restored.

It took longer to regain her calm than it should have, so to keep herself busy as she was wrangling in her emotions, she continued her perusal of the room. When she realized that the last vestiges of dizziness had been tamed, she breathed a sigh of relief.

Then her eyes locked onto Tony's framed bachelor's degree diploma that hung proudly on the wall. Her stomach lurched uncomfortably as her heart sank to her toes. Tears welled in her eyes and a deep feeling of sadness permeated the very marrow of her bones. One second she was calm and collected—the next she was drowning in a sea of despair, overwhelmed by a tremendous sense of loss, a sureness of a life wasted, of talent left untapped.

Odd. Vanessa was very proud of Tony and his accomplishments. She had no reason to feel sad. The very fact that the diploma was framed on the wall was proof that his talent was not going to go to waste.

The room spun again, but this time only for a split second. And just like that it was all clear. It was *her* talent that was being wasted. There should be a second framed diploma on the wall next to her husband's. But this one should have Vanessa's name on it.

Vanessa squeezed her eyes shut for several seconds as she tried to squeeze out the strange thoughts. Women didn't get diplomas! This remnant of the dream had to go. It was time to pull herself out of that unusually potent dream and get her brain back to normal.

Vanessa shook her head like a dog shakes his

favorite toy, but instead of it clearing her
mind, she was once again treated to a case of the
whirls. When the crazy motion finally stopped and
everything settled down, her brain was suddenly
flooded with a lifetime of memories.

They were her memories, yet they couldn't be.
Not when they included things like jobs, university
degrees, and even driving! Yet those odd memories
were strangely comfortable. They fit like a pair of
old gardening gloves she used to—

Vanessa paused mid-thought as she realized
she'd never gardened a day in her life. She'd never
been allowed to try.

Or had she?

To say that Vanessa was confused was an
understatement. Her brain was more scrambled
than an egg—

The thought stopped mid-simile as her brain,
frantic to clean up the chaos, kicked into high gear
and categorized everything—normal memories to
the right, crazy memories to the left.

And those left-hand memories truly were
wacky. One of them, a big one that stuck out
awkwardly, almost like it refused to be hidden
away, had her stepping through a time portal four

years ago, before the birth of her fourth child. The memory was exciting, fantastic, wonderful, and thoroughly unforgettable.

But Vanessa knew that it was also one hundred percent fiction since this portal was supposed to be located on the University of Washington campus, a place she had never visited since women weren't allowed on college campuses.

A series of memories, refusing to be swept aside, moved to center stage in her brain. There she was, alone late at night in the basement lab. Her muscles ached from hours spent perched on an uncomfortable lab stool as she studied pottery shards, old bones, and broken rocks. Her eyes, red and itchy from strain, begged for rest. Her stomach, angry at the lack of food, growled a warning.

But even with all of this discomfort she was happy. She was working hard to become an archaeologist, to fulfill one of her life's goals. The satisfaction she felt as she completed assignment after assignment made her feel strong, successful— nearly invincible.

Vanessa found that she liked the feeling. She wanted more of it.

Had she gone crazy? Women have never, and

would never, be allowed to pursue a degree. Only the craziest, most irresponsible fathers allowed their daughters to be educated past the point of rudimentary reading. It was too much of a risk.

Tony's accident must have shocked her system more than she had realized.

When she turned her thoughts back to her well-categorized brain, she realized that those strangely seductive memories of a life of study still sat center stage. She shook her head, hoping that the whirls would return to put everything back to normal. She wanted to get rid of those extra memories that had taken over her brain. They confused her.

But no matter how hard she shook, there were no more whirls.

Then it hit her. She wanted to learn, to exercise her brain, something she'd always been taught was unhealthy.

Vanessa climbed out of bed, threw on a robe, and headed to the kitchen to make herself a cup of coffee. She desperately needed coffee. It would help her dig all the way out of that dream.

She stopped along the way to check on the kids and was amazed to find them all still sound asleep in their beds. Proof positive that the world was wonky.

As soon as she had a steaming mug of coffee in hand, she curled up on the couch to think. If she applied herself, she was pretty sure she could banish the dream, and all its baggage. She could get rid of those intruding memories that kept stomping through her brain and trespassing on legitimate memories.

Vanessa sat on the couch and mentally browsed through events she could never have been a part of, much as a librarian might browse through a file cabinet of old newspaper articles that needed to be weeded. She'd pull out a memory, examine it for inaccuracies, and place the impossible ones in a pile to the side to be discarded.

She was at it for over an hour. Things did not play out as planned.

As the pile grew, so did her suspicion that these memories were not as alien as she first thought.

She'd had dreams before. Wonderful ones that she wanted to capture and cherish. But invariably, the more she examined the dream, the wispier and less substantial it became. Dreams were like cotton candy. They looked solid and abundant, but melted

away at the slightest touch. All that was
left behind was a sticky mess with no substance.

But these memories that she had assumed were from the dream were of a different caliber. She could touch them, pull them, and bounce them around all she wanted. They stayed solid. No wisp, no melting, no sickly-sweet sticky residue left behind.

The strangest memory she found, packed away among the time travel adventure, claimed that her children invented time travel. They were destined to do wonderful things, important things, things that contributed to society and changed the world.

Vanessa's head ached as she fought to maintain order in her brain.

Her children, her four daughters, could never contribute anything important to society. It was a cruel fact of human anatomy.

They were girls, and would grow into women. Women were not allowed, had never been allowed, an education past the sixth grade.

It made sense. Everyone knew about those famous studies done by scientists that proved, beyond a shadow of a doubt, that the female brain was incapable of higher learning. It had something

to do with hormones. When puberty
kicked in, schooling had to end. The female brain
was incapable of logical thought. It did odd things
to the neural pathways and made women crazy.

Except Vanessa knew this was not true. Even
before the disturbing dream with its over-vivid
memories, she'd never swallowed that whole
women-are-too-fragile-to-be-educated thing. She
had helped Tony study for all of his tests and had
discovered that she had just as good a memory as
he did, often better. And when she helped him find
facts for his dissertation, she found she had a knack
for research that Tony did not.

As far as she could tell, her neural pathways
were fine.

Unless Vanessa was too confused and crazy to
know she was confused and crazy.

Chapter 8

PHILIP SLAMMED THE DOOR of his apartment, tripped over a throw rug, and stumbled to his favorite chair. As he dropped into it he groaned, allowing all the frustration, fear, and worry into that one sound.

During the many hours he had spent looking for his wife, Philip had come to realize that the changes to the timeline went deep, much deeper than his little step into the past should have caused.

The entire layout of the city had changed. Buildings that should have been built had not been built, including Annabel's childhood home. Parks, buildings, monuments, streets—even the color scheme of the city—were all foreign to Philip.

The real shock came when Philip went to the DTA lab to search for Annabel. Instead of being concerned that she was missing, the men at the lab just laughed. It felt like they were laughing at him. As if they were part of a secret club that he knew nothing about, and they found his very cluelessness hilarious.

Then on his way home, he realized that he had not seen a single feminine form since he got back from his trip into the past. It was as if women did not exist.

He needed to find his wife. He missed her, but more importantly, she was the person most likely to be able to fix this whole mess. He understood the theory of time travel, but she was an expert on its practical applications.

Which was not surprising since time travel was in her blood. Her family had invented it. Or at least, they had invented the method used for it, conducted the first exploratory journeys, and wrote the manual. Not to mention that handy gene they all shared.

But try as he might, Philip could find no sign of his wife, or even her family. Which was confusing. The DTA lab existed, so Annabel's family must have been around to invent the technology. But he could find no sign of them.

He almost gave up when he could find no record of Annabel's birth until he noticed that only male children were recorded. Society thought so little of women that they did not even think it worth a line on a piece of paper to record the addition of a female child.

Which made him change his focus to history. What he found there stunned him.

Not only was there no historical record of any woman being given credit for any invention, scientific breakthrough, or literary work, no women were even listed. Ever. A traveler from another galaxy could be forgiven for thinking that such a thing as a woman had never existed.

Someone, somehow, had done the unthinkable. They had changed something so significant, so important, that the repercussions reverberated throughout time.

But to what purpose? Why would anyone, anyone at all, want to create a world in which women virtually disappeared from society?

History had never been his strong suit, yet even he knew that women had always been huge

contributors to society. Take away their
input and Earth quickly became a much different
planet.

Chapter 9

As THE DAY WORE on, the rogue memories solidified and strengthened until they felt just as authentic as Vanessa's real memories. In fact, the "other" memories, the ones that had snuck into her brain while her head twirled around like a cat on a merry-go-round, were now more real to her than the ones for her current life.

Whoa there, Vanessa thought, current life indeed!

If anyone knew that thought had even popped into her head, the guys that carry the stylish white jackets with arms that tie in the back would find their way to her door. They were always on alert for any woman whose brain had become unhinged due to too much thinking.

Vanessa found it odd that even with the extra set of memories clogging up her brain, she felt no confusion. After that first bout of the swirls, she had quickly became adept at recognizing which set of memories belonged where.

Still, it was strange that she had to deal with so many remnants of an overly vivid dream. Because that's all they could possibly be, right? To get memories this in-depth, this complete, she'd have to have lived an entire but totally different life parallel to the life she'd lived.

But that would be confusing, not to mention impossible!

Almost as confusing as this strange feeling she couldn't shake that there was something huge in her world that she needed to fix.

"Mommy! I need Koala Toala."

Audrey, Vanessa's youngest, was perched atop the back of the couch. She was amazingly graceful, like a professional circus acrobat. She was four, climbed like a monkey, and performed one stunt after another. Only to her they weren't stunts, just her normal method of getting around.

"What, sweetie?" Vanessa asked. Then she remembered her motherly duties and added, "Get

down from there. I told you not to climb
up the back of the couch."

"I didn't climb the couch," the little sweetie replied with the simple logic of a four-year-old, "I climbed the table. I jumped to the couch."

"But—" the tired mother began, but stopped as she remembered that four-year-olds only understood four-year-old logic, so she might as well save her breath. "Oh, never mind. Get down from there. Let me help you—"

She reached toward Audrey and untwisted her legs, but before Vanessa's foot so much as touched the floor so she could stand, the daredevil munchkin jumped as high as she could, bounced once on the couch on her rear, and landed safely on her feet on the coffee table.

Vanessa sighed as she thought about the family nickname Audrey had acquired. Stunt Monkey. It was so appropriate.

"No feet on the table, Audrey. You know Mommy's rule."

"Yes, Mommy," Audrey said sweetly as she gracefully hopped off the table.

Vanessa pulled the little munchkin into her lap to give her a mommy-loves-you hug. No matter

how surefooted Audrey was, Vanessa had
a mother's fear that something might go wrong.
That instead of a safe landing, the little monkey
might trip and hit her head. Or slip and break a leg.
Or an earthquake might open the floor beneath her
feet and—

Well, there was no need to go over the million
and four things her worried brain imagined could
happen. It was best to leave it that she was always
happy to see Audrey's little feet planted firmly on
the ground.

"Mommy, I need Koala Toala," Audrey repeated
as she placed her little hands on her mother's
shoulders and looked pleadingly into her eyes.
"Becca won't help me find her."

Vanessa smiled. She couldn't help but smile.
Nothing put the world into perspective as quickly
as looking at it through a child's eyes. What an
adult thinks of as a mere speck in a world of
basketball-sized problems, the child sees as the
biggest problem the world has ever known.

And of course, it works the other way, too. An
insurmountable problem blocking the path of an
adult was utter nonsense to a child, not even a blip
on the child's radar.

Of course, what mattered right now was that it was the most important thing in the world for this little girl was that she be reunited with her beloved toy.

Who was Vanessa to say that she was wrong? Aubrey had gotten the bear for her first birthday and it had always been one of her favorites. In her world, it was of the utmost importance. It calmed her when she was upset and cheered her when she felt sad. It was a quiet friend who never argued but was always there for her. So the fact that it was missing, that cuddly little bear that loomed so large in her life, was catastrophic.

"Becca," Vanessa called to her oldest daughter as she gave Audrey one more hug, set her own her feet, and pointed her toward the other room, "please help your sister find her bear."

"Mom?" came the question from the other room.

"Her Koala Toala. Help her find it. I've got some thinking to do."

Becca walked into the living room, looked first at her youngest sister and then at her mother.

"You want me to find what for her?" Becca's forehead crinkled in confusion, but Vanessa knew what this really was. The teen years were coming

111

and she was practicing that all-important skill of purposeful misunderstanding. Vanessa was not having any of it.

"Becca," she said sternly, "find Koala Toala for your sister."

"Mom said!" Vanessa heard her littlest angel say from the kitchen. She looked past Becca in time to see Audrey cross her dimpled arms in front of her chest and glare at her older sister.

Maybe her nickname should be Stealth Monkey instead of Stunt Monkey, Vanessa thought. When did she go to the kitchen?

"Find what?" Becca asked, unfazed by her bossy little sister.

"Becca." Vanessa put every drop of seriousness she could muster into her voice. She needed her oldest child to understand that now was not the time for that newly developed innocent act. "I really need your help here. Please just go find the toy for your sister."

"I would, if I had any idea what she was talking about!" complained twelve-year-old Becca. "What is a Koala Toala?"

Vanessa sighed and rolled her eyes. If Becca got away with this new attitude, Becca's parents would be in for a mountain of trouble when the girl fully hit those teen years. She had gotten too good at this too fast.

"Becca," Vanessa said in her sternest voice, determined to let the preteen know she meant business, "take your sister into the other room and help her."

"But—"

"Please, Becca. I need to think."

Luckily, Becca was still young enough not to want an all-out battle. She simply nodded her head, grabbed her sister who was scrambling up the side of the china cabinet, and carried her into the kitchen.

Vanessa breathed a relieved sigh and returned her focus to her current problem. Were those strange memories caused by that over-vivid dream? And if so, was it simply that her brain liked the dream too much to let it go?

Or was something else going on?

Vanessa had always thought that the so-called study that proved women's hormones made it impossible for them to process knowledge was a bunch of gobbledygook. That it was bad science by bad scientists, manipulated to back up even worse laws.

Now Vanessa was worried. Her brain seemed to have slipped a cog or two. She had to wonder if her foray into education had created a perfect storm of chaos in her brain that refused to be calmed.

It was a sobering thought, especially since she had never felt the least bit stressed. In fact, she had always enjoyed those opportunities when she could share in her husband's studies. It had made her feel alive and useful, rejuvenated, ready to take on the world.

But now she was worried. Had she poured so much into her brain that it had overloaded? Was her brain experiencing one of those critical meltdowns that everyone feared?

Or was there a scenario that made it logical for her to have memories that were foreign to other people?

Now Vanessa was in a real predicament. In order to figure out what was going on in her head, she needed to do some heavy thinking. But if science was correct, it was the heavy thinking that had created the problem in the first place.

What a mess! As her brain tiptoed around the convoluted logic, the unmistakable sounds of an imminent battle began to register. The kitchen seemed to be quickly turning into a war zone.

"My bear. My birfday present!" Vanessa heard her youngest yell in frustration.

"You got Miranda the Panda for your birthday," Vanessa's oldest replied with more calmness than could reasonably be expected. Dealing with an irate four-year-old was a challenge most adults avoided, yet Becca remained unfazed. When had she gotten so mature?

"Not that birfday! Other one!" Audrey yelled, punctuating her words with a foot stomp.

Vanessa's motherly instinct kicked in and her own problems were instantly forgotten. Audrey's temper rarely flared. If she was stomping her foot that meant she was in deep distress. Vanessa tiptoed to the doorway to listen, ready to jump in at a moment's notice.

"Maddie." Becca turned to address her closest sister, who was painting her fingernails at the kitchen table. "Will you please tell your little sister she doesn't have a koala?"

"You don't have a koala," eleven-year-old Maddie complied calmly. So calm, in fact, that she

115

didn't even look up from the mini masterpieces she was busy creating at the end of her fingertips.

"Axshully, you didn't get any toy animals for your other birthdays," eight-year-old Zoe piped in, always ready to put in her two cents. "I remember because I've wanted a toy dog for years, but didn't get it. I was hoping you would, but you didn't either."

Becca looked at Zoe and blinked a few times, which encouraged Zoe to throw in another tidbit.

"I still want the toy dog, you know," Zoe said hopefully. "Maybe for my next birthday?"

"Not this birfday," Audrey said with a stomp, "the other one."

"My next—" Zoe began, but was stopped by Becca.

"She's talking about her own birthday," Becca reminded Zoe. Then she turned back to her youngest sister.

"What other one?" Becca asked calmly. "You've only had four."

"The birfday before. Mommy put on the big black dress and punny hat."

"Mom doesn't like black dresses, and I've never

seen her wear a funny hat," Becca said patiently.

"Memember? A man in a dress gave her a box with a piece of paper in it."

"A man in a dress? Audrey!" Becca seemed to lose a little of her patience and couldn't help rolling her eyes.

"It was like Mommy's! Mommy was so happy. She pramed the paper and put it on the wall."

"Sounds like a crazy dream to me," Maddie said as she scrutinized her nails.

"In her bedroom," Audrey continued stubbornly.

"You and I know it was a dream. But how do we convince her?" Becca sighed at the thought of having to explain dreams to a stubborn four-year-old.

Becca shook her head at her younger sister. Audrey was usually a happy child, but that didn't stop that mile-wide stubborn streak. Once she set her mind to something, it was never easy to convince her to change it. And her mind was dead set on that imaginary koala.

"Memember!" Audrey commanded. "Mommy said we should cellbrate her gradashun. She got us ice cream. I had chocolate."

Vanessa almost fainted and had to grab the wall for support. She stumbled over to the couch and plopped down on it so her children wouldn't have to scrape her off the floor.

That memory, the one Audrey had just described, was one of her favorites. But it wasn't real. It belonged on the crazy dream team.

Which made no sense. It was impossible for Audrey to know anything about that memory. Audrey had no access to Vanessa's dreams.

Unless—

Vanessa gulped as logic did a U-turn and drove home the only possibility. The memories had to be real. They were not just the product of an overactive imagination.

She was flabbergasted, shocked, surprised even. She needed answers. She needed—

The Internet. Someone, somewhere, must have written about this very phenomenon. All she needed to do was a quick Internet search and she'd have the answers she needed, or at least an answer. The Internet was built to research quirky questions.

"Becca," Vanessa had to call rather loudly since the noise from the kitchen hadn't gotten any quieter, "go get my laptop out of the bedroom."

"Your what?"

Vanessa could tell that the teen years were not going to be fun. Becca had a perfectly straight face. She was entirely too good at acting like she didn't understand.

"My laptop, you know, shaped like a skinny book, electric, connects us to the World Wide Web."

Becca continued to look at her mother like she was speaking a foreign language.

"Becca," Vanessa said sternly, "go! Now!"

"Mom, I don't—"

"Fine. Be a teen. Maddie, go to my room and bring me my computer. I need to do research."

"Mom, I—"

"Maddie, get the laptop so I can do some research. Now. Don't give me any flack. You're too young to become a teen yet. I've got at least a year before you can start all this. Go do as I say without another word."

Maddie looked at Vanessa for a few seconds, her face blank as she quickly thought through her options. Then she grabbed Becca's arm and pulled her to the bedroom.

Good. Maddie would talk some sense
into her older sister. Peer pressure would be a great
tool to encourage Becca to behave.

The girls were gone about five minutes. When
they returned, both were loaded down with books
of all kinds.

"Very funny, girls!" Vanessa forced a smile. "But
I'm serious. I need to do research. Bring me my
laptop."

Becca plopped her pile of books onto a chair and
moved to the right of her mother. She placed her
hand gently on Vanessa's shoulder. Maddie put her
pile onto the coffee table and moved to the left,
mirroring her sister.

"Mom." Becca's face was more serious than
Vanessa had ever seen. "We love you, and we're
worried about you."

"We'll help you do whatever research you want.
We brought you the books you wanted, the ones
you can put on top of your lap."

Vanessa's brain must have been doing some
heavy-duty sorting, because suddenly it all clicked
into place. The truth slammed into her like a freight
train.

Timelines. She had memories from two different timelines. In this timeline, computers had not been invented. There were no laptops, no Internet, no online databases.

Her sweet, sweet daughters were not being sassy, disrespectful, or teenagery.

They were trying to keep a crazy mom happy — and calm.

They were doing whatever they could to get for her whatever she wanted, even if what she wanted did not exist.

Three cups of coffee (for the caffeine-addicted adult), twelve hot chocolates with miniature marshmallows (three apiece for each of the girls), and one boo-boo later (Audrey climbed on top of the refrigerator, and when Vanessa pulled her down she accidently bumped the little monkey's head on the cabinet), Vanessa finally had it all figured out.

It was about time travel. It had to be.

At first Vanessa couldn't figure out why Audrey also had the extra set of memories, until she remembered that according to those other memories, the child had also traveled through time, before she was even born. Vanessa had been pregnant with baby Audrey while she zipped back and forth between the present and the future. So whatever had happened to Vanessa to retain memories from the other timeline had also happened to Audrey.

Did that mean that Audrey also had dreams about time travel?

Just as she was trying to imagine what a time travel dream of a four-year-old would look like, the *trill* of the phone broke into her thoughts and she jumped up to answer.

She was on the phone for less than a minute, but it changed her whole life.

The call was from the hospital informing her that Tony's injuries had been worse than they had realized. Unknown to them, he had had extensive internal bleeding. They regretted to inform her that Tony had slipped away.

Vanessa's husband, the father of her children, the love of her life, was gone.

The shock of it was too much for her brain to handle so she did what any self-respecting woman would do when she got this big of a shock. She blacked out.

The next thing she knew she was on the couch. Becca was fluffing a pillow behind her head, Audrey was on her lap watching Zoe pat her cheeks, and Maddie was in her face saying, "Mommy, Mom, Mama," over and over again.

It took quite a few minutes for Vanessa to convince her children that she was okay. Then it took several more to get the older ones to take the younger ones into the other room to play. Becca and Maddie were old enough to know that something serious was going on. They were past the age where their mother could play off bad news like it was nothing important.

But Vanessa wasn't ready to tell her children that their father was dead. Not when she had that other set of memories where he was alive and well.

No, this was not the way it was meant to be. So much was wrong.

Vanessa needed to think. And not the type of thinking that was expected of women in this timeline. She needed to bury herself so deep in thought that an earthquake wouldn't register.

She made a fourth cup of coffee and dumped in a spoon of the powdered hot chocolate she usually kept for the girls. She wanted the extra *oomph* the chocolate would give her. Then she took her sweetened drink to the couch to dig in and figure out what she should do next.

The answer hit her before her rear end hit the couch. There was no need for deep thought. It was so obvious she was surprised she even had to make coffee.

A trip down memory lane was in order, or at least the part of it that would lead to the future. Vanessa needed to go back to the time and place she had visited while pregnant with Audrey, the place called the Department of Temporal Adjustment, that lovely department of the future that was charged with handling all travel through time. She'd have to find that nice doctor who had told her about what her children were destined to do, and ask him to find the idiot who had been messing with history.

The sooner she got started, the better it would be for everyone. Someone had changed a perfectly good timeline and destroyed her life, and most likely the lives of countless others.

And once the good doctor figured out the idiot's name, Vanessa wasn't going to wait around while some bureaucratic department formed a committee and wasted time deciding how, and if, it should be fixed.

Vanessa would take matters into her own hands. She would be the woman she was meant to be, the one she was in the other timeline. She knew she could do it. She had memories to prove she wasn't afraid of a little adventure.

Vanessa would fix things, restore history, and get her husband back.

Just let anyone, from any timeline, try to stop her.

Chapter 10

DECIDING THAT SOMETHING NEEDS to be done and doing it are two very different things.

But Vanessa had always been a good planner, even before she remembered that she had a brain. So the first thing she did was to work out each and every step she needed to make during her jaunt to the future.

Vanessa thought through scenarios, made contingency plans, searched for possible roadblocks, and listed everything that had even the slightest chance to go wrong.

Her result was a plan book that rivaled a couple of classic novels she had once seen on her father's bookshelf. One had been called *Moby Dick*, and the other a *Tale of Two Cities*.

By rivaled, she of course meant in size.

She had no clue about the content of those two books. In the other timeline, Vanessa had no interest in those books. In this timeline, women were allowed to read cookbooks and flip through magazines about fashion. Anything else would cause a catastrophic disturbance to the brain.

Vanessa had a little internal laugh about that whole catastrophic disturbance nonsense. She couldn't help herself. Those memories she had access to, the ones from the other timeline, made it abundantly clear that education did nothing to harm anyone's brain, male or female.

So now, after several hours of dangerously deep thinking, Vanessa's plans were made. Every contingency was accounted for except for one. She had no clue what she should do with her children. The thought of taking them on such a potentially dangerous journey did not appeal to her in the least. But she couldn't leave them alone. What if she traveled to the future and failed to fix history? And what if for some unforeseen reason, she was unable to get back to them? Her children would be alone and unprotected.

The problem was that while her husband was in

school they had been living in student family housing, far from friends and family. They were in a strange place among strange people. They had been here less than a month, not nearly enough time for Vanessa to know who could be trusted with her precious children.

So she shivered at the thought of taking her children with her on such a dangerous journey. Then she shivered even harder at the thought of leaving them behind.

Vanessa's brain and heart battled back and forth for several moments until her brain conceded defeat. Stubborn as it was, it knew that her only true option was to take her children with her.

Because while there was a chance that traveling though time might prove dangerous for her little monkeys, it was certain that leaving them behind would put them in danger.

Another shiver ran through Vanessa's body as she thought of what might happen to her children if she left them unprotected as she traipsed through time. The world was not a safe place for young girls. They'd be alone and vulnerable, prey to—

Her brain nearly shut down as images from news stories flashed through her head. Picture after picture of girls—just like her daughters, only broken and lifeless—whose parents had been unable to protect them from the many evils lurking in the world. It terrified Vanessa to know that her children had only her around to defend them.

But Vanessa could not go there, not now. She needed to remain strong and push away the grief. She would get Tony back. She had to. The alternative was too painful to think about.

"Mommy, can we go visit Daddy soon?" Zoe's voice asked, very, very loudly, in her ear.

When a person is so deep in thought that she's forgotten what zip code she lives in, there's nothing, absolutely nothing, like a yell in the ear to jolt her back to the present. It's an invigorating experience, but one that Vanessa would not recommend to the faint-hearted.

So startled was Vanessa that she jumped about a mile and a quarter, all while flailing her arms about like a demented octopus. Some mommy instinct must have been in play because she managed to refrain from hitting Zoe, but her coffee cup, still half full of lukewarm chocolate coffee, went flying across the living room in a beautiful arc that would have made any quarterback proud.

"I caught it, Mommy!" Maddie called from across the room.

Vanessa reeled in her flapping arms and convinced her shaky legs to bend. As she resumed her perch on the couch, she took a look around. Across the room her star receiver, Maddie, had the coffee cup in her left hand while she licked the sticky chocolate that had splashed down her right arm. Becca was smiling at Vanessa from the middle of the room, where she sat with Audrey in her lap. Audrey, crayon in hand, was happily adding roads and rivers to a book of maps.

"How long have you girls been in here?" Vanessa's heart was still pounding so loudly she could barely hear herself speak.

"Audrey wanted to watch you. The only way to keep her quiet," Becca replied, hugging her little sister, "was to bring her in here,"

"We've been here hours!" Maddie exclaimed.

"No, days!" Zoe piped in.

"Years!" Maddie said.

"Months!" Zoe countered.

Maddie shook her head. "Years are bigger than months. You need something else. Something bigger."

"Okay," Zoe conceded with a tilt of her head. "What's bigger than years?"

"Well, there are decades, and eons, and—" Becca began, but Vanessa held up her hand to stop the list from growing out of control.

"I get it. You girls have been in here for a while," she said.

Vanessa looked at the window and grimaced. It was already dark. She had spent the entire day planning and plotting and had neglected her children. Now it was time to get out of her head and turn on mommy mode.

"I'm hungry, Mommy!" Audrey jumped up from her sister's lap and ran to place her pudgy little hands on her mother's arm. "Can we have dinner now? Tumbly is mad."

"Mad?"

"She's growling at me," Audrey explained, her face one hundred percent serious.

Vanessa smiled as she reached down and grabbed the munchkin's hand.

"We don't want Tumbly to be mad, do we?"

Audrey crinkled her forehead and shook her head.

"Do you think if we gave Tumbly some food she

would stop being mad?"

The forehead crinkles disappeared at the mention of food.

"Should we cook dinner?"

The crinkles returned as Audrey shook her head.

"You don't want dinner?"

"Tumbly is really, really mad. Dinner takes forever."

"How about cheese toast and soup. Would that make Tumbly happy?"

Audrey put her hand on her belly, as if to ask it a question. A happy smile broke over her face and she nodded enthusiastically.

"How about the rest of you girls? Are you also—"

Directly behind Vanessa a *WHOOSH* of monumental proportions sucked the words she was about to say out of the room along with most of the air.

Vanessa spun around to find her daughters had vanished. They were indeed hungry, and the mention of food had rocketed them into the kitchen so fast that they had created a vacuum in their wake.

With a shrug, Vanessa took Audrey's little hand and together they went to the kitchen. It appeared

that at the moment the most pressing need
was to put food in her children's bellies. Everything
else would have to wait.

As she prepared a quick meal for the hungry
children, her mind continued to work on the details
of the upcoming journey. Her first obstacle was the
trip to the portal. In order to get there, she would
need to find transportation to the university
campus, as well as appropriate disguises.

They certainly wouldn't get very far dressed as
they were. Every article of clothing they wore
screamed femininity.

Vanessa opened a can of tomato soup, poured it
into a pan with milk, and slowly stirred its creamy
depths as she inspected her options.

The inspection didn't take very long, since as far
as she could tell, there was only one. She and her
daughters needed to pretend to be something that
they weren't—males. If they were caught, the
punishment would be severe.

But there was no way around it. Under the guise
of being pampered and protected, women were
restricted by both law and culture.

Freedom, the kind they needed to reach the
campus, was only available to the male population.

So she needed to become a man. On the outside, at least.

Heck. They should all become their male counterparts. It was about time her daughters learned that there was more to life than the overly confining strictures they had grown up under.

"Becca, take the cheese toast out of the oven," Vanessa called. "And Maddie, get out the bowls and set the table."

Vanessa watched her daughters follow her orders without question and realized that she was just as bad as the doctor. She was keeping information from her daughters because they might not be able to handle it.

But two of her daughters were old enough, and smart enough—and the two younger ones resilient enough—to handle much more than society gave them credit for.

"Mommy?"

Vanessa turned to find the table set, all four of her hungry children seated, and the soup bubbling over. She quickly grabbed the pan from the stove and dished out the hot soup.

Vanessa sat down at her place and studied each child in turn.

They must have realized that something odd was happening because, hungry as they were, not one of them touched so much as a morsel of food. All eyes were on Vanessa.

"Mommy," Becca asked, worry evident in her voice, "is everything okay?"

"It will be," Vanessa answered with a determined smile. "Or at least, it can be."

Becca and Maddie exchanged confused looks, Zoe stared at her mother with scared eyes, and Audrey dipped her finger into the hot soup before plunging her burnt finger into her mouth.

"Listen, girls, I have a story to tell you."

"Oh, good! I wuv stories! Does it have a princess?" Audrey's face beamed with pleasure at the thought of a princess story.

"No sweetie, there's no princess," Vanessa answered her youngest.

"Does it have a happy ending?" Zoe wanted to know.

"This is a different kind of story," Vanessa explained, hoping that she would be able to explain in a way that wouldn't scare them. "It doesn't have an ending yet."

"No ending?" Maddie questioned, shocked at

the mere thought. "What kind of story doesn't end?"

"It's our story, darling."

"Boring!" Becca scoffed. "I already know our story."

"No, you only *think* you do," Vanessa said firmly. Now was not the time to allow Becca to practice her teenagery attitude. "So dig in and eat your dinner. I have a lot to tell you."

Audrey picked up her toast and took a bite. But Zoe looked unsure, and Becca and Maddie were sending silent messages to each other with their eyes.

"Eat!" Vanessa ordered. "I want your tummies happy so you can focus on what I'm about to tell you."

"My tumbly's already happy, Mommy. She likes cheese toast," Audrey said.

"Don't talk with your mouth full, Audrey."

"Yes, Mommy," Audrey tried to reply. But the noises that came out were barely recognizable as words since her mouth was closed tight so Vanessa wouldn't see that it was still full of cheese toast.

All of a sudden Becca's eyes grew to the size of saucers and she went pale. She turned anguished eyes toward her mother.

"Becca? Are you okay?"

"Oh, Mom!" Becca said, panic just below the surface. "Am I adopted?"

"You are not adopted."

"What about me?" Maddie asked quickly. "Am I adopted?"

"None of you are adopted," Vanessa reassured her children. Not that the youngest even cared. She was too busy scarfing down her food.

Vanessa glanced at Zoe to see how she was doing. She probably hadn't even heard the exchange about adoption, she was so focused on Audrey's antics with her food. After Audrey enjoyed a particularly loud slurp of soup, Zoe, fascinated, took an equally loud slurp.

Two on their way to full bellies, and two to go.

"Please Becca, Maddie, eat."

Becca and Maddie looked at each other, nodded, and each took a bite of cheese toast. Their timing was so perfect that it was as if Vanessa had just watched the birth of a new sport—synchronized eating.

"Good," she sighed. "I've got a lot to tell you."

Vanessa started talking, and kept talking.

She told them about the other timeline, and continued to talk through the unbelieving guffaws of her two oldest daughters.

She spilled the beans about her previous adventures in time travel, and ignored it when Maddie and Becca rolled their eyes in disbelief.

Vanessa even kept talking when Audrey, bored by the princess-less story, decided to explore the cabinets above the refrigerator. Vanessa never let her mouth stop moving as she climbed a step stool, grabbed the little monkey out of her hiding place, and set her safely on the floor.

It was a lot of talking. More talking than she had ever done before. But it was no more than was necessary to explain time travel to her four children.

Becca and Maddie were simply humoring their mom until she finally gathered the courage to blurt out that in this timeline, their father had died. As the words left her mouth Becca and Maddie both blanched so white that Vanessa feared they would faint. The next hour was full of tears and more questions than could be answered by a full set of encyclopedias.

When the final tear was shed and all the emotion had been drained, Vanessa got the surprise of her life. It seemed that Becca had a much more logical mind than she had ever been given credit for.

Becca had thought through the whole Koala Toala episode and had come up with her own theory. Once she stopped fighting it, her brain naturally accepted the existence of time travel and she easily grasped its complexities.

After Becca accepted it, Maddie soon followed suit. Zoe would do whatever her older sisters wanted, and Audrey, at four, was just along for the ride.

Vanessa had to admit that having her daughters in on the action, having them available to help with the brainstorming, certainly made things easier. She would have never remembered that a neighbor down the street had several sons of varying ages, or that they were lazy in nature and tended to leave their wash out on the line overnight.

It has been said that the true depth of a person's character only becomes visible when she is tested. That certainly was true with Vanessa's children. She would have hesitated to sneak out to steal five sets of clothing, but Zoe and Maddie thought it an adventure.

They went to bed that night not as a family overcome by grief because they had just lost a well-loved father, but as a close-knit team of warriors who were prepared to fight to regain what was rightfully theirs.

After a full night's sleep, Vanessa spent several hours cutting hair, packing food into a backpack, and talking a shady neighbor into letting her borrow one of the many cars he had parked in his backyard.

Sure, he thought that Tony would be doing the driving, but what he didn't know couldn't hurt him.

Vanessa was proud of her daughters. They had shown real fortitude in a challenging situation and they had displayed more intelligence than she had given them credit for, in either timeline.

Even little Audrey caught on that what they were about to do was important. She was on her best behavior and Vanessa only had to scrape her off from the top of the china cabinet once. It was a new record around their house.

Chapter 11

"NO!" VANESSA YELLED. "PLEASE! You must listen to me."

Yelling was not something Vanessa did often, but what choice did she have when the white-coated men who surrounded her little family were laughing so hard they drowned out all other sound?

It had been a you-can't-win-for-losing type of day. One frustrating experience after another, and when Vanessa and her children finally made it to the DTA lab, nothing she said or did seemed to make the scientists take her seriously.

It reminded her of a day Tony had told her about. He had gotten to work late because of traffic but was relieved to find that there was still one vacant parking spot left in the lot. It was only after he'd pulled into it that he realized that it was a visitor spot with a two-hour limit. Which wouldn't work very well since he knew he'd be at work at least eight.

Tony was an easy-going guy so he shrugged and made plans to find another spot later in the day. After he had finished that important presentation he was supposed to give in front of his entire team, which included the big boss.

The presentation could be a career changer, if he did a good enough job. Problem was that the oh-so-important career-changing opportunity was scheduled to happen in a mere five minutes.

So he gathered the gigantic armload of papers he'd spent hours preparing and headed to the building. Arms full, he maneuvered to open the door. He'd done the maneuver a million times, only since it was one of those days, something snagged on his coffee cup and over it went, right onto all the papers and his previously pristine white shirt.

Tony found it was rather difficult to make the

right kind of impression with soggy handouts and a splotchy shirt.

For Vanessa, the first inkling it was going to be one of those days happened before she even had the chance to leave home. At the very last possible moment, her shady neighbor backed out of letting her borrow the car. She had just taken the keys from him when she was hit by a sudden memory of driving cross-country, the wind blowing through her hair and music blaring from the radio.

It was, of course, a memory from the other timeline, and it reminded her how much fun driving a car could be.

A laser beam of excitement must have shot out of her eyes and sliced through the neighbor's usual self-centered attitude because before Vanessa could open her mouth to thank the man, his demeanor changed.

He snatched the keys out of Vanessa's hand so fast that she was honestly impressed.

"What's the deal here?" he growled.

He must have suspected that she planned to drive, and that suspicion had activated every latent sexist bone in his body. Unprincipled he might be, but not enough to let a lowly woman drive his precious car.

One minute he was a disreputable rule-bender whose main goal in life was to be left alone to do whatever he wanted to do, and the next he was a self-righteous citizen, enraged that a mere woman had the audacity to use his car to break the law.

Vanessa opened her mouth to allay his fears, to convince him that she was perfectly capable of driving a car. But the look on his face made her snap her mouth shut without uttering a single word. It would have been pointless.

Several weeks earlier, she had taken the girls on an outing to the zoo and her attention had been drawn to a man in the snake house. Crowds of people moved around him but he took no notice. He simply stood staring, mesmerized by the snakes.

At first she had assumed that snakes were his favorite creatures, until one of the slithery creatures moved toward the glass and the man shivered as he took a quick step back. That was when Vanessa looked closer and realized distrust and loathing were the basis for his fascination.

Vanessa's neighbor had the same look on his face, as if she were a deadly creature that needed to be locked up in a glass case for the good of mankind.

No, the only way this neighbor was going to give up one of his cars was if he could place the keys in Tony's hand himself. He trusted her about as much as he would trust a snake with his pet rabbit.

"Come on, girls. It seems our plans have changed." Vanessa herded her daughters back home as the neighbor stomped away. She pasted a smile on her face and shrugged.

So the car was out and public transportation was too risky. As much as Vanessa disliked the notion, their only option was to walk.

It was two miles to their destination. But with children, even two miles could be undoable. Becca and Maddie were old enough and reliable enough that they would have no problem with that distance. Zoe and Audrey…well, they were another story altogether.

It turned out that Zoe was a good hiker and could have tackled a much longer distance. Audrey, on the other hand, was not.

Audrey began the two-mile long trek hopping and skipping, as was her habit. But after ten minutes she suddenly decided that she was too sleepy to continue and lay down on the sidewalk for a nap. Becca, Maddie, and Vanessa each took turns carrying her on their backs the rest of the way while she snored gently in their ears.

Four-year-olds were sweet, funny, and one hundred percent self-centered. They were also nearly impossible to reason with, so Vanessa always picked her battles carefully. It was better to hunker down in this stage of the journey and wait it out rather than to try to understand the bewildering logic that rules the narcissistic little world of a four-year-old.

So on they trudged, the sound of their footsteps punctuated by snores. Vanessa's daughters shuffled along at her side, too afraid to make a sound, their shoulders hunched in fear. They were true products of their culture—little mice, scared to do more than scramble for cover at the first sign of danger.

But children are adaptable creatures, even girl children.

They passed a group of boys wrestling on the ground like a squirmy pile of puppies. To Vanessa it was obvious they were entertaining themselves as they waited for the school bus, but her daughters cringed and scurried away, intimidated by this

146

public display of rambunctiousness.

But Vanessa noticed Maddie turn to look back at the boys several times. And when one boy pinned another and whooped in joy, Maddie couldn't help but smile.

Several blocks later they came across a second group of boys, also waiting for a bus. But instead of wrestling these boys had chosen to kick a soccer ball around. It got away from one of them and rolled over to Maddie, who kicked it back without thinking.

"Good one," the boy yelled. "Want to play?"

"Mom?"

Vanessa nearly laughed aloud when she saw the strange combination of fear and wonder on Maddie's face. She motioned Becca to give her Audrey. Becca looked like the extra weight of her sister was getting to her.

"Mom?" Maddie looked so hopeful, but Vanessa knew her daughter could never pull off being a boy for very long. She was sure to giggle, or some other feminine thing, and then they'd be caught. Best to keep on the move.

"Sorry darling. Maybe later."

Maddie's shoulders slumped and she shook her

head at the boy, who gave her a wave and went back to his friends to practice passes.

"I've always wanted to play," Maddie sighed. "Usually they act like I'm not even there." She looked down at her clothing. "I guess they thought I was a boy."

"Well, you're not," Becca said sternly as she stretched out her shoulders. "But I'll kick the ball around with you when we get back home."

"Thanks, but it's not the same. You don't even like to play, and you're not very good."

"But I'm all you've got."

"Maybe—"

"You know they won't play with a girl." Becca assumed the Wonder Woman stance, which she could do now that she didn't have extra weight on her back.

"I could dress like a boy."

"But you're still a girl."

"They wouldn't know."

"It's just a silly game."

"I really like soccer."

"If you get caught"—Becca pulled her shoulders back even further—"they might lock you up."

"They should let girls play too!"

"Boys don't like it when girls don't act like girls."

"I just want to play soccer!"

Becca relaxed her superhero pose and placed a hand on each of Maddie's shoulders. "Girls don't play soccer," she said softly. "Girls watch soccer."

"I know." Maddie turned forlorn eyes to her mother. "Why'd I have to be born a girl? Girls don't get to do anything!"

The pain in Maddie's eyes was too much for Vanessa. She used one arm to support the sleeping child on her back and held out her other arm to Maddie, who ran to her. Zoe, who had been studying a rock, saw Maddie's heartbroken tears and ran to join in. Becca tried to keep her distance, but the sight of her sisters' tears was too much for her and soon she was blubbering with the best of them.

Vanessa hated that her daughters had been raised in a world where men ruled and women obeyed. Brainwashed from birth into thinking they were lesser creatures, taught their whole lives that they must quash their dreams and settle for whatever crumbs society might toss their way.

Vanessa mourned the lost world of that other

timeline. So much potential—the intelligence and creativity of more than half the population—discarded like trash.

What a waste!

The world was broken, and no one even knew it.

Except for Vanessa. So it was up to her to fix it. She would do whatever it took to restore balance to the world so all that dormant talent, including that of her children, would not be wasted.

And when the world was restored, that whole mistake that took Tony from her would never have happened.

It was a daunting task, but it didn't scare her. Well, maybe a little. But what's a little fear when the fate of womankind, and therefore humankind, was on the line?

About halfway to the university, Vanessa began to silently thank her jerk of a neighbor for making them walk. If they had driven to the portal, her daughters would never have been forced to dress as boys, and they might not have noticed how much freedom men claimed as their right.

It was a mind-blowing revelation for her daughters.

Here they were, strolling down the street, and

not a single person questioned their right
to be there. No one asked where they thought they
were going. No one treated them as second-class
citizens.

It was an empowering experience.

Everything went smoothly...until they hit
campus. That's when things got a little dicey.
Vanessa's fascination with the other timeline had
caused her to forget the presence of the military
camped out in the quad. They walked right into an
encampment before they realized it was there.

Luckily, Becca and Maddie were thoroughly
enjoying their "undercover disguise" and strutted
around like they owned the world. Without
hesitation they befriended one of the younger
soldiers and convinced him to show them the way
to their destination. Having one of the soldiers
along made moving through campus a breeze.

As Vanessa stepped into the basement of Denny
Hall, she felt like she was home. It was the strangest
sensation, but as soon as Vanessa walked through
the door, she knew it was exactly where she was
meant to be. She belonged in that musty basement
the way only someone who had spent a lot of time
in the place could belong. She knew, without a

doubt, this this was her home away from home.

The last smidge of doubt, a tiny sliver that had splintered away and embedded itself in the corner of her mind waiting to fester, didn't stand a chance. Even if she had not already known that this timeline was wonky, the feeling of rightness she got from Denny Hall would have told her. After all, how could she feel so at home in a place where she was forbidden to be, if all was well with the world?

After a sigh of relief she herded her daughters to the portal door and told them to step inside. Becca and Maddie balked and looked so horrified that Vanessa knew they suspected she had gone crazy. Which made sense since she was asking them to step into a janitor's closet. But after a few nudges the family joined hands and stepped through the portal into the future.

Vanessa had such high hopes for the future. And why shouldn't she? She had been raised on such platitudes as "Time heals all," "Good things come to those who wait," and "Human nature is inherently good."

So Vanessa dragged her daughters through that portal fully expecting to be welcomed with open arms as full-fledged, thinking humans.

Surely enough time would have passed so that the convoluted mess that had created a world where a full half the population was treated as half-people would have been fixed.

So much for expectations. Instead of one of the good platitudes, Vanessa found herself embroiled in the one that warned, "Out of the frying pan and into the fire."

Not that she'd fully appreciated that particular saying before. Until she found that the problems she faced getting to the portal were nothing compared to the ones she and her daughters faced after stepping through it.

It certainly felt like they had landed in the fire when the portal plopped them unceremoniously onto the floor of the lab. They landed in a pile, with Vanessa on the bottom. As they struggled to unravel themselves, they were surrounded by a group of about twenty men who obviously thought they were the funniest things they had ever seen.

"Ignore them, they're just being rude," Vanessa had whispered to her children. "Zoe, if you put your leg through here, I think Becca can free her arm." How they had managed to get twisted together in such an unusual manner Vanessa couldn't fathom.

After a few final twists and pulls, Vanessa and her daughters separated their limbs. She took a moment to look over each of her daughters to make sure they were okay. Everyone was unharmed, and Audrey had slept through the entire thing.

Audrey could sleep through practically anything, even the raucous laughter of the uncouth men who surrounded Vanessa's family.

Vanessa's children currently lived an over-structured existence that would never allow them to grow to their full potential. The only way to counteract that was to allow them to experience a multitude of new situations, ones that would expand their horizons and teach them that there was more to the world than their own little corner.

This was not one of them.

Vanessa remembered the other timeline well, and the future that went with it. Those people had had their act together. They were professional, and skilled, and could be counted on to fix whatever was wrong with the timeline.

Not at all like this howling group of baboons.

Vanessa, tired of all the nonsense, decided to

hunt for the head baboon.

She spotted a man slightly to the side who had an air of authority about him. As she took a step toward him the group quieted, as if waiting to see what was next.

"Hello, my name—"

But she got no further. The entire group exploded in laughter so loud that it actually woke Audrey. The startled child rubbed her eyes with her little fists and looked around in confusion.

"That's great! Funniest thing I've heard in years," a man with reddish hair said between guffaws.

"His voice—it's so high and squeaky!" another man chortled.

High and squeaky? These men acted like they had never heard a woman speak.

"They're so little," a man said as he poked Vanessa's shoulder. "Do you think they're actually human?"

Vanessa jerked her shoulder away from the man's finger. She had spent hours planning every detail to get to the DTA, only to have these scientists treat her and her daughters like they were performing monkeys hired to entertain at a birthday party.

"Probably Russian. I heard they were having trouble with their tech."

"Yeah, but this?" Again the man's finger approached Vanessa, but this time he refrained from touching her.

It was obvious something catastrophic must have taken place between Vanessa's time and this one.

"Think they know English?"

Vanessa opened her mouth to prove she knew English—

"Nah. Russians don't speak English."

—But closed it with a snap. Would it be to her benefit to pretend to be Russian? Would it make the scientists accept her and her daughters?

"Can't be human," a man yelled from the back of the group. "Look at their heads. Too small for fully functioning brains."

"I thought it was agreed that rejects were to be destroyed immediately," another man yelled.

"Yeah," a man in the front row agreed, "we have to protect the gene pool from contaminants."

"Who sent them here?" a voice yelled.

"Is this a Russian attack?"

Suddenly every scientist in the group seemed to be jumping around and yelling, which only helped to reinforce Vanessa's view that they were a bunch of baboons.

Vanessa looked at her daughters. Audrey was perched on her oldest sister's back, her eyes wide with fear and her little hand holding tightly to her sister's ear. Becca's face was pinched and worried. Maddie and Zoe had closed ranks to toss eye spears at the men who continued to yell and point at them. The two middle girls didn't look so much scared as mad as hornets.

As Vanessa watched, Maddie's eyes narrowed to mere slits and her face suffused with red, both signs that a loud, violent, earsplitting tantrum was imminent.

Vanessa stepped to Maddie's side. It had taken years of consistent work to teach her child how to control her emotions. Vanessa had no intention of letting all that hard work go to waste simply because a group of fools had no manners.

A hand touched Maddie's shoulder and she turned, ready to attack whoever dared to touch her. But the hand on her shoulder belonged to her mother, and as their eyes met a message came through loud and clear. Maddie was not alone. Whatever troubles came her way, Maddie had her family by her side. They would stick together no matter what.

Maddie closed her eyes for a second as she drew in a deep breath, then she smiled at her mother. Her eyes, calm and steady, told Vanessa everything she needed to know.

Tantrum averted, Vanessa turned her attention back to the problem at hand. She must somehow convince this group that the "Russian rejects" were intelligent human beings that might have a thing or two worthwhile to say.

A brilliant idea sprang into Vanessa's head, probably sparked by the threat of a tantrum. She needed to do something that would have the opposite effect of a tantrum. Something that brought people together, gave them good feelings.

Music had that power. It inspired, elicited feelings, and had the ability to bring people together like nothing else. So if she sang a song, any song, she should be able to get through to these people. Prove to them that they were not "Russian rejects"—whatever that was—but normal people, just like them.

Not that it would be easy. Vanessa
never sang in public. Ever. Her voice might not be
the screechy, fingernails-on-a-chalkboard type, but
it still wasn't particularly good.

But if her daughters could act like cocky young
men to get help from a soldier, she could sing.

It turned out to be much easier than she had
expected.

Vanessa started by walking up to the baboon
king and tapping him on the shoulder. He turned a
surprised face to her and several of the men
stopped shouting to look her way.

So she sang. She would have liked to say that she
choose a song full of passion and angst that was
sure to pull at the heartstrings. But Vanessa was too
nervous to spend much time thinking through her
choices. She sang the first song that came to her
head, which happened to be from a Disney movie.
She closed her eyes and poured her soul into a song
that talked about flapping her fins and how much
she wished she could live on land.

Halfway through the song she felt a touch on her
hip and she looked down to see her daughters had
moved in close to her, seemingly enthralled by the
spectacle of their mother belting out a mermaid

tune in the midst of an angry mob.

Vanessa continued to sing as she shifted her gaze to the crowd around her. There was not an angry face in sight, only confused and worried ones. Two men in front were whispering as they pointed in her direction. Several others fidgeted uncomfortably as they watched her performance.

She had gotten their attention, without a doubt. But had she proven anything?

The high-pitched treble of a child's voice broke into her thoughts and Vanessa realized she was no longer singing solo. Audrey had climbed down from Becca's back and now stood on her own two feet, pouring every bit of her four-year-old being into the song.

Mother and daughter finished strong side-by-side, eyes closed and heads thrown back.

Vanessa grabbed Audrey for a hug before she looked around to see the effect of the song.

"Where'd everybody go?" she asked.

While she was pouring her heart out in song, her audience had quietly deserted her. Vanessa and her daughters were alone.

It was too much. The dam broke and out poured frustration, grief, and fear in a flood of tears that still fell short of matching the horrific day.

Blinded by the waterfall as she was, she could still feel the little hands of her daughters as they patted her back in an effort to console her. Even in her anguished state, she had just enough wits about her to count hands.

A mental picture of Tony playing catch with Zoe flashed through her mind, immediately followed by a pain in her heart so intense it brought shivers to her body. Her daughters must have felt that shiver because the pats stopped and they wrapped their arms around her instead. Then one pair of arms disappeared.

Before she could stop blubbering long enough to check on her missing child, all the arms let go as a much larger hand took her arm and led her away. She brushed frantically at her eyes. She needed to know what was going on. But nothing could stop the wall of water that continued to pour from her. All the world was a blur.

Vanessa should have known that holding back her emotions was a mistake. But this breakdown came as a total surprise to her. She'd been overwhelmed by emotion before; the problem was the broad range in such a short amount of time.

Fear, anger, hope, and despair—all in the matter of a few short minutes.

So instead of navigating a river of tears, she was drowning in an ocean of sobs. It was full tidal wave mode. Only time could calm the tsunami.

Before she knew what happened she was seated in a chair with a cup of cool water in her hands.

The first gulp of the water helped Vanessa tone her wails down to mere sobs, the second calmed her shivers, and by the time she got to the bottom of the cup, her sniffles were under control.

As she swallowed the last drop, her overabundance of emotion drained away, leaving exhaustion in its place. Total, bone deep, inescapable fatigue. So deep was the weariness that Vanessa would have given her bottom right molar for a quiet place where she could curl up in a ball and sleep. Until the whole nightmare was over.

But there would be no quick trip to the dentist. Vanessa had to dig deep and find the energy she needed—she had a mission, and until it was completed, she had to keep going.

Vanessa gulped back a few extra tears that had hidden in the corners as she turned to the man in a white lab coat standing uncomfortably behind a desk. Surprisingly, it was not the man she had assumed to be in charge, but a very tall man she had never before seen.

"Sir, I—" Her words were interrupted by the biggest, loudest *hiccup* known to mankind.

Vanessa blushed in embarrassment. But she pulled herself together to give it another try. That her body could so rudely gasp for air was not going to stop her mission. The life of her husband was at stake, as well as the wellbeing of every woman on the face of the earth.

"Pardon me!" she managed to say. "I—"

A loud, obnoxious, uncontrollable *hiccup* replaced what should have been well-chosen words.

Vanessa looked at her children. Becca and Maddie had their hands in front of their mouths, most likely to cover smiles. The two little ones were giggling like an invisible tickle monster was on the prowl. She turned back to the man to try again.

"Last time—"

Hiccup.

"I was here—"

Hiccup.

The man's discomfort increased with each of her

hiccups, and if the look in his eye was any indication, he fully intended to bolt. She needed to keep his attention and make him understand.

But she was practically voiceless. Vanessa's body refused to let her get a coherent sentence out. If she didn't do something soon, this man, the only person she'd seen here in the future with a smidge of empathy, would leave. And with him would go their chance of getting help from people who actually know about time travel.

It was a gamble, but as far as she could see, her only option was her children. So she speared the two oldest with her eyes until their hands dropped and she knew they were paying attention.

"Becca—"

Hiccup.

"Maddie—"

Hiccup.

The hands jumped back up to their mouths and both girls broke out in giggles.

"Important—"

Hiccup.

If anything, the giggles got louder.

"Your dad—"

Hiccup.

At the mention of their dad, the giggle brigade lost the desire to laugh. Maddie and Becca exchanged a look, a nod, and then gave Vanessa their full attention.

"Please tell—"

Hiccup.

"—Dr. White Coat here—"

Hiccup.

"—about me and the p—"

Hiccup.

"—the portal."

They did a surprisingly good job of explaining.

Vanessa didn't know how they did it. They had no memory of the other timeline, yet they were calm, poised, thorough, and very organized.

They certainly did not come across as uneducated females. If she didn't know they were eleven and twelve years old, even she might be excused for judging their ages as much older, they were so composed.

So surprised was Vanessa by how put-together her own children were that it was only the continued presence of hiccups that kept her mouth from hanging open. She turned to see the man's reaction to her daughters' narrative.

His mouth was hanging open. Until he saw Vanessa looking at him and he snapped it shut.

"So you see," Becca concluded, "someone has been very busy changing the timeline. And they've done such a horrible job of it that every person on the planet has been adversely affected."

"Adversely affected," Dr. White Coat repeated under his breath. He looked at Becca like she was an alien from outer space.

"We have to fix time," Maddie added. "We have to put things back the way they should be."

"Fix time," he muttered as he scrutinized Maddie's forehead for evidence of alien antennas.

"Back to how it should be," Maddie reiterated with a decisive nod.

Dr. White Coat stared for several more seconds at Maddie, who calmly returned his gaze. Then he turned his attention to Becca. Becca, like her sister, maintained complete calm under his scrutiny.

Who were these two young women? Vanessa's daughters were children, mere babies. These young women were mature beyond their years and exuded a level of composure and confidence they'd never been given the chance to develop in the life they'd lived.

Dr. White Coat, whose shoulders had been pulled up so high he looked more like a turtle than a man, suddenly relaxed and gave a loud guffaw.

"Good one!" he yelled as he used his long legs to close the distance to Vanessa.

"You almost got me with this one," he continued with a slap to Vanessa's back so hard it cured her hiccups and sent her staggering. She regained her balance and turned to glare at him as he continued. "Who set me up? Was it George? 'Cause I got him good last week."

"What are you talking about?" Vanessa asked, not even trying to keep the irritation out of her voice.

"This prank," Dr. White Coat answered. He pointed at the girls. "Where did he find these guys? These ones are so little…"

"They're kids. Of course they're little." Vanessa was still so upset she could barely keep her voice at a reasonable level.

Dr. White Coat crinkled his forehead, confused.

"They're my daughters," Vanessa explained. When Dr. White Coat still seemed confused, she couldn't help but roll her eyes. "You know, children. I'm their mother. They're little because they still have some growing up to do."

"Did you say 'mother'?" Dr. White Coat gulped and looked ready to faint when Vanessa nodded her head.

"So you really are from the past? You really did come through the portal?"

Vanessa again nodded her head. Dr. White Coat opened his mouth to speak, but something about Vanessa's face caught his eye. He grabbed her chin and turned her face to look at it from different angles. Vanessa slapped his hand away and glared.

As Dr. White Coat looked from Vanessa to her daughters, he turned so pale he had to lean against the wall to remain upright.

"This is bad," he said. Blood rushed to his face and he sprang away from the wall and began to pace. "Very bad."

"I want Daddy!" Audrey yelled as she balanced precariously halfway up a nearby bookshelf.

"Hush, Audrey," Zoe shushed her sister and pulled her off her perch. "Stay by me."

The man looked quickly at Audrey and Zoe.

"Children—" Dr. White Coat muttered.

He shook his head as he looked at each of them

as the cogs in his brain slowly began to turn and the pieces fall into place.

"Girl children—" he began. But his mouth refused to accept what his brain surmised, so he snapped it shut.

He paced back and forth, his brow crinkled with worry, his long legs making short work of distance. Every so often he would pause to look at Vanessa and her children and shake his head before he continued his journey across the room.

"Maybe I should—" he began after one of these pauses, but whatever he thought he should do, he left unspoken.

Becca opened her mouth to speak, but Vanessa shook her head and put a finger to her own lips. The man needed time and quiet to process all they had told him.

After enough loops around the room to wind up the biggest yo-yo ever imagined, Dr. White Coat paused in front of Vanessa and searched the depths of her soul. Or at least, that's what it felt like to Vanessa as he stared intently into her eyes.

What he saw there must have reassured him, because after what seemed like a lifetime, he gave a decisive nod.

"You have no idea how hard this is to believe," he said.

"I might. I've been through my own version of this, you know," Vanessa replied, thankful that her hiccups had been banished.

"You're female."

"I understand. I grew up in this timeline too."

"No, I don't think you do," he said with a quick shake of his head. "Several hundred years ago— "

He looked at each of them again and turned the sickliest, greenish shade Vanessa had ever seen. Vanessa scanned the room and spotted what looked like a trash can. A useful object to have on hand if Dr. White Coat's stomach was as upset as his face was green.

"The scientists, scientists like me—" Again he stopped mid-sentence. He stumbled to a chair and dropped into it.

Vanessa again eyed the trashcan. It was obvious the man was ill. Rather than wait for him to spew his breakfast all over—

Dr. White Coat grabbed his hair with both hands and groaned. It was not the groan of physical pain, but emotional. So Vanessa, always sympathetic to another's pain, tiptoed the few feet to his chair.

"In one of the timelines I, too, was raised to believe that women were to be protected. That their inferior brains weren't capable of thinking like a man." Vanessa gently put a hand on his shoulder. "I understand."

"No, you don't understand." He jerked his shoulder away from Vanessa's hand and gave her a look with so much anger that she had to take a step back.

"They don't exist!" he yelled.

"Okay." Vanessa employed the same level tone she used when her children were upset. "You are angry at me, why?"

"I'm not angry at you," the man in the white lab coat admitted. His shoulders slumped, either in defeat or anguish.

"The other timeline," he asked, looking up quickly, "the one you say is the right one."

"It *is* the right one. What about it?"

"You said you visited this time in that timeline. Did you see any women?"

"Sure. Plenty of them."

The man in the white coat shivered and his face contorted in pain. Then he straightened his shoulders.

"There are things you need to know. About my time. This time."

"I'm listening."

Dr. White Coat sighed, grabbed his knees with his hands, and stared at them.

"I have to go back several centuries to explain. It was cancer. Everyone was looking for a cure. Everyone wanted a cancer-free world."

"Understandable."

"Scientists discovered the gene that allowed uterine cancer to happen."

"Go on," Vanessa prompted.

"Look, no one knew it would turn out like it did." Dr. White Coat turned pleading eyes to Vanessa. "Scientist just wanted to give every woman a chance to live a long life. They thought they were doing a good thing."

"What did they do?" Vanessa demanded.

"Honestly, they thought they were helping."

"What did they do?" she repeated more sternly.

"Gene therapy. Geneticists used gene therapy to eradicate uterine cancer," he blurted quickly, as if the quicker he said it, the better it would sound. "They modified the gene. It was a huge, world-wide program."

Vanessa blinked rapidly as she let it sink in. Modifying the genes of billions of women was huge. But that still didn't explain what so disturbed the doctor.

"For the first few generations, everything was great. Until the female babies started being born mute," Dr. White Coat continued, shifting his eyes again to his knees. "Scientists tried to reverse it, but everything they did made things worse."

"That's horrible! Women lost the ability to speak? All of them?"

"Worse. Fewer and fewer females started being born. We barely had time to create technology to continue humankind before females died out altogether."

"What do you mean…died out altogether?"

"They're extinct. No women. Haven't been any for hundreds of years."

Vanessa was too shocked to stand and had to find a chair.

"Nowadays, most men don't even know that women once existed. Or children. Our technology creates full-grown men. That's why the men thought the little ones were so strange."

"But you seem—"

"I'm a history buff. I've read old books about the time when women existed."

"What about when your people travel back in time? Don't they wonder—?"

"Oh, we haven't time traveled for centuries—" Dr. White Coat interrupted. "Budget cuts."

"Then what do you do here?"

"Weather. We have the best and the brightest working here to balance it for optimal pleasure and productivity. And let me tell you, somebody is always complaining that it's too wet, or too hot, or—"

"Got it. You've got a tough job. Want to help us with an even tougher one?"

"Like—?"

"Putting the timeline right again. Restoring real balance to the world."

"I don't know."

"Well I do. It's time to talk plans," Vanessa decreed.

"Now wait a minute—"

"Why should I?" Vanessa poked him in the chest with her finger. "A rogue time traveler has changed the lives of billions of people. Ensured that a full half of the population has become extinct."

"I didn't do it." He blocked the finger
that had continued to jab his chest and looked at it
pointedly. She dropped her hand and moved away.

"Sorry," Vanessa apologized. "But I had counted
on finding the DTA."

"But you did find us! This is the DTA."

"Department of Temporal Adjustment?"

"Not Temporal, Tropospheric. The good, old
Department of Tropospheric Adjustment.
Established to fix weather in—"

"Stop!" Vanessa had no intention of starting a
history lesson.

"You don't like history?"

"I don't like that I traveled all this way to get
help from time travel experts and all I can find are
a silly bunch of meteorologists."

"Hey! No need to get nasty about it.
Meteorology is a noble field." Dr. White Coat
straightened the front of his lab coat.

"You're right. I shouldn't take it out on you.
You're the only decent person we've met here."

"Like I said"—Dr. White Coat smiled—"I'm a
history buff. I have an open mind."

He looked the four children, who were laughing
and playing clapping games together.

"You know, the five of you don't follow my concept of what women from ancient times were like. I mean, the way your youngsters laid out that story."

"They were rather impressive."

"How old are they?"

"Becca is twelve, Maddie eleven, Zoe eight, and Audrey four."

Dr. White Coat looked at the children as he shook his head.

"They're smaller than I thought they'd be. I've read about children, but I didn't imagine them so little, so vulnerable looking."

"That's why there are parents to protect them. Parents…" Vanessa stopped when she realized by the look on his face that the man had no idea what she was talking about.

"Right. No kids, no parents. Got it."

"Look. I'm part of a group. History buffs like me. I'm sure they'd love to meet—"

"We're not staying."

"Of course, of course. I only meant—"

"Whether you help us or not, we've got a mission."

"I understand. You need to get back to your life."

"Wrong."

"Wrong?"

"We're here to save the world. That's our mission. So will you help us?"

" I don't know if—"

"Don't know if what? If you've got the guts? If you're man enough? If—"

Dr. White Coat raised his hand to stop her words.

"I don't know what I could do. The Department of Tropospheric Adjustments doesn't change history, we don't know how. We fix the weather."

"Someone has to know."

"No one has even attempted time travel for over fifty years. I don't know if the machines even work."

"We're here."

"Right. The machines do work. But no one knows how to operate them."

"Find the manual. It has to be around here somewhere."

"Maybe. But I don't think—"

Dr. White Coat stopped, unsure and uncomfortable, as he noticed that not one, but five pairs of eyes were aimed in his direction.

Quietly, while Vanessa and Dr. White
Coat were busy discussing the fate of the world,
Vanessa's daughters had noticed that their mother
needed support. So they did what every child
learned to do in times of stress. They aimed their
heat-seeking eye missiles at their target.

Poor Dr. White Coat had no experience with
children and therefore no defense against a child's
most deadly weapon, the stare. It was a foregone
conclusion that Dr. White Coat would lose this war
of wills.

Several minutes went by with Dr. White Coat
steeling himself to speak, only to snap his mouth
closed as he chickened out under the heat of the
glares. And each time he snapped his mouth closed,
his face grew redder. After the tenth or so time,
sweat formed on his brow and he had to use the
sleeve of his lab coat to brush it away. Finally he
raised his hands in defeat.

"I give up," Dr. White Coat admitted.

"You'll help us?"

"Yes." He nodded. "Whatever you want."

"You'll help us with the time portal?"

Dr. White Coat pulled his collar away from his
neck to let some of the steam that had built up

escape.

"Dr. White Coat? You'll help us with the time portal?" When Vanessa raised a questioning brow, Becca and Maddie followed suit. Zoe and Audrey kept their glares solidly focused on Dr. White Coat.

"Okay!" Dr. White Coat cringed. "Call them off. I'll help."

"Let's be nice to the man, girls," Vanessa smiled at her daughters before looking pointedly at Dr. White Coat. "He's going to help us fix things."

Dr. White Coat grudgingly nodded.

"Great!" Vanessa rubbed her hands together and smiled. "The way I figure it, the change must have occurred—"

Dr. White Coat held up his hand.

"We're not doing anything without the manual."

"But—"

"But nothing." There was no indecisiveness in Dr. White Coat now. "I know where it must be."

"Look, Dr. White Coat—" Vanessa began.

"I wish you'd stop calling me that. It's Dr. Wilson. Roderick Wilson."

"Okay. Dr. Wilson it is."

Dr. Wilson stared at Vanessa a full minute, deep

in thought. Then he offered her his hand to shake.

"I don't think I ever got your name."

"Vanessa, Vanessa Rossi."

"It's nice to meet you, Vanessa." He turned to the girls. "And Becca, Maddie, Zoe, and Audrey. Right?"

"Right. And now that we've got the introductions out of the way, it's time to get to work. Where's this manual?"

"I'm pretty sure it should be in the history room."

"History room? Boring!" Becca declared. "I'll stay here."

"Not me! I like history," Maddie exclaimed. "I want to go. I want to see what happens in a few years. I mean a few years my time."

"I'll stay with Becca," Zoe said, her words overlapping with Maddie's.

"I want to go with Maddie!" Audrey piped in. "I like books. My paverit story is Cinderella. I like the pairies."

"Oh, Audrey," Becca said. "They won't have those kinds of books. The books they'll have will be stuffy and dull and—"

Suddenly the room was filled with voices as each of Vanessa's daughters voiced her opinion.

"Pairies are the best! They ply around..." began Audrey.

"It's not pairies, it's fairies, with an 'f'..." Maddie corrected her sister.

"I'm with Becca. I don't like history either!" Zoe exclaimed.

"Pairies, pairies, pairies!" Audrey shouted.

"How would you know, Zoe?" Becca asked her sister.

"You need to practice saying the 'f' sound..." Maddie continued.

"You've never even seen a history book."

"I can say pairies if I want!"

"Girls! Enough. You're scaring Dr. Wilson."

The girls stopped talking and turned to look at the doctor, who seemed to have lost any desire to work with Vanessa and her children. His back was to the door and his hand gripped the doorknob.

Vanessa tamped down the giggle that struggled to escape. Dr. Wilson's world, childless as it was, must be a very boring place.

"I think I'll just step out—"

"Wait," Vanessa pleaded. Then she turned to her children. "Girls, apologize to the doctor for scaring him."

"We're sorry," the girls called out in unison.

Then Audrey climbed into Maddie's arms, and Zoe and Becca gave each other a hug.

With that, the sibling tiff was forgotten.

"Is it over? Their voices are so high they hurt my ears," Dr. Wilson whispered.

"It's over." Vanessa nodded.

"In that case" —a tentative smile replaced the grimace on the doctor's face—"I will explain about the history room. First of all, none of you will be going in."

"Wait a minute." Vanessa's patience was wearing thin. "If you think—"

"Just listen. We call it a room, but it's actually a wormhole that we tap into."

"How does that work?"

"You don't really need to know that."

Vanessa raised an eyebrow and Dr. Wilson sighed.

"Okay. So I can't explain it because I don't know. But I've read that it's very stable, and inside the wormhole, time doesn't exist."

"How can time not exist?"

"All I know," Dr. Wilson said with a shrug, "is that the history room was set up, back when we did travel a bit, as a failsafe. Whatever was put into that room remained unchanged no matter what happened to the timeline."

"So you *do* know something about time travel!"

"Only what I've read in history books."

"What happens to people who go into the history room?" Maddie asked. "If time doesn't exist there?"

"Ah, that was one of the problems. Early on, before anyone knew there might be a problem, one man went into the history room and didn't come out for nearly thirty years."

"Oh, no!" Vanessa looked horrified.

"You got it. He went in to retrieve a single piece of paper. But he had gotten to work early and there was an earthquake that day. No one realized he was inside. Men were missing all over the city."

"What happened?"

"As I said, no one knew he was in the room. It was right when a budget crisis hit and protesters shut down the department. Time travel was suspended for decades. If it weren't for a document that needed to be retrieved, who know how long it would have been."

"So no one went in?"

"Right. It was minutes for him, but several decades for the rest of the world."

"His family?"

"His what? Oh, right. We don't have families. But by the time he got out, all his friends had moved away and the DTA had switched to weather control. He wasn't very happy."

"How horrible!"

"So when I go in to get the manual, I'm going to wear a tether and have all my friends holding on to me. I don't want to find myself in the wrong time."

"Like us?"

"Yes." Dr. Wilson nodded thoughtfully. "Just like you."

Chapter 12

DR. WILSON FILLED OUT a requisition form for the key to the history room. As head of the DTA he could pop in, retrieve the manual—fully anchored, of course—without anyone being the wiser.

It was one of the perks of being in charge. He could do things others couldn't.

Except there were two things he neglected to take into account. One, that people were inherently curious creatures. And two, that the Department of Tropospheric Adjustments was a bureaucracy, and bureaucracies were built on redundancies that made secrets nearly impossible to hide.

Before the requisition form hit the archivist's desk, everyone in the building knew the history room door was going to be breached. By the time the archivist had dug the key out of the dusty safety deposit box where it had been kept for more than fifty years, a committee had formed to choose a delegation of ten men to accompany Dr. Wilson.

Then, as Dr. Wilson was supervising the gathering of the tethers and other supplies, he overheard a group of men planning what they would do to "those Russians" if given a chance.

There was a longstanding dislike of Russians ever since it was discovered that their method of research consisted of stealing technology from as many countries as possible. The weather department had had a number of proprietary machines stolen or copied, and some of the most innovative had been repurposed as weapons. Everybody in the weather department hated Russians.

The only way Dr. Wilson could keep Vanessa and her children safe was to keep an eye on them at all times. So he added them to the list of those who would make the trip into the history room. It was a very unpopular decision.

It didn't help the popularity of Vanessa and her daughters much, either. Even while being escorted by Dr. Wilson, they had to push, shove, and elbow their way through the grumbling mass of manhood to the door of the history room. Not one of the twenty or so men stuffed into the little anteroom, or the thirty more crowded in the hallway leading to the anteroom, had any intention of making things easy for the Russians that had been sent to their department to steal all their new technology.

But getting to the history room door was only the first step in the journey. The next was to actually open the door, which proved more problematic than expected. Because the door had remained shut so long, the hinges had rusted over.

One mild-looking scientist in a blue lab coat stepped forward and motioned the others to give him room. He was known as one of their best problem solvers, so the crowd respectfully stepped back to give him room to work.

He began simply enough, rattling the doorknob and giving it a quick pull. But when that didn't work, he became increasingly frustrated and before anyone knew what he intended, he had both hands wrapped around the knob and a foot on the wall as he pulled with all his might. Sweat poured from his forehead as he strained every muscle in his somewhat puny body, obviously determined to be the man to get the door open. Finally he pulled so hard that his sweaty palms lost their grip and he went flying into the eagerly watching crowd.

Pandemonium broke out as each man voiced his opinion about how to solve the human puzzle in the middle of the floor. As the scrawny scientist worked to untangle his arms and legs from those of his coworkers, a muscular man in an orange jacket stepped forward.

"You're going about this all wrong," the brawny man yelled over the deafeningly loud crowd. "The door needs to be taken out. Knocked down entirely. I can handle that." And he flexed his muscles.

For about five seconds a deaf man could have heard a pin drop, everyone was so quiet. Then the bomb of voices exploded as the discussion about the brawny man's proposal began.

The crowd quickly split into two groups. One group, made up mainly of men in orange jackets, was adamantly for breaking down the door. The other group, primarily men in blue lab coats, argued strongly against it.

Things got very heated very quickly, and before anyone knew what was happening, fists began to fly. Vanessa pulled her children close and looked around for a safe harbor out of the melee.

The only place that was clear of flying arms was a sitting area just to the side of the door to the history room. She guided her kids there to wait until the fight was over and tempers had cooled.

It wasn't a long wait. By the time Vanessa had all four girls safely seated and had taken a seat herself, the show was over. One of the sprinklers, the one directly over the biggest knot of men, turned on and began to spurt cooling droplets of anger management. It was magical how quickly a little moisture turned a seething mass of angry men into a bunch of contrite puppies.

Vanessa had no idea grown men could look so ashamed. One by one they picked themselves up off the floor, straightened their clothes, and shuffled off to the side.

"Now that that's out of the way." Dr. Wilson slammed closed a panel labeled with the words *IN CASE OF HEATED DISCUSSION.*

So much for the oft-held belief that the future was a more civilized place!

"Removing the door by force is out of the question," Dr. Wilson continued. "The door must remain intact. An uncovered wormhole entry point is too dangerous. We can't risk it."

Vanessa rose from her seat by the door. "I know how to—"

The sound of her voice stirred up the wildlife and Dr. Wilson scowled. Vanessa remembered that these men believed she had been sent to steal from them and she shut her mouth. If she wanted help fixing what needed to be fixed, she absolutely had to keep quiet. Otherwise, the heads of these men might explode, which would create an even bigger mess.

So she shut her mouth, shrugged, and plopped back down in her seat, secure in the knowledge that she could have that door open in under a minute. She had dealt with much worse than rusty hinges in the past, both of her pasts.

Certain things were consistent in both timelines, like the fact that she and Tony had their share of hard times. Money was tight when the primary breadwinner was also a fulltime student. Add four little ones determined to outgrow their clothes before they had a chance to wear them, and money quickly became a finite commodity.

Which was why when something broke, stuck, or simply stopped working, Vanessa fixed it

herself. There was no money in the budget
to hire someone to solve problems.

Vanessa's first experience with DIY-ing was a window that refused to close. Tony had left Vanessa, eight months pregnant and nervous, alone with one-year-old Becca while he flew out on a mission.

As luck would have it, as soon as Tony got safely out of town a sudden, violent storm hit and what had been a beautiful spring day turned nasty—run-for-the-hills sideways rain kind of nasty. Vanessa grabbed Becca and rushed to slam all the windows shut, until she got to the-window-that-would-not-close. She attacked that window with everything she had. She pulled, pushed, and pried, but no matter what she did to the-window-that-would-not-close, rain continued to pour in. Everything in the room was drenched, including her and her daughter.

That first DIY opportunity got the better of Vanessa. She was unable to figure out how to close the window so she used a garbage bag and tape to block out the rain. It worked, even if it wasn't pretty.

Then, in the months that followed, she spent

most of her spare time reading books and magazines that explained how to fix things around the house. Her favorite was a rather hefty book titled *10,001 Household Fixes*, a hefty tome that covered everything from stained shirts to how to build a henhouse. If it wasn't in the book, it probably was not worth fixing.

So the next time Tony went on a trip and a lock refused to click closed, Vanessa fixed it. And when the toilet overflowed, a pipe burst, and one of the faucets developed an obnoxious drip, she fixed them all.

She had conquered a multitude of repairs over the years, most of them much tougher than a mere rusty hinge. She was quite handy and knew exactly what needed to be done to make that door pop open.

Unfortunately, Vanessa was less important to these scientists than a mustard stain on their favorite lab coat, and twice as annoying. They had decided she was a Russian, and that Russians were the scum of the earth.

What would they think if they found out she was a woman? Or had the concept of womanhood completely faded by this time?

Did they even know half of humanity had been lost?

She looked at her daughters, entertaining themselves as they completely ignored the melee building around them. They were strong, and wonderful, and young. Given a chance, they could grow up—

"The children," Vanessa whispered as the truth hit. Blood drained from her face and the cacophony of men's voices faded away as the full significance of what had happened to the world slammed into Vanessa like the proverbial ton of bricks.

Ever since she discovered that women had been "scienced" right out of existence, she had wondered exactly what effect it had had on the world. Since scientific and technological breakthroughs were usually built on the work of others, it was often hard to pinpoint exactly who had been the most instrumental.

The problem was that, although she knew women brought a different way of thinking to the table, she had never been able to determine if that way of thinking had been created by nature or nurture. Did women look at the world differently than men because their bodies were different than

men's bodies, or were they trained to think
that way by society?

She had been so caught up in her own musings about how womankind contributed to the world that she had not paid attention when Dr. Wilson had said that all attempts to recreate the female sex had failed, as had the attempts for children who would grow to adulthood. The technology that allowed humanity to survive provided fully formed adult males ready to enter the workforce.

So it wasn't only women who had become extinct, but also children.

What had humankind done to itself? No childhood memories. No families. No siblings. No lifelong connections forged by the bond of childhood.

She looked at the men milling around, grumbling about their wet clothes as they jostled their way to the front to have their turn at the door. As human as they looked on the outside, Vanessa felt they might as well be robots. It was the insides that made humans human, and how could these creatures be real humans when they had never faced the rich emotional experiences created by family life, the glue that held humanity together?

This world was broken in ways she had never imagined possible. All she wanted to do was grab her children and leave—the quicker the better.

But the thought of escaping back through the portal to her time only lasted about two seconds. That was all the time it took for Vanessa to realize that if the tampering occurred before her time, she could not simply go back to her own time to set things right. And if she didn't fix things, humanity was doomed.

She'd be darned if she'd sit idly by and let humanity be ruined.

Dr. Wilson had said that everything in the history room was impervious to changes to the timeline, and that many of the books were about history. So all she had to do was research. Find that one single event among millions. No pressure. No pressure at all.

Especially since finding which event had been changed was only the first step. Then she needed to figure out how to use the time portal to go back in time, undo whatever had been done, and get her children safely back to their own time so they could live normal lives.

Vanessa sighed. She hated cleaning up other

people's messes. It was one of her least favorite things to do.

"One step at a time, Vanessa. One step," Vanessa muttered.

"Did you say something, Mommy?" Becca asked.

"Not really, sweetie. What are they doing now?"

"Still trying to figure out how to open the door." Becca snickered. "It's kinda funny."

And it was. These men—who should have been the brightest of the bright—were laughably inept.

"Mommy?" Zoe bit her lower lip to keep from smiling.

"Yes, Zoe?"

"How many scientists does it take to open a door?"

"I don't know, sweetie. How many scientists does it take to open a door?"

"A gazillion, zillion, because they can't open a door." Zoe giggled. She pointed to the men, who continued to push each other out of the way so they could get a shot at the door. "Look at them!"

"Good joke, Zoe," Vanessa smiled. "What do you think, Audrey?"

"They're punny," Audrey said with a serious

look on her face. "Like monkey clowns."

Which was good enough for Vanessa. Anything that kept Audrey amused also kept her out of trouble.

Dr. Wilson shoved everyone aside as he noticed the rusty hinges. He called a young man in a white lab coat over and pointed at the hinges, then he made several odd gestures with his hands.

"Look," Vanessa whispered to her daughters. "He's sending that young man to get oil for the door."

But whatever Dr. Wilson had planned, it wasn't as simple as sending the man for oil. Because as soon as Dr. Wilson gave a whispered order to the young man and sent him on his way, he changed is mind and called him back. A low volume discussion became a heated one, and before long, several more men were called over.

The oddest part was that Dr. Wilson seemed to not want Vanessa to know what he was doing. Every time a voice was raised, Dr. Wilson would look at Vanessa, almost as if he were embarrassed.

But what was he doing that could make him so embarrassed?

Vanessa leaned closer. If she could just catch a

few words—

Dr. Wilson glanced her way, glared, and pulled the huddle across the room.

"What's he up to?" Vanessa wondered aloud.

She took a moment to count heads. There were only three.

"Becca, where's Audrey?" she asked in a panic.

Zoe tugged on Vanessa's sleeve and pointed to a high shelf above Dr. Wilson's head.

Vanessa's heart dropped into her shoes as she spotted Audrey, comfortably perched where she could swing her legs back and forth as she watched the discussion below.

It wasn't just the child's altitude that worried her. Some of the scientist believed them to be Russian spies. Audrey's current perch, perfect for spying, might inflame the more hotheaded of the group. Vanessa had to find a way—

Chaos broke out among the scientists before the worried mother could come up with a plan. One moment they were in a huddle, the next they had scattered in every direction like cockroaches exposed to the bright light of day.

Vanessa waved her hands in the air to attract Audrey's attention, but Audrey only had eyes for

the five men who raced in with cans that
they lined up in a row in front of Dr. Wilson.

Audrey leaned forward to get a better view and Vanessa's heart nearly fell out of her chest. Even a little monkey like Audrey couldn't survive a tumble from that height without a major injury.

Thankfully, as Dr. Wilson moved down the line inspecting each can in turn, Audrey got bored and looked for her mother.

"Audrey!" Vanessa whispered as she frantically motioned the child to climb down from the ledge. "Audrey, come here!"

When Dr. Wilson looked Vanessa's way, she quickly turned her hand motion into a friendly wave. She tried to accompany the wave with a smile, but she was so upset that she was sure it was more of a grimace. Dr. Wilson gave her a funny look before he continued with his inspection.

"Please don't choose this moment to start the Foolhardy Fours," Vanessa whispered. "Please, Audrey. Come to Mama."

But it looked like the Foolhardy Fours had indeed begun, because instead of climbing down from that high shelf to her mother's lap, Audrey crossed her little arms and shook her head. It was

abundantly clear she liked where she was
and had no intention of leaving her perch, at least
not soon enough to keep Vanessa's heart from
darting about like a drunken lizard.

"It's okay, Mommy," Becca reassured the
worried mother. "She's been that high before. She
never falls."

"She'll come down when she's ready," Maddie
added.

Vanessa nodded, well aware that she had no
choice in the matter. All she could do was watch,
wait, and hope for the best.

Vanessa looked directly below her daughter to
Dr. Wilson as he reverently took a can from one
young man and passed it carefully to a pack of men
in blue. With all the ceremony usually afforded
only the most important moments in a society, the
blue coats took their precious little can and
solemnly oiled the rusty hinges.

The ceremony lasted until the chosen one took
the doorknob in hand, turned it, and, a smug look
on his face, pulled. When the door remained closed
he jiggled the doorknob and pulled harder. After
that, chaos erupted again as every man in the place
thought he was obligated to take a turn at the door.

Soon all the scientists were capering around like monkeys wired on caffeine.

"Is that what they mean by manhandling something?" Maddie asked.

"Looks more like ape-handling to me," Becca answered with a shake of her head.

Vanessa also shook her head, amused by how silly they looked. Until one brute of a man shook the door so hard Audrey had to grab the shelf to keep from falling.

"Stop that! You're going to make her fall," Vanessa yelled in a panic. But the noise level was so high no one heard her.

So she did what only a mother in a desperate situation would do. She climbed up onto that little shelf to rescue her child.

"Mom, let me do it," Becca yelled as she grabbed her mother's shirt and tried to pull her back down.

"Let go, Becca. I've got to get Audrey."

"I'll go, Mom. You're afraid of heights."

"My child, my responsibility."

"She's my sister."

Vanessa simply shook her head. Becca looked at the anguish in her mother's face, let go, and nodded.

As soon as Vanessa began to crawl along that oh-so-high shelf, she almost regretted her decision to rescue her daughter. It was very narrow, and looked almost too flimsy to hold the weight of a grown woman.

"One inch at a time," Vanessa muttered. "I only need to go one inch at a time."

Some of the men began to throw themselves against the door, which made the shelf shake so much that twice she had to lay flat to keep from tumbling off. When she finally reached Audrey, the child was in tears, and Vanessa had to pry her little white-knuckled hands away from the shelf so she could take the sobbing child into her arms.

But Audrey was a brave little thing, and it didn't take much to convince her to crawl back to the spot where they could climb safely to the floor. Especially since Becca had climbed up to the shelf and was waiting for her there.

Audrey crawled out of the precarious safety of her mother's lap and scuttled toward safety. Vanessa started to follow, but a loud *THUMP* made her look down at the doorway below. That's when she saw it.

The simple but effective reason none of these

geniuses had been able to open the door was a slide bolt located above the sightline of the men, at the very top of the frame.

"Who would've guessed?"

Not these capering scientists, with their scuffles for dominance and chest beating. Not one of them had enough common sense to check if it was locked before they tried to use brute force to open the door.

Best and brightest, indeed!

Audrey and Becca reached the floor and Becca scooped up her sister. Once all four girls were safe on the couch, Vanessa turned her attention back to the door.

The men seemed to have forgotten her existence as they discussed a new way to shake the door open. Vanessa stretched out her arm, grabbed the lock, and pulled. The bolt slid smoothly, without the slightest sign of rust. The door was unlocked. She scuttled back to her children and the relative safety of the couch.

She'd barely had a chance to sit before an orange coat and a blue coat got into a shoving match. As their respective teammates pulled them apart, Vanessa looked at her daughters.

"Are you girls tired of this?"

Four heads nodded in unison.

"Should we—?" Vanessa pointed to the door and mimicked turning a doorknob and opening it.

Four heads again nodded in unison, only this time the nods were accompanied by huge grins.

"What about the whole Russian spy thing?" Becca whispered.

"Let them think what they want. They'll probably just be glad we opened the door."

"Will they let you?" Maddie's whisper was so quiet Vanessa could barely hear it.

Vanessa looked at her four daughters. A man in orange stepped back toward the couch, and Vanessa watched in dismay as three of her daughters cowered from him.

It was obvious that the confidence her daughters had gained on the way to the portal was slipping away. All the testosterone in the room was rather unnerving.

It was time to set a good example for her daughters. Time to show them women could do things, things that mattered. She owed it to her daughters, and to the sisterhood, to fan the sputtering flame of confidence, before all this overt manliness extinguished it like a candle flame deprived of oxygen.

Vanessa motioned the girls to sit tight as she waited until the ten feet between the couch and the door was unblocked. Then she straightened her shoulders, marched directly to the door, and grabbed the knob.

"Hey, get away from there," a deep voice behind her yelled. Vanessa turned her head to see a tableau of frozen men with all eyes pointed her way.

"Don't touch that—"

Vanessa ignored the command as she balled her hand into a fist, chose a spot near the doorframe, and gave it a quick, hard hit.

A gasp went up from the crowd. With as much flourish as she could muster, Vanessa turned the knob and threw open the door.

Only, before the opening could get more than five inches wide, a man shoved the door shut. Then he gently pulled it open an inch and reclosed it, as if to check that it worked properly.

Immediately, two men in orange jackets swooped in, picked Vanessa up by her underarms, and deposited her on the couch next to her children.

"Sit," one man ordered with a growl.

Vanessa watched the orange, blue, and white

coats mill around the doorway, slapping each other on the back and grinning as if they had opened the door. Vanessa and her children had been shoved aside and dismissed, the part they had played instantly forgotten.

It made her fume. How dare these men order her around like a dog? If she hadn't unlocked that stupid door, they would still be cavorting around like a bunch of monkeys—

"Vanessa," Dr. Wilson said in an authoritative voice. She looked up, startled to find him standing in front of her. Then he winked and whispered, "Bring your daughters. It's time to put on the safety harnesses."

She had been so focused on her anger that she hadn't noticed what was going on around her. A set of very solid looking hooks had been installed on a concrete wall and long, thick ropes attached. Several men already had ropes tied around their waists.

Vanessa suddenly wondered if *history room* was a misnomer. These men were prepared for a grueling climb up Mount Everest, not a visit to a room filled with books. Vanessa certainly never wrapped a rope around her middle and tethered it to a piece of steel when she took a trip to the local library.

What exactly were they expecting on the other side of that door?

Motherly anxiety reared its ugly head as Vanessa imagined an invisible vortex waiting on the other side of the door, a hidden trap that would suck Vanessa's children to a far galaxy.

In a panic, Vanessa realized that a rope tied around her children's waists would do absolutely nothing to keep them safe. The slightest tug and those supple kid bodies would slip right through like well-oiled noodles.

"Vanessa?"

Dr. Wilson looked down at her expectantly. She opened her mouth to voice her concern about the rope, but Dr. Wilson quickly shushed her. She opened her mouth again, and again she was shushed.

"Not a word," Dr. Wilson whispered as he pointed at the men milling around. "They're scared enough of the history room to let me take you inside. But they don't trust you."

Vanessa twisted around so only the doctor could see her face, and she kept her mouth stiff as an added caution.

"We might not want to go inside," Vanessa whispered. "Those ropes won't stop my daughters from being sucked away."

"Not a problem." Dr. Wilson looked toward the door. "We need to get moving."

"No, you don't understand—"

"They'll be safe," Dr. Wilson said firmly.

Vanessa was conflicted. Dr. Wilson had no reason to purposely endanger her family, so if he thought the ropes would keep her daughters safe, she should trust him.

But those girls were her children, her responsibility. As much as she wanted to visit the history room, their safety was more important. She had already put them in jeopardy by dragging them to the future—

"Don't worry your pretty little head," Dr. Wilson muttered as he absentmindedly patted Vanessa like a puppy.

That pat cleared her mind like nothing else could. A pat on the head to an adult human was the ultimate sign of disrespect.

Before Vanessa could think of an appropriate response, the door of the history room slammed

open and out poured the brightest blue
light she had ever seen.

It was as if a vacuum had sucked all the sound
from the room, the silence was so complete. No
scuffle of feet as each man vied for a better view. No
sibilant whispers as neighbor turned to ask
neighbor what was going on. Not even the ragged
sound of panicked breathing could be heard. So
deep was the silence that a feather daring to sweep
across the floor would have sounded like a sonic
boom.

A gargantuan figure stepped into the doorway
and cast a menacing shadow over the crowd.
Vanessa grabbed her kids and hugged them close.
Whatever this monster was that they were about to
face, her only goal was to keep her children safe.

Vanessa closed her eyes and took a deep breath
as she realized she might be overreacting. This
whole scenario of the history room was new to her,
but all she needed to do was follow the lead of the
scientist who knew the most about it. Dr. Wilson
would know exactly what to expect. He would be
prepared for whatever creatures the wormhole
might connect to his world.

This thought gave her comfort until she shot a

quick glance at Dr. Wilson's genial, serene face and found instead a man with a twitch who was unable to pull his terror-stricken eyes from figure in the doorway.

There was no comfort to be found in the sight of the good doctor, only a reason to panic. And panic she did. Her heart pounded like a steam engine racing to prove it was still a valid technology.

Her panic was only heightened when she realized that there was no *bam, bam, bam* of her heart as it pounded against her chest, and no *whoosh* of blood as it raced past her ears. The world was eerily quiet.

Vanessa gulped as she recalled the rusted hinges and the hidden lock on the door. Someone, at some time, had wanted that door to remain closed. Someone had known about the monster, and that same someone had taken steps to protect the world from that thing standing in the doorway.

Vanessa had unlocked that door. Whatever happened next, it was her fault.

A quick scan showed her that there was not a calm face in sight. Every man in the room shared Dr. Wilson's dread of the creature.

The monster stepped out of the doorway and a

whoosh of air blew past Vanessa's arm. Out of the corner of her eye she saw a streak of white disappear around the corner and she knew what had happened.

They had been abandoned, ditched, left to fend for themselves. Every man in the room, including Dr. Wilson, had turned tail and run.

Vanessa and her daughters were alone with the monster.

Terror grabbed hold of Vanessa's heart and squeezed it like a lemon as the creature pounced into the room and seized the doorknob with its massive claw.

For about the fifth time Vanessa panicked. The only escape out of the room was past that creature, so she did what any mother who feared for the safety of her children would do. She shoved them onto the floor and tossed herself on top of the pile. If they were lucky, the monster wouldn't notice them. But if it did, at least it would have to go through her before it got to her kids.

Chapter 13

THERE WAS A SLIGHT change in air pressure followed by a gentle *CLICK* as the door latched.

"Funny guys, real funny," a woman's voice said. "Who's the jokester who locked the door?"

Vanessa's tense body twitched. That voice. Why did that voice sound so familiar?

The mass of arms and legs below her writhed and shifted. A small arm shot out of the pile. Vanessa shoved it back in.

"Ouch, Zoe! Watch your elbow," Becca yelled. "That was my face!"

"Be quiet," Vanessa whispered into the squirming pile beneath her.

"It wasn't me," Zoe shouted back. Either she hadn't heard the plea for silence or she was ignoring it. "I'm by Maddie. That was Audrey's elbow."

"Shhh," Vanessa hissed, this time loud enough that she knew all the girls had heard.

"Be quiet!" Maddie was in a helpful mood, so her whisper was loud and clear. "Mommy said to be quiet."

"Why?" Audrey demanded from just below her ear.

"Girls," Vanessa tried again, "hush."

She finally got through to them and for a full five seconds all four of the girls were both still and quiet. Vanessa strained her ears. She needed to figure out—

"The monster's coming!" Zoe screamed.

With those three panicky words, any chance Vanessa had of maintaining control flew out the window and chaos flew in to take its place.

"Monster? What kind of monster?" Maddie grabbed Zoe's head and tried to move it out of the way so she would have an unobstructed view.

"I want to see," Audrey yelled. Being a four-year-old, she didn't think to get one person to move out of her way—she was determined to get everyone to move. So she employed a method that had worked for her in the past: She kicked her arms and legs in every direction and made contact with more soft tissue than should be humanly possible.

"Ouch! Audrey, stop! That hurt," Becca

complained.

"Stop it, Audrey!" Maddie yelled.

"I got her leg!" Zoe shouted gleefully.

"Let go!" Audrey yelled, and gave a particularly vicious kick aimed at Zoe's stomach.

That sent things from bad to worse. No punches were held back. Arms, legs, and words flew about in every direction.

What exactly was happening, Vanessa couldn't tell. Her daughters' voices were too similar for her to be able to make out the individual words, but it was obvious that anger had taken over. And when anger comes to town, fear heads for the hills.

Not that Vanessa could blame them. She had thrown her children into an uncomfortable pile without any explanation, and then thrown herself on top. And then for some reason she had expected them to lay guietly, again without explanation. She had expected them to mimic a stack of old rugs, instead of the living, squirming children they were.

Vanessa gasped as a knee to her stomach knocked the breath out of her. Audrey's military grade weapons, the ones usually disguised as knees and elbows, were working at full capacity. She would need to—

A hand on her shoulder stopped that thought and she froze in fear. The monster had found them.

"Need help?" said a voice in her ear.

Vanessa blinked several times. It wasn't just that monsters don't speak. That voice. That friendly, helpful voice, it reminded her of—

"Erica?" Vanessa twisted around to look at the creature that stood beside her. Only...it wasn't a creature, it was an old friend, a woman who had been a fellow student in another place and time.

Erica smiled as she reached out a hand to help Vanessa rise from the squirming mass beneath her. As soon as her weight no longer pinned them down, the jumbled mess of arms and legs untangled itself and became Vanessa's four daughters.

Vanessa wanted to properly greet her old friend, but before she could so much as draw a breath, Audrey created a situation.

True to her four-year-old code of ethics, Audrey jumped off the pile without a care in the world and landed on Zoe's stomach. Zoe reacted as anyone would and sat up quickly, which threw off Audrey's balance. Becca, ever conscious of her big-sister duties, caught Audrey before she could hit the ground.

"Why'd you do that?" Zoe yelled. "She deserves to fall. She hurt me!"

"She hurt me, too." Becca brushed a footprint off her pants and stoically ignored the bruise she felt forming on her leg. "But she's still our little sister."

Becca stood Audrey on her feet and turned her to face Zoe.

"Tell Zoe you're sorry," she ordered sternly.

"Am not sorry!" Audrey yelled. To show she wasn't in the least bit sorry, she stomped her foot, barely missing Zoe's leg. Zoe glared daggers at her stubborn little sister.

Maddie was always ready to join forces with Becca in the war to rule younger siblings. So she quickly joined her, and they subconsciously did the best imitation in the history of imitations. Each put her hands on her hips, lifted one brow, and gave Audrey that special *behave-or-you're-gonna-get-it* look Vanessa reserved for bad behavior on special occasions.

Which, when Vanessa thought about it, made perfect sense. What occasion was more special than a visit to a wormhole hundreds of years in the future?

Not that the thought lasted long. Two little Vanessa's reprimanding one sister while protecting another was more than she could handle. Vanessa couldn't help herself. She burst into laughter.

Becca and Maddie looked at their amused mother, who was laughing hard enough that it would have been impossible for her to talk. Then, eyebrows still raised, they looked at each other. Vanessa was looking at them the moment they got it. A flash of surprise quickly followed by a dash of embarrassment, then their well-developed sense of humor took over and they, too, broke into laughter.

It was lucky that the two girls were old enough to see the comedy in the situation and not get offended by their mother's laughter. That might have been a bit awkward.

Zoe, on the other hand, was younger, more sensitive, and less able to see the humor in the situation. She scrambled to stand beside Audrey as she glared at her two laughing sisters.

"Are you laughing at me?" she asked suspiciously. Then she did the worst thing possible. She put her hands on her hips, raised an eyebrow, and gave her sisters *the look*.

Becca, Maddie, and Vanessa lost it. They laughed so hard they had to sit on the floor to keep from falling over. It was wonderful to have all the fear and anger that had built up over the last few days bubbling out in the form of laughter. It felt fantastic, until Vanessa looked up and saw Zoe's confused face.

Zoe's eyes were getting shinier by the moment as huge pools of tears formed. She was not in on the joke. They were laughing at her. She was devastated that her mother and sisters could be so cruel.

"No, sweetie," Vanessa cried. She grabbed her little hurt daughter into her arms, horrified at the pain on her face. "We aren't laughing at you, not really. We're laughing at ourselves."

One look at that baffled little face and Vanessa knew the child had no clue what she meant. Vanessa racked her brain, determined to find a way to make the little munchkin understand. But before she could come up with anything, the munchkin's older sisters came to the rescue.

"Watch how funny we are, Zoe," Becca snickered.

"We're just like Mom. Look." Maddie was

obviously holding back giggles.

As Zoe watched, Becca and Maddie assumed the position—hands on hips, eyebrows raised, "the look" in place. They could only hold it for a split second—it was just too funny for them not to break into laughter—but it was long enough for Zoe to realize what had amused them all. Vanessa breathed a relieved sigh as Zoe broke into a grin and nodded happily.

But Audrey was still in her angry stance. Vanessa hated to see the little munchkin in such a bad mood, especially when the rest of the group was so cheery. She was about to try to lighten the youngster's mood when all three of the little one's sisters swooped in with a tickle attack. Audrey immediately broke into giggles, unable to withstand a full-blown, thirty-digit tickle-fest. Having the full attention of all of her sisters didn't hurt, either.

"I see your daughters inherited your sense of humor," Erica yelled above the happy sound of childish laughter.

Vanessa had been so caught up in daughter drama that she had almost forgotten her old friend. She turned to her.

There was a confidence in Erica's eye that assured Vanessa this woman was from the true timeline, the timeline Vanessa would do everything in her power to restore.

Vanessa had no choice but to succeed. Her daughters must be allowed to grow up in a world where women were contributing members of society, not fluff pieces only useful to decorate a room. Her daughters were fully capable of making their way in the world. All they needed was to be educated, to be allowed to flex their mental muscles, to fail or succeed on their own merit.

Vanessa looked closer at her old friend and realized that Erica was very different than she remembered. Vanessa had been Erica's closest friend, study buddy, and confidant. They had bonded over pottery shards, homework, and discussions about the male gender bias prevalent in most archaeology textbooks.

Erica had the same brown hair, the same serious face. She no longer wore glasses, but the change went deeper than that. The Erica Vanessa had known was meek, mousy, and seemed younger than her actual years. This Erica was mature and exuded a confidence that would make a pride of lions proud.

It was obvious that when Vanessa and Erica had stumbled through the portal into the future on that long ago day and Erica had decided to stay, her decision had been a good one.

"Erica." Vanessa gave her a huge hug. "It's so good to see you!"

Erica returned the embrace. Then she pushed her old friend away at arm's length and looked her in the eye.

"Tell me the truth, did you lock me in?" she asked suspiciously.

"*Really*?" It may have sounded like a question, but the addition of a roll of Vanessa's eyes made it much more of a statement.

Erica searched Vanessa's face. Vanessa raised an eyebrow, which brought a smile to Erica.

"Right. So where is everybody? My team is waiting for my research. There was a question about whether—"

Erica stopped short and looked around. "What's going on here?" she asked, her forehead crinkled in confusion.

Vanessa's daughters had finished with the tickle-fest and moved on to clapping games. Erica grabbed Vanessa's arm in alarm.

"Wait. Why are your daughters here? What happened to—?"

The brave horde of manly scientists chose that moment to make an excessively awkward and slow entrance. For some strange reason they looked more like a pile of marbles jammed into socks than men.

Vanessa had to watch for several seconds to figure out how they managed such a strange effect. Smaller guys had been shoved to the front as cannon fodder and were being pushed forward by the bigger guys, who stayed in the rear. But the guys in front didn't like the idea of being sacrificed for the greater good, and kept digging in their heels. So the forward momentum was very slow, and every so often a fortunate soul would manage to roll across the front row and spin away to the back of the group.

The terror on the faces of the men would have been funny if it hadn't been so pathetic.

Vanessa watched Erica's face and saw the exact moment when it dawned on her that there wasn't a woman in the group. She looked at Vanessa quickly.

"Someone changed the timeline?" she whispered.

Vanessa nodded.

"How bad is it?"

"Really bad," Vanessa whispered back.

"How so?"

"A world without women," Vanessa sneered in disgust. "Due to gene-therapy gone bad, we've been erased from the species."

Erica blinked a few times and scrunched up her forehead in a way Vanessa remembered very well. It was nice to catch a glimpse of the old Erica.

"They recognize we're different, so they've decided we're mutated Russians sent to spy on them."

"Good grief!" Erica shook her head. "And me?"

"You," Vanessa began, grinning, "are a monster that came through the wormhole to gobble them up."

Erica looked at the scuffling group of men. The men in the back looked brave enough, until they got shoved to the front. Then all that bravery turned to terror and panic.

"At least that gives me some leverage." Erica wrinkled her nose. "Do you know who's in charge?"

"There." Vanessa pointed to the middle of the undulating crowd. "Behind that tall guy in the orange jacket."

Erica peered at the group and gasped. A mischievous smile spread across her face.

"Get your children ready, we're going into the history room," Erica whispered. "As soon as I get that 'man in charge' to join us."

"Do you think you can? They're terrified of you."

"I'm counting on the terror."

"Are you sure we need him?"

"I've got a few questions for Dr. Wilson."

"You know—?"

"Get ready."

Vanessa motioned her daughters to join her and hold hands. Then, to be safe, she picked up Audrey. Whatever happened next, having Audrey in hand would remove the chance she'd have to climb a ledge, jump a table, or crawl under a couch to retrieve the active child.

"Roderick Matthew Wilson, front and center," Erica's voice rang out.

There was a moment of complete silence, then as

if by magic Dr. Wilson was left standing alone. Someone must have either decided he would be a good sacrifice or that as the boss he needed to face the problem head on, because someone gave him a tremendous shove from behind. He stumbled away from the cowering group of men and landed on his knees directly in front of Erica.

How could one woman be so scary?

"Come here," Erica commanded again, but this time she pointed to a spot by her side.

Dr. Wilson gulped as he looked at his friends and coworkers huddled together in a tight-knit group. Two men motioned for him to stand, several others gave uneasy grins meant to give support, but most of them simply closed their eyes and looked away, too uncomfortable to watch.

Dr. Wilson cleared his throat as he struggled to his feet. He again looked at his men. He wiped his sweaty palms on his pants, pasted a smile on his face, and reached out a welcoming hand toward the scary creature he feared was a monster.

Before anyone knew what was happening, Erica grabbed his arm, opened the door, and pulled him inside the history room. Vanessa was glad Erica had given her a head's up, because she was able to quickly grab Zoe's hand and follow, pulling her children through the door daisy chain style.

Vanessa caught the door and did a quick head count. The world through that door was too messed up to take the chance one of them might be left behind.

But she had no need to worry. All four had made it through the door, unharmed and ready for an adventure. She let the door close with a satisfying *CLICK*.

Chapter 14

THE ROOM BEHIND VANESSA was quieter than a tomb.

"I want down, Mommy," Audrey yelled, shattering the silence with her high-pitched little girl voice. Then when Vanessa didn't immediately respond, she squirmed like a piglet that had spotted its dinner.

"In a minute, sweetie." Vanessa kept her voice low in an attempt to calm the child. "Mommy wants to look around first."

But the calm-voice method only worked sometimes, because when Audrey wanted down, she wanted down *now*. The little monkey did a few quick twists that caught Vanessa by surprise and slipped right out of her mother's arms. Luckily the child had that cat-like ability to land on her feet so there was no need for tears.

But Vanessa could also be quick, so as soon as Audrey's feet hit the floor, Vanessa grabbed the little monkey's hand and held it tight. They were in a wormhole after all, and with Audrey's propensity to climb where she shouldn't, who knew what kind of trouble she might get into, or what strange creatures she might encounter.

"*Mommy*!" Audrey whined as she tried to pull her hand out of her mother's firm grasp.

"You are NOT to leave my side," Vanessa ordered sternly. To make sure Audrey knew she was serious, she lifted one brow.

Audrey looked from her mother's mouth to her raised eyebrow and gave up on her plan to explore, for now at least. Mommy's brow only chased her hair like that when she was cranky. And a cranky Mommy was no fun.

"We'll look around together," Vanessa smiled mischievously.

Audrey sighed. As much as Mommy's smile promised fun, Audrey knew exploring on her own would be more fun. Mommy only looked at the low things. Up high was where all the good stuff was.

"Audrey?" The brow again jumped up to the hairline.

"Okay, Mommy," Audrey said, and she was sincere. Every fiber of her four-year-old being ached to please her mother—even if that meant missing out on the good stuff.

Satisfied, Vanessa looked with interest at the history room. She'd never been in a wormhole before and expected great things.

But Vanessa was disappointed. Other than a strange blue glow emanating from the walls, the room looked—well, boring. Beige metal file cabinets lined the walls, interspersed with shelves filled with normal, everyday books of every sort. There didn't even seem to be a method in how they were shelved. She saw cookbooks next to history books, mysteries mixed in with chemistry books, and it looked like picture books had been crammed in wherever there was an extra quarter inch.

"Erica, how do you find anything?" Vanessa asked over her shoulder as she ran her fingers across a shelf that had Edward Gibbon's *The History of the Decline and Fall of the Roman Empire* next to A.A. Milne's *Winnie the Pooh*. "The way these books are shelved makes no sense."

"Mom," Becca whispered.

When Vanessa didn't respond Becca grabbed

her mother's shirt and gave it a good, hard tug.

"What is it, Becca?" Vanessa reluctantly pulled her thoughts away from the mystery of the oddly arranged books and turned her attention to her oldest daughter.

Becca pointed across the room. Vanessa turned to see what so enthralled her daughter and got the surprise of her life.

Erica had her arms wrapped firmly around Dr. Wilson and was squeezing him, bear hug fashion, like she had no plan to ever let go.

Dr. Wilson, for his part, had no clue how to handle the situation. His eyes were huge pools of fear as he held his arms, ramrod straight, at his sides. He appeared to think Erica was a bear that would eat him for dinner if he made the slightest wrong move.

Vanessa smiled as she shifted her attention back to her old friend. Erica had matured during her time here in the future. The Erica Vanessa had known and mentored was studious, shy, and would rather jump off a cliff than wrap her arms around some random guy in a wormhole.

Or talk to that same guy. Based on the

movement of Erica's mouth, she was having quite the one-way conversation with Dr. Wilson. Dr. Wilson certainly was not responding; whatever words were coming out of Erica's mouth had petrified him faster than normal fear ever could.

Vanessa kept her eyes firmly on her friend's mouth as she tried to quietly inch forward. If she could just make out—

A scuffling sound to Vanessa's right made her twirl, fists raised as she prepared to fight the monsters from another realm she was sure were about to attack.

But there were no intergalactic invaders, only her very curious children.

Vanessa barely had time to register that it was her own brood before a domino effect was set in motion. Zoe jumped back to avoid Vanessa's flailing elbow, which made her step on Maddie's toes.

Maddie howled and grabbed her foot, which made her slam into Audrey.

Lightweight little Audrey didn't have enough mass to hold her ground, so she was sent flying across the room.

Becca heroically dove through the air to save her little sister, landed on her back, and skidded to a stop, Audrey safely perched on her stomach.

The smile on Becca's face allowed the worried mother to once again start breathing.

"I plew, Mommy! See me?" Audrey was too excited to have been hurt. Vanessa scooped her off Becca's stomach and gave her a quick hug.

"You did fly, darling. Right through the air." Vanessa ruffled the little monkey's hair.

"How about you, Becca?" Vanessa offered Becca a hand. "Are you okay?"

"Okay? I'm great! Did you see that?" Becca's stunned look said it all. "I snatched her right out of the air."

"Yes, you did." Vanessa smiled. "It was amazing!"

"It was…it was…it was like something in a circus," Becca continued, still too surprised by her own accomplishment to notice the hand stretched her way.

Vanessa's outstretched arm was getting tired. So she flapped her hand in front of Becca's face to pull her out of her shock-induced daze. It worked, and the young girl grabbed her mother's hand and was soon upright.

By the time Vanessa had Audrey and Becca safely on their feet, Zoe and Maddie had joined them. Any casual observer would have thought they had just won a tournament with the congratulations that flew around.

Vanessa looked in Erica's direction and was surprised that all the commotion had gone unnoticed. Erica's arms were still wrapped around Dr. Wilson, her mouth still moving at the steady pace of a consummate storyteller. Dr. Wilson, for his part, was still doing a rather good imitation of a statue.

Vanessa glanced at her children, huddled together, deep in conversation. They were sufficiently occupied; she was free to continue on her quest for answers. So she took a few steps toward Erica and Dr. Wilson. If she could get close enough to hear—

"Ready?" Vanessa heard Becca ask. She froze. Who was supposed to be ready, and for what?

"Maddie," Becca continued with a confidence Vanessa would normally like to hear in her voice. "Push hard when Audrey jumps. Make her go really high. Zoe, you count to three."

Vanessa whipped around. Audrey was perched on Maddie's shoulders, ready to spring. Becca was crouched on the floor a few feet away, all set to dive for another big catch.

"One, two—" Zoe began.

"Stop!" Vanessa yelled. She quickly snatched Audrey from her sister's shoulders before the little monkey could jump. "What are you doing?"

"Practicing," Zoe replied calmly, as if tossing a little sister sky high was the most normal thing in the world.

"We're coming up with a stunt," Becca explained.

"For a circus," Maddie added.

"I want to ply like a bird." Audrey flapped her arms like bird wings.

"No," Vanessa said firmly. She pulled Audrey into her arms and hugged her tight. "It's too dangerous."

"Don't worry, Mommy," Audrey said as she gently put a little hand on each side of her mother's face. "Becca will catch me."

"I'm sure she would, darling," Vanessa said. She gave Audrey a kiss on the cheek and set her down.

"If she got the chance, which she won't."

"Oh, Mom!" Becca and Maddie wailed together.

"Let's see," Vanessa said calmly, "We're in a wormhole, in the future, in a lab, and there are sharp edges everywhere. I don't think you girls need to work to create more danger."

Becca and Maddie both sighed and rolled their eyes.

Vanessa focused her attention on her two oldest. "Becca, Maddie, I expect both of you to set a good example."

"I will, Mommy," Maddie said as she straightened her back, proud to be asked to take on such an important role.

"Yes, Mother," Becca grumbled with just the slightest touch of sarcasm, even as her shoulders slumped in despair. She turned sad eyes in her mother's direction.

Maddie noticed Becca's slump and expression and immediately followed suit. Which, of course, brought on a chain reaction of shoulder slumps, and before Vanessa knew what had happened, she was in a stare-down with four sets of *you-stole-my-puppy* eyes.

"Great," Vanessa whispered under her breath.

She sighed and rolled her eyes. She couldn't help it. There was nothing harder for a parent than to deny her children what they really, really wanted, and those eyes screamed for pity. It was obvious the circus stunt was important to her children.

But no matter how much those eyes might pull at her heartstrings, she absolutely could not let them do circus stunts. Not here. There might be consequences well past a few bumps and bruises. It was a wormhole, after all.

Vanessa, being the good mom she was, decided to give them hope of future fun.

"Tell you what," she said as she kissed each forehead, in turn. "As soon as this is over, I'll take you someplace where you can practice your stunt. Safely. Someplace where the ground is soft and there aren't file cabinets everywhere. Deal?"

That got Vanessa a lot of hugs. Some of the hugs were so tight she had to turn into a tickle machine to make them let go. Not that she wanted them to let go, but the world wasn't going to save itself. Vanessa and her daughters had a job to do.

But first they needed to find out what was going on with Erica and Dr. Wilson. She looked at the couple that was still locked in that awkward embrace.

"Girls, hush!" Vanessa whispered at her giggling daughters. Why she made the effort to whisper she wasn't sure. Neither Erica nor Dr. Wilson so much as noticed that there were other people in the room. Even when a bomb of girly giggles exploded behind Vanessa, it elicited no response from the pair.

Vanessa motioned the girls to be quiet but they frankly didn't even notice her. Becca and Maddie had created their own tickle machines and were busy torturing their little sisters.

"Girls," Vanessa called.

Nothing but giggles.

"It's time for seriousness."

Giggles.

"We need to focus."

More giggles.

"C'mon girls! We need to save the world!"

Zoe, who was Maddie's target, started laughing so hard she fell to the floor at Audrey's feet and curled up into a ball. Becca stopped tickling Audrey and grinned.

"Power boost?" Becca asked Audrey.

When Audrey nodded, both girls turned their attention to the vulnerable sister on the floor. Soon Zoe's giggles had become screams of laughter.

"Becca!"

Vanessa might as well have been talking to a wall. There was no sign she had even been heard.

"Becca," Vanessa pleaded. "Your dad."

Her voice had been low, but her words had somehow penetrated through the wall of mirth and reached Becca's ears. Becca sat back and looked at her mother.

"We need to get him back."

Becca whispered in Maddie's ear. Now the tickle machine only had one set of hands.

"The tickle machine is off," Becca said as she grabbed Audrey around the waist and pulled her away from Zoe.

"Why?" Audrey asked.

"Yeah, why?" Zoe echoed. She uncurled and stood up. "I don't mind it."

"Daddy" was Becca's one-word answer.

Zoe blinked several times. "Daddy," she whispered.

"Tickle machine is on," Audrey yelled gleefully

as she held up her fingers and rushed toward a now serious Zoe. But Maddie snatched her up.

"Put me down!" Audrey yelled. "I want to tickle."

"We'll do it later," Becca consoled her. "Zoe's all tickled out right now."

And Zoe, who was thinking about her dad, did look all tickled out. So Audrey nodded and Maddie set her on her feet.

The whole tickle machine episode had been loud, the stressed-kids-need-to-blow-off-steam kind of loud that has been known to make sensitive ears bleed.

But Erica and Dr. Wilson hadn't noticed a thing. The two were so caught up in their own little drama that they were oblivious to the world around them. They had created a personal space bubble around themselves so strong that anything outside the bubble might as well not exist. A tidal wave the size of Seattle could sweep through the wormhole, obliterate every bookshelf and file cabinet in sight, and they would remain perfectly dry.

Whatever this was, it was important to Erica. Since Vanessa knew that only two things mattered to Erica—her career and her family, and she had left her family in the past—this must be a career-related conversation.

Or so she thought until she moved close enough to hear.

"When I stepped through that door to find things changed," Erica said into Dr. Wilson's chest, "I thought I'd lost you forever."

Dr. Wilson's eyes looked ready to pop out of his face.

Vanessa slapped her forehead with the heel of her palm.

"What is it, Mom?" Becca asked. Vanessa turned to find all four of her daughters crowded beside her.

"Shh."

"Why?" Maddie asked. "They can't hear us."

"They might," Vanessa insisted. "Besides," she continued, "I can't hear."

"Oh, Roddy," Erica pleaded into Dr. Wilson's chest, "you have to remember me. Remember us."

"What a horrible friend I am," Vanessa sighed. "This is that guy."

"What guy?" Becca asked.

"The guy Erica fell in love with. The one that

convinced her to stay here in the future instead of going back to our time."

"We have children, Roddy," Erica continued. "You remember our children, don't you?"

As soon as she mentioned children, a memory of Erica popped into Vanessa's head. It was on Vanessa's last trip to the future. Erica had been happy, besotted with her job and the man she married, and very, very pregnant.

Vanessa looked at Dr. Wilson's face to see how he was taking the revelation that he and Erica had children together. It wasn't pretty. He was so white it was a miracle he could still stand. So much blood had left his head that Vanessa was surprised he didn't drop to the floor like a sack of potatoes in a French fry factory. *Splat!*

"This is heartbreaking," Vanessa whispered. "He's ready to faint any second, and when he looks at her it's like she's some kind of monster who's going to gobble him up."

"Your daughter," Erica continued, her voice almost panicked as she searched for a way to reach him, "little Rodrica—"

"Stop!" Dr. Wilson croaked. He grabbed Erica by her shoulders and pushed her away—pasty, but stoic. "Enough of this nonsense."

"But Roderick—" Erica began, only to find herself speaking to Dr. Wilson's palm.

"Whatever game you're playing, I want no part of it," Dr. Wilson said with a voice so shaky, no one could be accused of exaggeration if they said he was sure to collapse at any moment. "History is one thing. This is something else."

The thought that she should intervene flitted through Vanessa's mind, then right back out again. This was a great opportunity to learn more about the dynamics of timeline changes.

Mainly she wanted to know if love was the catalyst that allowed memories to break through the veil of time. She had remembered a different timeline—was it because of her love of Tony?

Vanessa looked at her kids, worried that all this heart-squeezing drama might traumatize them, but they were perfectly fine. They had plopped down on the floor, totally enthralled.

"Remember our wedding?" Erica asked quietly. "Your mother said—"

"I've never had a mother," Dr. Wilson interrupted quickly. "Or a father for that matter."

"I don't know why you're being so stubborn."

Erica huffed. "Your mother spoke at our wedding. She told everyone—"

"Stop!"

"—About a story you wrote when you were eight."

"There was no wedding. I have no mother. I was never a child. This never happened."

"It was about space—"

"You can't know about that story."

"—A wormhole—"

"Stop talking," Dr. Wilson pleaded. "Please."

"—Aliens," Erica continued, ignoring Dr. Wilson's distress, "came through this wormhole—"

"Please stop," Dr. Wilson begged.

"—And took over the world—"

Dr. Wilson shook his head and paced.

"They tricked humanity into trusting them."

"I don't want to hear anymore," Dr. Wilson said as he stopped pacing and covered his ears with his hands.

"No, Roddy," Erica begged, as she raced over to grab Dr. Wilson's hands. "Just listen—"

"Stop calling me Roddy. No one calls me that." Dr. Wilson jerked his hands out of Erica's.

"But Roderick, I'm your wife!"

"No, " Dr. Wilson said as he shivered and took a step back. "You're a monster. Like the story I wrote my first year."

"The story I somehow know about. Now, Roderick. Do I look like a monster to you?"

Dr. Wilson blinked so fast as he looked Erica over that his eyelashes looked more like hummingbird wings than anything human.

"Well?"

"I don't know," Dr. Wilson admitted with an uncomfortable shrug. "But the aliens in my story were monsters. And I didn't make them up. I dreamed them."

Dr. Wilson looked closely at Erica's face, then his eyes widened in shock. "Oh!"

"Roddy!" Erica said with a relieved smile. "You remember me—"

Dr. Wilson shook his head, clearly conflicted.

Vanessa looked around to see if there were any snacks handy. She was getting peckish, and if she was hungry the girls probably were too. Unfortunately, there was nothing.

Where was the popcorn when a mother needed it?

Erica reached out her arms to Dr. Wilson, but

instead of moving toward her he backed away in the opposite direction. He would have retreated all the way across the room if a file cabinet hadn't gotten in the way.

"Roddy?"

"You. You were in the dream. You're one of the aliens—"

Dr. Wilson grabbed his head and slid to the floor in apparent pain as memories of that long forgotten dream resurfaced.

Erica and Vanessa immediately rushed to his aid. Erica turned his face toward her, but he closed his eyes as if the sight of her face gave him even more pain.

"Don't fight it, darling. Just relax," Erica soothed as she put a calm hand on Dr. Wilson's shoulders. "Let your brain make structure from the chaos."

"What's happening to him?" Vanessa asked.

"He's remembering the other timeline," Erica replied calmly.

"That's possible? Then that means—"

"Slow down. Only a small percentage of people, about one in ten million, have the mutation that allows them to travel through time without any adverse side effects. They also have the ability to remember alternative timelines, if they're given the right stimuli."

"Dr. Wilson has this mutation?"

"So do you," Erica said, "and your daughters."

"You were the reason we discovered the mutation. It was why we couldn't shield your memories. Your brain is just too adaptable."

Vanessa glanced at her daughters. Maddie stood stiffly as Audrey demonstrated to Zoe the best way to climb onto her shoulders.

"Becca," Vanessa called with a raised eyebrow.

"No jumping or throwing, Mom. I promise. We're just practicing climbs," Becca reassured her.

Vanessa sighed and shook her head. Then what Erica had said sunk in.

"Wait a minute. My daughters have this mutation?"

"All four of them."

"So, with a little help, they too could remember the other timeline?"

"It's not that simple. Their brains haven't matured yet, so it might be harder to find the trigger. I lucked out with Roddy. Sure, I knew about that story he wrote as a child. But I didn't know it was from a dream. Luckily it still worked as a trigger."

"Mommy, look!" Zoe called excitedly.

Vanessa twirled to find her perched atop Maddie's shoulders.

"I climbed, just like Mulan!" she yelled.

"No, you didn't," Becca corrected her. "Mulan climbed a pole using weights. You climbed Maddie using her arms."

"Well it's almost as good, isn't it Mommy?" Zoe asked from her perch atop her sister's shoulders.

"Every bit as good, Zoe," the distracted mother called back. "But no jumping. Save that for later."

"Do you think—" Vanessa turned back to Erica, but was halted by a realization.

"Do I think what?" Erica prodded. "Do you have an idea?"

Instead of answering, Vanessa allowed her mind to run with a crazy idea. Could what she was thinking be true? Could—

"Vanessa! Talk to me!" Erica grabbed Vanessa's shoulders and gave her a little shake. "Snap out of it."

"Learn a little patience," Vanessa replied as she calmly removed Erica's hands from her shoulders.

"Do you really think this is the time for

patience?"

"It's always time for patience."

"So says the mother who has her children with her. I don't know where my children are, or if they were even born."

"Erica, I'm sorry!"

"At least I'll have my husband back soon. He's coming out of it."

It was true. Dr. Wilson, who had been writhing on the floor holding his head in pain, was now slowly sitting up as he looked around in confusion.

"So back to my question," Erica said, "what is your idea? Do you think you could figure out the trigger for your girls? It might take quite a bit of time. There are four of them, after all, and each might have a different trigger. We could start with the oldest—"

Vanessa shook her head.

"The youngest?"

She again shook her head.

"One of the middle ones? But why would—?"

Vanessa grabbed Erica by the shoulders and twirled her around so she could watch the four girls building a human pyramid.

"Look at them."

"I'm looking."

Erica watched for several seconds, then shrugged.

"Don't you get it?" Vanessa said. "They're climbing around like a bunch of monkeys."

"So? What's wrong with that?"

"Nothing. Absolutely nothing. They're confident, adventurous."

"Okay. I would think you'd want them to be confident and adventurous."

Vanessa's frustration came out as a semi-restrained roll of the eyes.

"What?" Erica asked.

"Those references to *Mulan*?"

Erica was confused and her body language showed it.

"The movie was about a girl who proved she was every bit as good as a boy."

"Still don't get it." Erica shrugged.

"Do my daughters look, or act, like they grew up in a society where girls aren't allowed to walk outside alone?"

Erica's eyes widened as she looked from Vanessa to the four girls.

"You mean—?"

Vanessa nodded happily. Erica did an excellent imitation of an owl as she processed the thought.

"How?" she finally asked.

"Don't know," Vanessa replied. Then she smiled. "Frankly, I don't care."

"But when—?"

"I'm pretty sure their memories have been coming back, gradually, all day."

Erica watched a few moments while Vanessa's daughters huddled up. She turned to Vanessa.

"So what now?"

"I think—" Vanessa's train of thought was interrupted when Dr. Wilson grabbed Erica, whirled her around, and gave her a big kiss.

"Hello, gorgeous!"

"Roddy!"

"Sorry I didn't remember you," Dr. Wilson said as he continued to hold his wife close. "And just so you know, you are in no way monster-like. I've missed you."

"I was beginning to think I wouldn't get you back," Erica said as she squeezed him like she had no plans to ever let go.

"I remember," Dr. Wilson said. He gazed at

Erica like he hadn't seen her in years. "I have a whole life of memories without you."

"How was it?"

"Lonely. Let's never do that again."

"Dr. Wilson," Vanessa said, hating to interrupt the blissful reunion. "Don't we have a world to save?"

Dr. Wilson gave a goofy, puppy-dog-love look to Erica before he answered.

"Right," he said. "And call me Roderick."

"Okay, Roderick. So where's the manual?"

"The what?"

"The manual. We need it to operate the portal."

Roderick and Erica looked at each other and burst out laughing.

"What's so funny?" Vanessa asked.

"I don't know," Erica snickered, "probably the thought of using a manual to operate the portal."

"Well…" Vanessa raised a brow at Roderick. "He thought we'd need it."

"I did, didn't I? But that was before."

"Before?"

"Before I got my memories of the other timeline. Now I can operate the portal in my sleep."

"What about you, Erica? Do you know how to

operate it?"

"I'm not a time monkey, like Roddy—he was the top time adapter until they promoted him to administration—but I've done a few trips. I can work the portal in a pinch."

Erica craned her neck to see what Vanessa's daughters were doing. She smiled when she saw that they had figured out how to play jacks with paperclips and a rubber band ball.

"You know, your daughters are special," Erica said quietly to Vanessa.

"I know."

"Do you?" Erica motioned Vanessa to follow. She led her to a plaque proudly displayed on the opposite side of the room and read aloud.

"The Rossi History Room. Dedicated to Rebecca Rossi, Madeline Rossi, Zoe Rossi, and Audrey Rossi. Inventors of the Marz Portal and Marz Stabilizer and the first time travelers."

Vanessa reread the plaque several times, but she was having trouble absorbing what it said.

"Mars like the planet?" Vanessa asked.

"No, first initials."

Vanessa nodded her head in understanding.

"The Marz Portal is, well, the portal. You know

about that. The stabilizer is the technology that tames the wormhole and makes the history room possible."

Vanessa reached up and ran her finger over the engraved letters on the plaque. Then she turned to Erica.

"They time traveled?"

"They were the first. They thought their technology might be dangerous, so they put in over a thousand trips apiece before they let anyone else try."

Vanessa glanced at her daughters. They seemed to be enjoying their game while Roderick watched nearby.

"Your daughters founded and ran the DTA for years. They created the operating procedures, the safety protocols, and wrote the manual. They figured out a solution when it was discovered that not everyone could travel without side effects. They even named the department."

Vanessa nodded and looked across the room at her daughters. They had stopped playing jacks and were deep in conversation with Roderick, who had grabbed a clipboard and was frantically taking notes.

"What's he doing?" Vanessa asked.

"I don't know, but they are his heroes. He always wanted to meet them."

"Why didn't he just use the portal—?"

"Not allowed," Erica explained with a quick shake of her head. "There are people in the timeline who are off-limits. Can you imagine if someone talked to them as youngsters and accidently got them interested in another field?"

Erica shivered at the thought.

"Yeah, well, the timeline must be more resilient than you thought, because someone changed something, and now my daughters won't be allowed to invent a new hairstyle, much less a time portal. Yet the portal was invented. Can you explain that?"

Erica shrugged and shook her head.

"Okay then, can we fix it?"

"I don't think we have a choice."

"Maybe we should start by—"

"—Eating," Roderick interrupted. "The girls are hungry. Audrey says her tumbly is rumbly, whatever that means. They gave me a list of what they'd like to eat. I've never heard of most of it."

He turned the clipboard so Vanessa could see a

long list of junk food. She shook her head.

"You guys still have sandwiches?"

Erica nodded, realized she had no way of really knowing, and looked to Roderick for an answer.

"My favorite quick meal any time…line," he quipped with a smile.

∞

"Out of curiosity, who do people, in this timeline at least, think invented time travel?" Vanessa asked as she looked over a sandwich before taking a bite. It had been decided that it would be best if they stayed out of sight as much as possible, so Erica, Vanessa, Roderick, and the girls had hunkered down in Roderick's office and were eating a well-deserved meal of sandwiches and cookies.

"Douglas Whitfield," Roderick answered as he hungrily bit into his sandwich. "He made a fortune with that patent."

"How big of a fortune?" Vanessa asked mid-bite.

"Big enough to become one of the wealthiest men in the twenty-first century. And he was good at investing, too, so his line is still one of the wealthiest."

Vanessa put down her sandwich. "He did it!"

"Did what?" Roderick asked as he took such big a bite of his sandwich that a huge blob of mustard squirted out and plopped down on his pristine, white tunic.

"Darn! Mustard has always been my nemesis," Roderick grumbled as he grabbed a butter knife and began to scrape at the mustard.

"Roderick, focus. This is important!"

"So is this. It's my favorite tunic. I can't wear it with this big yellow blotch on it. It's unprofessional. People will think I've turned into a slob."

"Don't you think finding out who changed the timeline is more important than a little spilled mustard?"

"A little! Look at this," Roderick exclaimed. He pointed to the blotch of bright yellow. "It's bigger than my hand."

"Only because you're spreading it with that knife," Erica said.

"How else am I supposed to scoop up the mustard?"

"We don't care about the silly old mustard," Vanessa grumbled. "We have a clue to a who, that can lead us to a why, that could lead us to a when."

"Go on," Erica prodded. "What are you

thinking?"

"Once we know the who, why, and when, we can undo the damage. Repair the timeline."

"And you think Douglas Whitfield is the who?"

"Makes sense," Vanessa said with a shrug. "He's supposed to have invented time travel, but I didn't see any plaques about him in the history room."

"Well, if he changed the timeline for money," Roderick said as he watched Erica cut a sandwich in half for Zoe, "I'd say instead of doing an awful lot, he did a lot of awful."

"Can't argue with you there," Vanessa agreed as she took another bite. She chewed, swallowed, then added, "You should wash out the mustard in cold water and then soak it in hydrogen peroxide."

"What?"

"It'll get the stain out. Hydrogen peroxide will work wonders on that white tunic."

Roderick looked down at the stain.

"We can be planning."

Roderick thought a moment before he picked up a file to hide the stain.

"I'll be back in a bit," he said.

"You'll probably have to soak it for about an hour, but that should do the trick," Vanessa reminded the good doctor.

Roderick nodded. "While I'm gone, it would be best if you stayed in my office. Safer, since you're monsters and Russian spies, and all."

"Will do." Vanessa smiled. "We'll wait here until you get back."

Chapter 15

PHILIP SAT AT A table in the public library with his head in his hands. After several days of sleepless searching, he was no closer to finding his wife.

Not that all his hard work had been futile. He had uncovered who had made the changes, and why.

It all started when he walked into the lobby of the DTA and gazed at the plaque dedicated to his heroes, the four daughters of the Rossi family who had long ago made time travel possible. He often used the plaque as a focal point when he needed to think.

Only someone had changed the plaque. Instead of Annabel's relatives, this plaque was dedicated to a man named Douglas Whitfield.

"Douglas Whitfield," Philip had said under his breath. "Where have I heard that name before?"

He pushed it out of his head as unimportant, until he had stumbled across a statue in front of the main library. It commemorated the greatest inventor of all time, Douglas Whitfield, and the face on the statue was that of the man who had bought him dinner and drinks during that failed trip to the past. Philip knew beyond a shadow of a doubt that the statue had not existed before his trip.

His stomach churned at the thought of what else might be different. He had to know the worst, so he rushed into the library to dive into some heavy-duty research.

What he discovered shocked him. Almost every major invention of the early twenty-first century was credited to Douglas Whitfield. The wealth he accumulated by strategically leasing those inventions was immense. He had even used that wealth to start a corporation, the Whitfield Institute for the Greater Good of Humanity, tasked with genetic manipulation targeted at flaws in the

human race. The WIGGH was credited
with eradicating baldness, cancer, and high-pitched
voices.

It was only after Whitfield's death that it was
discovered that the WIGGH had used very suspect
experimentation practices. The government shut it
down.

The thought of WIGGH's successes temporarily
pulled Philip out of his funk. He gingerly touched
the thinning patch he had noticed on the back of his
head a few years earlier. It was gone. The hair was
thick and full, just as it had been when he was a boy.

After several pats to the back of his head, he
excitedly rushed into the library bathroom and
spent the next several minutes twisting and turning
to get just the right angle so he could see the back
of his head in the mirror. He finally succeeded with
the help of an extra shiny metal file box he found
lying on a shelf.

"Well, Whitfield." He nodded. "You got that
right. Let's see what else you did."

He returned to the books, but what he found
there made him sick. And the deeper he dug, the
worse it got.

At first he was surprised that a number of inventions had taken quite a bit longer to develop than they should have. The most glaring change was computers. They should have come into existence during WWII, but they hadn't been invented until the early 2100s.

It made no sense.

So he dug deeper and discovered that WWII had lasted an inordinately long length of time—instead of six years, it had gone on for more than forty.

"Good God, that means—"

"Quiet," the librarian behind the counter growled.

"Sorry," Philip whispered. He looked around and caught the glares of several other researchers, who obviously didn't appreciate loud exclamations. Philip shrugged and turned his eyes back to the book.

Not that he could read a word. His eyes refused to focus while his mind reeled with the repercussions.

Forty years of a worldwide war. So many people dead, people who should have lived productive lives, and had children who lived productive lives, who in turn had children who lived productive lives....

The damage done to the timeline was staggering, nearly unimaginable.

He had to find out how far back it went. He grabbed a book from the shelf, blew off the thick dust, and read the title. It dealt with the first half of the twentieth century, obviously not a particularly popular time in history.

Nothing seemed unusual until a paragraph about landmark laws caught his eye. In 1931 it became illegal for women to be employed or educated past rudimentary reading level. It went on to say that the law was so successful in the United States that many countries around the world passed similar laws.

Philip was reminded of the way some conquered nations were kept under control. Education and money were restricted, which made the conquered easier to keep in line.

But women? He was missing something, some important part of the pattern.

Based on the plethora of plaques and statues around the city, Douglas Whitfield had somehow found out about the time portal and used it to steal inventions.

Although Philip didn't agree with the ethics of it, he understood why Whitfield had stolen those inventions. Whitfield had seen it as a way to acquire wealth, power, and fame.

But that didn't explain women being denied basic human rights. Unless Douglas Whitfield had been harmed by a woman and wanted to get revenge by—

Philip bolted to his feet, knocking over his chair with a loud *CRASH*. He ignored the glares sent his way as he realized that Douglas Whitfield had done was exactly what he, Philip, had planned to do.

Only Douglas Whitfield had done it on a much, much larger scale.

Philip groaned loudly, which brought even more glares in his direction.

He didn't care, now that he knew that he was the cause of his own heartbreak. He should have been more careful with the settings of the portal. When he realized he was in the wrong time period, he should have immediately returned to his own time. He should have—

Philip suddenly remembered the brochure he had stuffed into his pocket immediately before his trip into the past. He slapped his pockets and threw books over his shoulder as he searched for the missing brochure.

"You need to leave," a gruff voice said in his ear.

"It has to be here!" Philip yelled, as he continued to toss books in every direction.

Without any further warning, several pairs of hands picked him up, carried him to the door, and tossed him out. By the time he had brushed off his pants and stood, the door of the library was tightly closed.

"I was just about to leave, anyway," Philip yelled at the door. As a response, he heard the lock of the door CLICK.

"My jacket!"

He hadn't worn the jacket since that fateful trip. He rushed home, searched his jacket pockets, but didn't find the brochure. So he frantically searched his entire, miniscule apartment from top to bottom. There was no sign of the brochure anywhere.

Philip sighed in self-disgust. The brochure, complete with schematics of the very first time machine, was gone. And since it had been in a zipped pocket, the most likely reason for its disappearance was that Douglas Whitfield had gotten his greedy mitts on it.

Had Whitfield searched his pockets while he slept?

Philip sat on the couch and focused on the time he had spent with Whitfield. He remembered the relief he had felt when Whitfield invited him to sit, his shame at having to admit he had no money, followed by relief when Whitfield offered to pay.

Whitfield was one of those people who made friends quickly and easily, and it had taken only a few minutes before Philip had felt totally at home. As Douglas kept the food and drinks coming, Philip's guard had lowered and all his worries about his career had spilled out. Whitfield slapped him on the back, laughed heartily, and told him that his career woes were a rite of passage. Every man went through a period of time when he had trouble getting the job he wanted. It was a necessary part of life. It made a man tough.

Then Whitfield had slapped him on the back again and bought him a half dozen miniature glasses of a liquid that he called Vodka shots. He told Philip that these shots were also a rite of passage, and that after he drank them, all his troubles would go away, for a while at least.

All the memories after Philip drank the
fiery liquid were a blurry haze. He could just
remember telling Whitfield about Annabel.

A memory of Annabel's sunny smile burned
away the haze and Philip had a clear memory of the
biggest mistake of his entire life.

He had not only bragged about his intelligent,
beautiful wife, but he distinctly remembered
fumbling around in his pocket and pulling out the
museum's brochure about the history of time
travel.

He had even gone so far as to wave it about,
several times so close to Whitfield's face that he hit
him on the nose.

He should have been more careful. He should
have emptied his pockets before he stepped
through the portal. He should have—

Philip stopped in the middle of his "should
haves" and groaned.

"What I should have done is not try to use time
travel for my own personal gain. I would have
eventually gotten a job. I should have had more
patience."

He reached into his tunic pocket and
pulled out the small metal box that contained the
only connection he had left with his wife.

"Oh, Annabel," Philip sighed as he clicked open
the lid. "What have I done?"

Chapter 16

"I REALLY, REALLY, REALLY have to go," Zoe whined as she squirmed the there-will-be-a-puddle-on-the-floor-soon dance.

Ten minutes had passed since Roderick had gone to remove the mustard stain from his tunic. The girls were fed, but they were also restless. Audrey had climbed every surface in the room at least three times, and her older sisters had amused themselves by shooting each other with rubber bands from the dismantled rubber band ball, usually with painful results.

Each time Audrey climbed too high, Vanessa pulled her down to safety. She had planned to let the rubber band war continue until the girls tired of the game, except they got sloppy in their aim and she and Erica got zinged several times. She confiscated the rubber band ball and all its babies and hid them in the pocket of her jacket.

As soon as the last rubber band baby was stowed in her pocket, Zoe decided she needed to go to the bathroom.

"Can it wait, Zoe? Just for a bit?" Vanessa asked.

Zoe nodded an affirmative, but scrunched up her forehead and continued with her squirmy little dance. Which told Vanessa that a bit was about as long as the child could wait. A bathroom needed to be found, and fast.

"How about the rest of you?" Vanessa asked. "Do you need the restroom too?"

Three kid-sized and one adult-sized head bobbed in unison.

"You too, Erica?" Vanessa asked the adult-sized head bobber.

"I did spend a lifetime in that history room." Erica shrugged. "About time I took a bathroom break."

"Guess it is. So where are women's bathrooms?"

"I know where they used to be," Erica replied. "But by my calculations a bathroom is just a bathroom in this timeline. You know, no women."

"Right. Believe it or not, I forgot."

"If the plumbing is the same in this building, the closest bathroom will be across from the portal.

Which is great for us, because since the portal is shut down…"

"…No one will be around! Good thinking. I'll take Zoe first; she obviously needs to go the most. When I get back you can take—"

"Mom!" Becca interrupted. She pointed at Audrey, who had moved a trash can next to Roderick's desk and climbed on top so that all she had to do was pull down her pants, squat, and—

"*Audrey*!" Vanessa yelled.

Vanessa sprinted to snatch the four-year-old off the desk.

"Audrey, sweetie, not there. We'll find a bathroom."

"Okay, Mommy." Audrey grabbed her mother's hand and pulled her toward the door.

"Wait, sweetie. I think Zoe should go first."

"No, Mommy," Audrey responded, her eyes growing bigger and sadder by the second, "I need to go. Now."

Vanessa glanced from Zoe, whose dance had become rather spastic, to her two older daughters. She raised a questioning eyebrow.

"Me too, Mom," Becca responded.

Maddie nodded, her eyes shut tight.

Vanessa bit her lip.

"Okay, when we leave this room we have to be very, very quiet. We don't want to draw any attention to ourselves."

"We can be quiet, Mom. Don't worry," Becca said solemnly. Then she smirked. "After all, we are Russian spies."

A very serious Maddie opened one eye as she nodded in agreement.

"And you two?" Vanessa asked her two youngest daughters.

"I can be quiet, Mommy." Zoe's whisper was loud, but at least she was trying.

"Me, too!" Audrey yelled. Then she sang, "Quiet, quiet, quiet. I can be quiet. Watch me be quiet. Quiet—"

"Nice song, Audrey, but we need a different quiet. Like we're going through a jungle that has big, scary lions. So we're going to—"

"Swords!" Zoe shivered in anticipation.

"What?" Vanessa was momentarily confused by Zoe's sword fighting stance. "No, I meant—"

"I'll fight the lions, one by one." Zoe raised an invisible sword and danced around as if in an intense sword fight. "I can save us."

"Me too! I plight lions too," Audrey yelled. She joined her sister in the fight against the invisible lions.

Erica watched the two little girls with amusement.

"I don't think this is what you wanted," she whispered to Vanessa.

"Actually, this will work great," Vanessa whispered back. "I'll just let them burn off a little energy first."

After several minutes of intense battle, the combatants slowed, a sure signal that their energy levels were depleted.

"Hey, girls, what about the bathroom?" Vanessa asked.

Zoe had just raised her arm to give the finishing blow to a cowering lion when a very upset Audrey stopped her.

"Wait!" Audrey yelled as she grabbed Zoe's arm. "It's a mommy lion."

Audrey pointed to the far corner of the office, tears in her eyes.

"Her babies. They need her."

Zoe looked in confusion from the invisible lion on the floor in front of her to the invisible cubs across the room. She was unsure what to do next and gave an audible sigh of relief when Vanessa stepped in to help.

"Stand back. She's getting up." Vanessa gently pulled her daughters closer, as if to protect them.

"What's that?" Vanessa tilted her head toward the invisible lion and watched as it rose to tower over her. Then she nodded.

"She says she doesn't want to hurt us, she just wants to protect her babies. Just like"—Vanessa bent down and hugged both girls—"I want to protect my babies."

Zoe and Audrey eyes remained glued to the invisible lion, even while they returned their mother's hug.

"What's that?" Vanessa asked the air in front of her. She slowly rose.

"We're sorry, your majesty." Vanessa curtseyed deeply. "We didn't know. Thank you, your majesty."

"Mom," Zoe whispered.

"Shush, Zoe. Her majesty is leaving," Vanessa whispered back. She stayed in a deep curtsey a few more moments. After a quick peek toward the door, she stood up.

"Well, that was close!"

"What did she say, Mommy?" Zoe asked.

"She said her kingdom is enchanted. A wicked fairy turned them all into lions. She said we can have safe passage through her land, but we must be quiet, very quiet. There are dragons outside that door that have been asleep for more than a hundred years."

Vanessa beckoned for the others and the six of them formed a huddle. Vanessa's face was its most serious as she locked eyes with each in turn.

"We can do this, if we're quiet. But if we wake those dragons...well, it won't be pretty."

Becca and Maddie exchanged a look that warned Vanessa that explosive laughter was imminent. She cleared her throat and raised a warning eyebrow when they looked her way. Becca scrunched her eyes closed as she nodded. Maddie bit her upper lip.

"I've studied dragons for years," Erica broke in, surprising Vanessa. The Erica who had been her study partner had been excessively serious and had rarely shown even a sliver of humor. Now she was ready to jump into a major flight of fantasy that required both humor and imagination?

Erica noticed the surprise on Vanessa's face and explained.

"My son is positively fascinated by dragons. He collects everything he can find, reads every book, and watches every movie. So of course I studied up on them."

"You have a son?" Vanessa smiled.

"Two of them. And a daughter." Memories of her children made her face glow with love.

Then she blinked as she remembered the changed timeline.

"Had. I guess they were never born."

Vanessa broke the huddle and gave Erica a quick hug.

"We'll get them back."

"I know." Erica nodded. "But before we can figure out what to do, we need to be comfortable. And to do that, we need a bathroom."

The huddle reformed.

"I know dragons usually sleep at least three hundred years," Erica continued. "So if we wake them early, they're going to be cranky."

"Fire-breathing cranky?" Zoe asked.

"Fire-breathing cranky," Erica answered firmly.

Zoe shivered excitedly, but Audrey was

concerned.

"Hot pire, like a stove?" Audrey asked.

At the age of two she had burned her hand on a hot stove after stubbornly ignoring her mother's caution. She had kept her distance from hot things ever since.

"Only if they wake up," Vanessa assured her. "Sleeping dragons aren't hot at all."

Audrey nodded. "I'll be quiet," she whispered, and amazingly that whisper could only be heard within a one-foot radius.

"Me too," Zoe agreed. She sheathed her sword in her scabbard. "Put up your sword, Audrey, so it won't clank. I need the bathroom before I fight dragons."

Audrey followed her sister's lead and sheathed her sword.

"Okay, here's what we're going to do," Vanessa said quietly. "We're going to walk out of here like we own the place, head straight to the bathroom, without one word to anyone."

Four heads bobbed an agreement. But Audrey's head tilted in thought.

"What if we see a baby lion, Mommy?" Audrey asked, her eyes big. "Can we pet it and say hi?"

"No, munchkin, we can't talk to anyone. Not even a baby lion."

"But it will be sad." Audrey's protruding lower lip mimicked the baby lion's extreme sadness.

"It will be sadder if we wake the dragons and the baby lion gets an owie." Vanessa pulled Audrey into a hug. Then she held the child at arm's length and looked directly into her eyes. "We don't want the baby lion to get hurt, do we?"

Audrey thought a split second before she shook her head. "No, Mommy."

"So no talking?"

"No talking, Mommy. Promise."

"That's my girl!" Vanessa gave her a quick squeeze and tickled her belly. Audrey giggled and wiggled free.

"Well now." Vanessa looked around at her little group. "All set to go?"

"The sooner the better." Erica pointed to a squirming Zoe. "Now that she's thinking about it again, I don't think she's going to last much longer."

Vanessa led everyone to the door, checked that the coast was clear, and slid through the doorway. When everyone was in the hallway, she quietly pulled the door closed.

It was eerily quiet. Not a voice, not a footstep, not even the distant sound of a motor could be heard.

"Where is everyone?" Erica whispered.

Vanessa shrugged. Every other time Vanessa had been in the lab, it had been a bustling hub of activity.

"Do you think it's safe?" Erica looked suspiciously down the long, empty hallway.

"At the moment, I don't much care." Vanessa jerked her head toward Zoe, who was twisting and turning in a very odd manner.

"Right. This way." Erica motioned for them to follow.

As they passed through the history room anteroom, Audrey's eyes lit up and she darted away from the group to climb onto the couch. With an ecstatic sigh and a huge smile, she kneeled to cautiously pet a dog-sized object no one else could see.

"A baby lion, Mommy, look!" Audrey whispered loudly.

"Hush, Audrey," Vanessa cautioned.

A movement out of the corner of her eye caught

her attention. Pretending to pick up something off the floor, she snuck a look toward the hallway they had just left. At the corner was a man in an orange jacket peeking around the corner, watching. He probably was spying on the spies.

Which created a problem. If he heard Audrey talking about invisible baby lions, he would report back to the others that the Russian spies, who were obviously genetic experiments, had become mentally unstable. To protect themselves, the group would swoop in, capture the crazy spies, and lock them away as dangerous to society.

Audrey turned excitedly to her mother to say more about the baby lion, but Vanessa silently mouthed the word "dragons" and pointed to a far corner. Audrey's eyes widened. Vanessa raised a finger to her lips for silence. Audrey nodded, gave a final pat to the invisible lion cub, and took her mother's outstretched hand.

Vanessa picked up another imaginary item from the floor. The man was still watching. So Vanessa motioned for the group to continue. As they turned a corner, Vanessa looked back in time to see the man turn to leave.

A few minutes later, the little group successfully

reached the bathrooms without any further run-ins with the lab workers.

The time spent in the stalls was actually rather short. When a girl's gotta go, a girl's gotta go. It really doesn't take that long.

But washing hands, that was a different story. No girl worth her salt would let all that lovely water go to waste without splashing a bit of it onto a sister, or three. Not after enduring that tension-ridden hike through the land of sleeping dragons.

So the girls had a water fight, complete with giggles and squeals. The wetter they got, the more carefree they became. Before long, all four girls were cheerfully laughing with the rowdy joy of childhood.

Vanessa watched as her two oldest daughters shared a conspiratorial whisper before gathering a handful each of water and pouring it onto Erica's head. In response, Erica scooped up a double handful of water and chased Becca twice around the bathroom, slipping and sliding all the while, before tossing the water directly into Maddie's face.

A movement caught Vanessa's eye and she turned to see the door to the hallway *CLICK* shut. The water fight had drawn attention. Hoping that it

was only Roderick who had come to check
on them but didn't want to disturb the girls' play,
she tiptoed to the door and slowly pushed it open.
Directly across the hall a man was doing something
to a keypad beside a door clearly labeled *Portal
closed. Keep Out!* As she watched, he opened the
door and raised his foot to step inside.

"Hey, what are you doing?" Vanessa yelled. She
threw the door wide and rushed across the hallway
to grab the man by the arm. At the sound of her
raised voice, Becca grabbed Audrey and Maddie
grabbed Zoe and the four girls ran after her into the
hallway, leaving a trail of puddles. Erica, not
wanting to risk being left behind, dropped the
paper towels she was using to dry her face and
rushed to join the others. In her rush she forgot
about the slipperiness of the wet floor and skidded
into Becca, who knocked Maddie off balance, and
soon everyone but Vanessa and the man were in a
heap in the middle of the hallway.

The pile of people at their feet took both Vanessa
and the man by surprise. Vanessa reached with one
hand for Audrey, who was teetering precariously
on top of the pile. The man took advantage of her
distraction to slide his arm out of Vanessa's grasp

and shoved the portal door wide. He disappeared into the bright light that spilled out of the opening. As the door swung shut, Vanessa had the presence of mind to stick her foot into the opening to keep it from closing. Because even though she might not know exactly how the portal worked, she was pretty sure it would not reset while the door remained open.

That man was not wearing a lab coat and was using a portal that had been shut down for centuries, both red flags. He was a very suspicious character, probably the scoundrel who caused the timeline glitch in the first place.

Erica and the girls looked like a wiggly plate of human spaghetti. As the arms and legs sorted themselves out, Vanessa turned her attention to following the man through the portal.

Erica gently pushed the last kiddy arm off her stomach and climbed to a standing position. As soon as she was out of the way, the four girls squirmed like a bunch of eels and sprung up like four jack-in-the-boxes with overwound springs.

"Girls, you okay?" Vanessa called.

"That was fun!" Zoe giggled. Becca brushed Zoe's hair out of her eyes.

Erica shook her head.

"I thought my boys were tough. These girls of yours might as well be monkeys."

"They're healthy and active. What can I say." Vanessa shrugged. "How about you? Any broken bones we need to worry about?"

Erica checked her arms and legs.

"Nope! I'm good. Where did Philip go?"

"Philip?"

"The good-looking man who was here a second ago. He's the husband of our best time monkey. She's as unfazed by time travel as your daughters are by a tumble to the floor."

"Oh. When he went through the portal, I assumed he was the one who messed with the timeline. But if it makes sense he's here—"

"Actually, it doesn't." Erica shook her head. "He's not a traveler, he's a theorist. One of the best, I've heard. There was a rumor he might become head of the department, but someone else got the job."

"Does him being here make sense?"

"Well, if he came to find Annabel—"

"Who's Annabel?"

"Philip's wife. Only the best time monkey that

ever lived."

"Why would he come to find someone who was never born? 'Cause in this timeline, there are no Annabels."

"Good point. Are you sure he went—"

Erica pointed toward the portal, and for the first time noticed Vanessa's foot wedged in the crack.

"Hey! What are you doing? Get your foot out of there. That could be dangerous."

"Can't."

"Why?"

"If it closes it might reset. If it resets, we might lose him. We've got to follow. To see where he went, and when. In case he was the one who changed things."

"No, not Philip. He's too smart. He knows an untrained traveler could cause all kinds of damage—"

Vanessa raised an eyebrow.

"He couldn't," Erica gasped. "He wouldn't."

"I think he did."

Erica opened and closed her mouth as she processed Vanessa's accusation. She couldn't have done a more perfect imitation of a fish if she had tried.

"Maybe you're right." She sighed and leaned against a nearby wall for support. "But that doesn't mean we should—"

"You can stay here if you want." Vanessa's chin jutted out stubbornly. "My daughters and I can save the world by ourselves."

Erica watched as the four girls, who had found paper and pens, crouched down on the floor to draw diagrams.

"But is it safe? For them?" Erica warmed up to her topic. "No data has been collected about the effect of time travel on a child's growth cycle. I mean it might—"

"If your children were here, what would you do?" Vanessa asked.

"I would hold on tight and never let go," Erica said sadly.

"Exactly. I have to go. So do they."

Erica nodded her understanding.

"The question is"—Vanessa squinted her eyes and stretched her neck, turtle fashion, to get her face as close to Erica's as she possibly could without taking her foot from the door—"what are you going to do?"

Chapter 17

PHILIP WAS BENT DOUBLE in Denny Hall basement as he fought to catch his breath. Only time monkeys, like his wife, could freely move through the timeline without significant physical consequences. The portal took a lot out of people. But even time monkeys would hesitate to sprint through the portal like he had just done.

He'd nearly had a heart attack when that woman yelled at him. It wasn't the yelling, although it had startled him enough that the detailed plans he had developed for this trip had scuttled away into some unknown section of his brain.

No, it was the children. There they were, laughing, playing, splashing water everywhere, and being very childlike. How had he not noticed the absence of children?

Perhaps the oversight was understandable since his focus was on Annabel. When he had failed to find her, he had spent every hour of the day and night searching, researching, and making a nuisance of himself. All to discover that anomaly that would help him figure out what had happened to the world.

And find it he had, because it had to be an anomaly that women had disappeared from society. They weren't in grocery stores, coffee shops, restaurants, or at the DTA. So he had gone to the library and found that several laws had been passed in the twentieth century that he was sure should not have been passed. Laws that claimed to protect the female population, but actually snatched away their rights and made them second-class citizens.

The end result was that they were kept hidden, out of sight. Probably viewed more as property than people.

He tried, but failed, to imagine Annabel in such a situation. His wife was simply too intelligent and spunky.

So where was she?

He had to get her back.

Whatever it took, he would put the
world right again.

For Annabel.

Chapter 18

VANESSA LET OUT THE breath she had been holding as she did a quick head count before she closed the portal door. The last thing she wanted was to leave someone behind.

"Good old Denny Hall." She squinted down the wide, shadowy hallway. Massive lockers lined the walls, blocking the meager light from a single bulb in the ceiling a few feet away. "I remember it much brighter."

"Safety certainly isn't a priority." Erica, who was cradling a very still Audrey, shivered. "It feels deserted, like no one's been here in years."

Vanessa bent to rub her hand across the floor and showed a disgustingly dirty finger to Erica.

"Seems that way. No self-respecting university would let a building in use get this dirty. There'd be a lawsuit."

Vanessa noticed the nostalgic look on Erica's face as she gazed at the sleeping child in her arms. She brushed the hair off Audrey's face.

"Wouldn't hold her breath, huh?"

"I told her it would keep her from passing out. Stubborn little thing, isn't she?"

"Just a normal four-year-old. It's a tough age."

"I remember. With my kids."

There was a long pause as Erica stared at an empty wall.

"Sooo…" Vanessa drew the word out to give Erica time to pull her mind away from her own children. "How long do you think she'll be out?"

"What?"

"Audrey. How long will she be out?"

"Ten minutes, at a guess." Erica shrugged. "She's got the gene. It shouldn't affect her too long."

"Why did no one ever tell me about the holding your breath thing? It would have saved me a ton of grief."

"Yeah. But the DTA had no reason to tell you to pressurize your lungs. They didn't want to make time travel comfortable for you."

"I know that. But it would have been nice if—"

"Mom!" Becca urgently whispered. Becca

pointed down the hall. "There's a man,"
she hissed, "sneaking around, over there. He's
watching us."

It was so dark at the end of the hallway that
Vanessa felt she needed night goggles. But after
staring for several seconds, she was able to make
out a dark figure, nearly, but not quite,
indistinguishable from the lockers.

"Hey, you!" Vanessa yelled. "What are you
doing here?"

At the sound of her voice, the figure bolted
deeper into the darkness. As she watched, a vertical
sliver of stars appeared, which she knew meant that
the door had been opened. The lower two-thirds of
the stars were blocked temporarily as the figure
slipped outside.

"He's getting away, Mom!" Maddie grabbed
Vanessa's arm and pulled her toward the dark
hallway. "Let's get him!"

"Maddie's right, Mom. I want to know why he
was watching us." Becca added her hand to
Vanessa's arm and pulled toward the darkness.

"No, Mommy, no!" Zoe cried, her lip trembling.
She grabbed Vanessa's other arm and pulled in the
opposite direction. "Dragons. They like the dark.

We need to go home."

"Girls!" Vanessa planted her feet firmly. "I'm not a rope, and this isn't tug-of-war."

All three girls abruptly let go. Vanessa wobbled back and forth a few times as she regained her balance. Then she turned to Erica.

"Philip?" Vanessa asked.

"Must be," Erica agreed.

"Load her on." Vanessa held one arm toward her sleeping child and used the other to point at her back. "C'mon, I've done it a million times. I can practically run a marathon that way."

Becca mouthed the word "adventure." Maddie giggled in delight.

Erica took one final look at the sleeping child in her arms and carefully placed her on Vanessa's back. Becca and Maddie tied a jacket in place to keep her from slipping.

"Ready?" Vanessa asked.

"Mama," Zoe whimpered, "what about the dragons?" She couldn't understand why her sisters were being so silly. Dragons were mean, horrible, scary creatures.

"Take Mommy's hand, sweetie, I won't let any old dragons hurt you." Zoe grabbed hold of

Vanessa's outstretched hand and immediately felt better.

"Quietly, girls," Vanessa warned as she tiptoed into the dark hallway. "Stealth mode time. We don't want to wake any dragons."

Zoe, eyes the size of saucers, nodded and managed a timid smile. But the further down the hallway they went, the darker it got. The darker it got, the more worried Zoe became. The more worried she became, the tighter she gripped her mother's hand.

By the time they were halfway down the hallway, it was blacker than a crow's feathers. Zoe's grip had become so tight that Vanessa could no longer feel her fingers.

They had made it most of the way through the pitch black hallway and were only five feet from the doorway when they heard a *CLICK* at the opposite end of the hall and a dim light came on. Erica just happened to be between the light and Zoe, and when Zoe saw a dark shadow suddenly loom over her, she whimpered and threw her free arm around her mother's waist.

"It's okay, sweetie—"

Something claw-like touched Zoe on the head

and she sprang into action.

"The dragons…they're awake! Run!" Which was exactly what Zoe did. And since she still had a firm grip on her mother's hand, Vanessa had no option but to run with her. Zoe flung open the door, pulled her mother to safety, and dropped her mother's hand so she could keep the door open for her sisters and Erica.

"Hurry!" she yelled. "Get out of there!"

As soon as everyone had cleared the door, Zoe slammed it shut and blocked it with her back. Her worst nightmares had come true. The dragons had come after them.

But they had survived. Everyone had gotten out in time.

"What happened in there?" Erica asked.

"Dragons, they woke up," Zoe explained, her eyes wide, but this time with excitement. "One of them grabbed me. I got us out of there."

Zoe pushed away from the door and swaggered over to Vanessa.

"That was a nest, Mom. I know it. They had us surrounded."

Becca looked to Maddie to see what she thought they should do. Maddie shrugged, unsure how to handle the situation. So Becca opened her mouth to tell Zoe exactly how wrong she was, only to be intercepted by a shake of her mother's head.

"Good thing I run so fast!" Zoe pulled her shoulders back until Vanessa feared she would fall backward. "I saved us from the fiery dragons!"

"You certainly did, sweetie." Vanessa brushed a wayward curl off Zoe's face. "You were very, very brave."

As she bent down to hug her brave little daughter, the jacket around her waist went slack. The sudden lack of weight on her back threw her off balance and she teetered gracelessly as she struggled to regain her equilibrium. For five whole seconds she flailed her arms in an attempt not to plummet to the filthy ground. When she finally regained the ability to stand upright, she twirled around.

"Audrey!" Vanessa yelled in a panic, fully expecting to see her sleeping child in a broken heap on the ground.

But instead, Audrey was perfectly fine, standing on her own two feet.

"You're awake!"

"Yes, Mommy. I waked up in the dragon's nest.

I touched a dragon. It was purry, like a dog."

"Furry like a dog—" Vanessa looked from Audrey's outstretched hand, which she held like a claw, to Zoe's fluffy head of curls and a smile spread over her face.

Now it made sense. Audrey was the owner of the claw that had touched Zoe's head and scared her into action. And the dragon Audrey had petted—well, Zoe's curls were rather "purry" and would seem dog-like in the pitch-black of the hallway.

Laughter bubbled up inside and threatened to pop her lungs like a couple of over inflated balloons. Her daughters were just so darn cute. Start with a dark hallway, add in a dash of dragons, and *WHAM*, it's an adventure.

Vanessa's heart melted as her two youngest children beamed up at her happily. Children were so amazing. The trek through the dragon's nest had made their day.

She decided to let her lungs burst rather than laugh at the little darlings.

"You girls are so brave," Vanessa grabbed the two little munchkins and squeezed them tight.

"We've had quite an adventure, haven't we?"

Both girls nodded. Vanessa gave them each a little tickle as she let them go, which brought the expected giggles. But what Vanessa did not expect was the proud way they held themselves, as if they had faced a mountain of their deepest fears and conquered them all. They had been tested. They could overcome anything.

No, Zoe and Audrey need not know the truth about their exciting run-in with a nest of dragons. Now all Vanessa had to do was keep her two older daughters from spoiling the fun of the two younger ones.

Zoe jerked as a squirrel jumped from a nearby bush to a tree. She looked back at the door to Denny Hall and gulped. It was obvious she had not completely overcome all of her fears.

Becca, Maddie, and Erica were deep in conversation but all three had caught the look of fear on Zoe's face. Erica slipped something into Becca's hand and the three shared a conspiratorial nod.

"Zoe, something's in your hair!" Becca rushed to lay the palm of her hand on Zoe's head. With her other hand she gently dug around in Zoe's curls, until she pulled her hand away to reveal a shiny silver chain with a small green jewel.

"That was in my hair?" Zoe asked, as her eyes grew wide.

"It wasn't in mine!" Becca replied.

"Dragon treasure," Zoe sighed happily.

"Becca—" Vanessa began, intent on a lecture about the danger of lies.

"Isn't it exciting, Mom?" Becca interrupted. She formed each word carefully. "The dragon tried to put the necklace on Zoe's head and it got stuck in her hair."

Maddie stepped forward and took Zoe by the shoulders. She bent down until she was eye to eye with her little sister.

"That dragon must think you are very brave," Maddie said solemnly. "Dragons don't give their treasure away very often. And only to the most worthy."

"The dragon thinks I'm worthy?" Zoe's face glowed with a mixture of pride, happiness, and awe.

"It must! We all know that dragon treasure is lucky!" Becca placed the necklace around Zoe's neck.

"Girls, I think—" Vanessa began again, but Becca turned and distorted her face with a wink so large Vanessa wondered if it hurt.

"You are very special, Zoe." Becca held the wink an extra long time for emphasis, then turned back to her little sister. "This necklace proves it."

Vanessa's mouth snapped shut. Zoe was the most nervous and cautious of her daughters. If a simple necklace could help the child find her courage, maybe Vanessa should play along.

So instead of a lecture to Becca, she gave a hug to Zoe and was rewarded with a beaming smile.

Then she hugged her even smaller daughter, who had joined the group to gawk at that oh-so-special necklace.

"It's so pretty, Mama." Audrey stared at the shiny trinket around Zoe's neck. "I want one too!"

She grabbed Vanessa's hand and pulled her toward the door, determined to get a necklace of her own from the dragons.

Quick-thinking Erica grabbed Audrey's arm.

"Audrey, wait! There's something in your hood!"

Audrey froze, too frightened to move.

"Is it," she whispered, "a spider?"

Audrey was a fearless child, except for spiders. For some reason, the little creatures terrified her.

"No." Erica reached for Audrey's hood. "It was shiny. I think it might be a ring."

"Pind it! Pind it!" Audrey skipped around with excitement. "I never had a ring before."

Erica made a big show of the searching through the bouncing hood. Now that the threat of a creepy crawly was over, Audrey could barely contain her excitement, which made Erica smile. Children were so easy to fool!

"I'll help!" Zoe yelled as she pulled the hoodie toward her.

"You're choking me!" Audrey never missed a beat as she grabbed the front of her sweatshirt and jerked it away from her neck. "Pind it, Zoe. Hurry."

Erica tried to slip a ring off her pinky and drop it into Audrey's hood, but Zoe was too close. She would see.

"Vanessa, you could—"

"Nope." Vanessa's smile was smug, but her eyes twinkled.

"But—"

Vanessa stubbornly shook her head.

Erica pursed her lips and drew her eyebrows together, as if to say she wanted help.

Vanessa responded by pursing her lips and making her eyes very wide.

Erica copied the eyes wide stance, and Vanessa was about to respond with an eye roll when Becca broke in with a suggestion.

"Turn Audrey upside down. I bet the ring would fall out then."

Erica blinked several times then asked, "Okay with you, Audrey?"

Audrey nodded.

"I'll watch down here," Zoe exclaimed, as she crouched low to the ground. "So it won't bounce away and get lost."

As Zoe crouched, Audrey held up her arms to be picked up. Erica turned slightly away and slipped the small ring from her pinky finger. She palmed it, lifted Audrey, and let the ring fall to the ground as she flipped the child upside down.

It hit the concrete with a satisfying *PING*. Zoe pounced on it and held it up triumphantly.

"I got it!" she crowed.

She handed the ring to Audrey, whose head was still lower than her feet. "Your present from the dragons! And look, it has a green stone, just like mine."

Erica righted Audrey and stood her on her feet. Audrey stared at the ring for several seconds before she turned with shining eyes to her mother.

"Can I wear it, Mommy? Please?" she begged.

"Of course you can, darling. It's your ring."

Audrey tried the ring on every finger, but it was too big for all of them.

"It doesn't pit, Mommy." Audrey's lower lip trembled and big, plump teardrops formed in her eyes. "They don't like me!"

"Of course they do, darling!" Vanessa gave her daughter a quick hug. "They just know you're going to grow bigger. They want you to have the ring forever."

Audrey blinked several times.

"Mommy can keep it for you, for now," Becca suggested.

"Put it on a chain for you, when we get home," Maddie added. "Until your fingers grow."

"You'll have a necklace, like me," Zoe chimed in.

Audrey looked longingly at the necklace around Zoe's neck. Zoe blinked a few times as she touched the green stone.

"I think the dragons made a mistake."

Zoe tilted her head in thought. "Maybe I was supposed to find the ring in your hood, and you were supposed to find the necklace in my hair."

Audrey's eyes were wide.

"Can I try the ring?" Zoe asked.

Audrey handed the ring to Zoe, who slid the ring onto her thumb. She smiled widely as she raised her thumb in the air so everyone could see that the ring fit perfectly.

"It pits!" Audrey exclaimed. "The ring must be por you."

"And the necklace"—Zoe touched the stone of the necklace gently—"must be for you. Can you help me, Mommy?"

Zoe stood still so Vanessa could unlatch the necklace. When the dragon's treasure necklace was safely transferred to Audrey, there were two very happy little girls.

"I should check your hair, Maddie, and you should check mine. I think the dragon probably left treasure for us too."

"Umm…" Erica shook her head. "I've heard that dragons never give up more than two pieces of treasure at a time."

"So, no jewelry for us?"

"Sorry girls."

"It was worth a try." Becca shrugged.

"Back to business." Vanessa put her hand on her hips as she scanned the dark landscape for figures creeping about. "Which way did he go?"

"That way." Maddie pointed.

Vanessa tilted her head at Maddie.

"I saw him go around the corner of that building when we first came out."

"Why didn't you say something? Now we've lost him."

"We were busy."

Vanessa opened her mouth to say that Philip was their top priority, but she caught sight of her two youngest daughters clicking the sparkly green stones of the necklace and ring together.

They were so happy, and so like their dad. Vanessa turned away.

"He's gone," she whispered into a bush.

"We'll find him," Erica said. She was so pleased with herself—that dragon treasure bit had been pure genius—she failed to notice Vanessa's normally upright posture had melted into a dejected puddle.

She slapped a hand on Vanessa's shoulder. "Do you think we should—?"

Vanessa turned, her eyes swimming in twin pools of despair as a river of tears cascaded down her cheeks. Her soul had been ripped in half. The pain was nearly unbearable.

This was not about Philip.

"Tony?"

Vanessa nodded.

"Oh, Vanessa! I should have—"

Vanessa gave a warning shake of her head and turned to face the bush. Erica reached out a hand but Vanessa flapped her away. Vanessa wanted to be left alone with her grief.

Erica's heart fluttered in panic.

If Vanessa fell apart, it would be left to Erica to fix the world.

But Erica was a normal person. She was no time monkey, like Vanessa. She had not been born with an innate sense about the timeline.

If it was left up to Erica, she was likely to make mistakes. Big ones. Ones that could end humanity. Ones that—

A tug on her jacket pulled her back to sanity. She looked down to see little curly-haired Zoe holding the treasured dragon's ring up to her.

"You can wear it if you want," Zoe whispered. Kindness beamed from her eyes. "It'll make you feel better."

Erica smiled as she took the ring and slid it on her little finger.

"You're right, Zoe," she whispered as she hugged the child. "I feel better already. Thank you."

Zoe nodded, smugly pleased with herself, and Erica realized that she did feel better. Not through any magic powers that the ring might possess, but because Zoe cared enough to share the dragon's ring with her.

Zoe ran to join her sisters, who had surrounded their mother with a family-sized bear hug. By the time the hug broke up, Vanessa's tears had dried and she was once again her normal, composed self.

And around her neck was the little necklace with the green stone. She touched it, looked at the ring on Erica's finger, and smiled. It made a mama proud when her children were so unselfish.

"How long should we keep them?" Erica mouthed when the girls weren't looking.

"Ten minutes," Vanessa mouthed back with a

shrug. Proper etiquette for returning dragon treasure wasn't that well defined.

"Should we—?" Erica wanted to ask how to properly return the trinket, but stopped when Becca stepped forward.

"We've been talking it over, and we have a plan."

"Okay." Vanessa blinked in surprise. "What sort of plan?"

"A really good one. First we go to the library—"

"We can't go to the library. No women are allowed."

"Okay, we'll pretend to be men."

"As soon as we open our mouths they'll know."

"So we won't talk. We'll just search the computers—"

"No computers in this timeline. We would need to ask the librarian for help. One word and we'd be kicked out."

"What if we—"

"Mommy, look!" Audrey yelled. "A head."

Everyone looked, and sure enough, a man's head peeped around the corner of the building.

"Erica?" the head asked.

"Philip?" Erica was very glad there would be no

need to chase Philip all over the timeline.

"Come meet my friends."

"Erica, I'm so glad to see you."

As Philip joined the little group, Erica was shocked by the extreme weariness on his face. "Philip, you look—"

"I know. I know. I haven't slept in a long time. I couldn't."

"Philip, answer me truthfully." Erica searched Philip's face. "Do you know what happened to the timeline?"

Philip squirmed under her scrutiny, then nodded. The guilt on his face told Erica part of the story.

"Spill it, Philip," Erica demanded. "We need to know everything."

Chapter 19

DOUGLAS WHITFIELD WAS SITTING pretty—very pretty indeed.

He could never have dreamed that his generous impulse fifteen years earlier would have paid off so abundantly.

Any normal guy who played the Good Samaritan would be lucky to get a timid "thank you" after he bought some poor sap dinner.

But Douglas was no normal guy. He had big plans but few resources. To get where he wanted to be in the world, he had to use those resources wisely.

Which was why each of his helping hands was carefully calculated to bring the highest rate of return. No handouts for poor slobs begging in the street. That would be a waste of money. Instead, he spent his cash helping well-dressed down-and-outers get back on their feet.

It was the surest way to open doors, gather information, and build a network of men who owed him.

The Good Samaritan act had worked well for him. He'd made a name for himself as a good guy, had gotten amazing stock tips from a Wall Street dude who couldn't hold his liquor, and even made a huge sale to an executive whose blood sugar had gotten dangerously low.

He had almost passed by that guy, Philip, with his odd clothes and painfully pretty looks. But Douglas was a good judge of people, and his gut had told him that Philip was likely to have at least a few good connections.

But Philip had more than connections. He'd been a veritable gold mine!

It had been boneheaded of Philip to carry around that extremely detailed brochure. It could have so easily fallen into the wrong hands.

Luckily, Douglas had found it in Philip's pocket and stashed it away. No one but Douglas had the combination to that safe.

Of course, when he first looked at that brochure he had been skeptical, until he'd stepped through that door and woken up in the future.

Good thing no one was around to see him. It had been fun, zipping through history, changing this and that so that his future was secure.

It had taken surprisingly little effort to claim the greatest inventions of his time as his own, especially when the future treated patents as historical documents.

Of course, in a few years when he had made all the changes he wished, he would announce to the world that he had been successful in his long and painful endeavor, the invention of time travel. He would be hailed as the greatest scientist and inventor that has ever lived, but more importantly, he would own the rights to the portal.

If anyone wanted to use his machine, they would have to pay dearly.

That whole business of passing a law against women in the workforce during the Depression had certainly been a stroke of genius. All he had to do was research who had the power and inclination to suggests such a law, get in good with the right men, and in one fell swoop a full half of the people he usually had to compete against were out of the running.

Or so he had thought, until he found out those

idiots in Congress repealed the law in the 1970s. So he made a trip to the 1940s, just before that whole Nuremberg business got people worried about ethics in human experimentation, and got hired as Dr. Jo's lab assistant. Once he was on site, it was the easiest thing in the world to tweak the results.

That he had needed to make a third trip into the past had been unexpected. But he had no regrets. The results were worth it.

It had been extremely satisfying to know that he had put that annoying Dr. Jones in her place. She not only had never become a scientist, but she never even graduated elementary school.

It was her fault. She should have applauded his fast thinking and intelligence, not fired him. He had not submitted falsified results, merely slightly fudged ones. Everyone did it.

If he were the sappy type, he might think another good brain gone, but why waste the energy? He had never liked the woman. And as for the rest of the women—well, the world was a much better place without women messing everything up.

His father had always been right all along. A

woman's place was in the home.

Of course, that whole computer business had been unexpected. Who knew that women were instrumental in the invention of computers? And who would have guessed that without the help of women, WWII would have lasted such a long time?

No matter. WWII eventually ended, and computers would soon make their appearance. A little discomfort was worth the end result.

Humanity was better off without input from women and their inferior brains.

It was a shame he couldn't announce to the world what he had done and be treated as the true hero he was. But he knew that even though every man in the world should thank him, not all men would. He had heard about several groups of men who were fighting to change the laws that kept women from working. They seemed to think women should have the same rights as men.

What idiots! They probably had pushy wives, mothers, or daughters egging them on.

He needed to do something fast or all of his hard work might go to waste.

He had already made a bundle with "his" inventions. Now was the time to put the money to good use.

Time to usher in the age of the computer.

Yes, with the help of a good computer, he could work on a little gene therapy. Do a little philanthropic work. Tweak a gene or two to make them healthier, and shut them up in the process.

He would keep women where they belonged if it was the last thing he did.

Chapter 20

"SO YOU SEE, IT'S *my* fault," Philip confessed. His chin dropped to his chest and the next words were barely audible. "I've lost Annabel, forever."

With those words, the devastating effects of despair and guilt were complete. Philip's thirty-five-year-old vibrancy was no more. He had transformed into a broken and withered old man right before their eyes.

Yet the sun continued its progress across the morning sky and spilled glorious rays of warmth through the solid ring of trees that protected the clearing from the rest of the campus.

When they first arrived at the grove, the three adults had claimed a spot under the four Greek columns that stood to one side, majestic but alone. But the children refused to be satisfied with just one spot. They wanted the whole grove. So Becca had tagged Maddie and started a game that sent the four children racing happily across every inch of grass. The grove was a favorite Rossi adventure and the sisters had spent many happy hours in it with their parents.

"If we work together—" Vanessa sought to console the man curled like a pillbug on the ground beside her. But before she could offer him hope, he brushed away the hand she had placed on his shoulder and turned angry eyes her way. She jerked back, surprised.

"You don't understand," Philip growled. "It's over. It can't be fixed."

"Of course it can! All we need to do—"

"Is nothing," Philip yelled.

At the sound of Philip's loud, angry voice, Vanessa's daughters stopped their game of tag and rushed to form a protective ring around their mother.

"Accept it," Philip shouted. "There's nothing we

can do. Nothing. We're out of time."

"But with the portal we can—"

"This is my second trip here without a sleep machine."

Vanessa opened her mouth to speak but Philip turned to Erica.

"You get it, don't you? What a second trip without a sleep machine means?"

When Erica nodded in response, he continued.

"I'm barely hanging on here. I haven't slept in ages, and the only reason I can remember anything is because of this picture." Philip reached into his pocket and pulled out a small photo of Annabel. He lovingly traced the face with his finger.

"But even this won't save me forever. The next time I go through that portal, I'll wonder where this picture came from and I'll probably toss it away. Then I'll go about my sad little life, without any memory of what I lost."

"Maybe we can find a sleep machine—" Erica began but stopped as Philip shook his head.

"They were never invented. So after three trips through the portal, our brains can't take the strain and will lock in whatever timeline is in play."

"We've only been through twice"—Vanessa

pointed to herself and her daughters—
"and this is Erica's first trip."

"You and your daughters aren't the problem. You're time monkeys."

"They're time monkeys?" Philip sat up and stared at Vanessa and her children.

"Shouldn't that make it easier? If we can keep our memories, we can go straight to the problem and fix things."

"If you know where and when to find the problem," Erica said with a shake of her head. "And you should know, the portal is locked into the DTA lab. All trips begin or end at the lab. And the lab's time continues, like normal. It's to provide some protection to the timeline."

"That was in the original timeline. In this timeline, it has been shut down for years."

"True."

"Philip." Vanessa's face brightened with a thought. "What if we went back to the day you took your first trip? If we could stop you ever going through the portal—"

"We can stand outside the door of the portal and make him, you, go back inside." Erica's eyes glowed. "That should do the trick."

The three adults looked at each other and smiled.

"It could work!" Hope radiated from Philip and he sprang to his feet, his vibrancy returned.

"We'll go back to the lab and reset the system. Philip, do you remember the exact day you did that first visit? We can—"

"It won't work." Becca looked like a little girl but her voice rang with authority.

"What did you say, darling?" Vanessa asked, surprised.

"Going back. Making him"—she pointed to Philip dismissively—"not make the visit. It won't work."

"Why do you say that, sweetie?"

"My sisters and I have been talking."

Vanessa smiled.

"About what happens when the timeline is messed with."

"Go on," Vanessa encouraged. She loved it when her daughters pretended to know what was going on. It was so cute.

"Well, we figured out that the way the timeline is now, Philip wouldn't even make that trip."

"Right," Maddie chimed in. "He wouldn't have

any reason to."

Philip groaned and slapped his forehead with his palm.

"Think about it." Becca turned to Philip. "You made that trip to make a woman choose a different career field. In this timeline, women don't even exist."

"So what reason would you have to travel back in time?" Maddie added. "None."

Philip turned so pale Vanessa was afraid he would faint.

"Philip?"

"Oh, God." Philip grabbed a nearby column as all the blood in his brain rushed to his toes.

"Philip!" Vanessa exclaimed as Philip's face grew whiter than the marble column. She grabbed him by the arm, guided him to the ground, and knelt beside him.

"What is it, Philip?" Erica asked, concerned that a preeminent time travel theorist like Philip could be so upset.

"A backward cascade."

"A what?"

"I thought it was just a theory." Philip shook his head.

"Snap out of it," Vanessa ordered. "What are you talking about?"

"The backward cascade."

"What is a backward cascade?" Erica struggled to tamp down her rising frustration. "I've never heard of it before."

"It's a temporal theory proposed by Dr. Jennsaro in the late—"

"Pretend we don't want a lecture and don't know a lot about time travel," Vanessa interrupted. "Give us the quick and easy version."

"Right. So we're very careful when we make a change in the timeline. We make a single tweak and see how it cascades forward through time."

"Go on," Vanessa encouraged, relieved to see color return to Philip's face.

"He leapfrogged me! Backward! He used what he learned from me to go further back and make even more changes. No concern about the mess he might be making."

"Okay, so how far back do we need to go?"

"Don't you get it? A backward cascade twists time like a pretzel. We'll never, never be able to put things back the way they were!"

"Are you trying to say we shouldn't try?"

"Mom." Becca handed a very complicated diagram to her irate mother. "He built his own time machine."

Vanessa looked at the paper in her hand and forced a smile for Becca. "Why thank you, sweetie. It's very pretty."

Becca frowned and turned to her sisters, who motioned her to keep talking.

Erica peeked at the drawing and whispered, "What is it, a tree?"

"If you look on the *time map*" — Becca shot a glare at Erica before she pointed to two squares on the narrow end of the diagram — "there's clear evidence of two separate portals, here and here."

"This one," Maddie said as she stepped forward and pointed to one of the squares, "is the portal we used. Its pattern shows signs that the portal itself has been changed. Made weaker somehow—"

"Less precise," Becca corrected.

"It's not the same portal that existed in the original timeline."

"The pattern is all wrong, it should—"

"Have strong, long lines—" Maddie said.

"But the lines are weak, instead. And short," Becca finished.

"But the pattern that radiates from here..." Maddie pointed to the second square.

"Is wavy, and strong. Definitely—" Becca said.

"A different portal," Maddie finished.

"One built, built—" Becca stopped as Philip snatched the paper out of Vanessa's hands.

"I don't understand," he muttered, seemingly mesmerized by the complexity of the design. With trembling fingers he gently traced the lines of the intricate diagram as if it were a precious piece of art that might melt away at his touch.

"Um, the signs of the second portal—" Becca tried to continue. But when Philip jerked up his head to stare at her it was more than she could take. She looked pleadingly at her mother. Vanessa simply shrugged her shoulders.

Philip looked at the paper then back at the sisters.

"How could you know—?"

Erica, curious what had so disturbed Philip, moved beside him to get a better look at the drawing.

It was a neat mixture of numbers, letters, and lines drawn into a tree-like shape, complete with a trunk, branches, and what appeared to be an infinite number of twigs. She looked closer and realized that the numbers and letters looked a lot like a complex mathematical formula she had once seen in a book, only without any recognizable mathematical symbols.

Meanwhile, Philip's stares at the children had grown even more intense, if that was possible. Before long, the girls felt like sideshow freaks. And since they didn't like the feeling, they bunched up behind Vanessa to use her as a shield.

"It's not possible." Philip stood a few feet from where Vanessa sat, her children cowering in a tight knot behind her. The girls' attempt to use their mother as a shield from Philip's stare failed miserably. "Could it be possible—?"

Vanessa studied Philip. Behind the pain was an odd mixture of fear and adoration. As if he had worked his whole life to prove the creature from the black lagoon existed, only to realize when the mythical monster crawled out of the swamp and shook his hand that it was a man-eater and ready for a snack.

"Mom?" Becca whispered. "What's wrong with him? Why does he keep staring like that?"

The sound of Becca's whisper triggered the well-known attach-to-mommy instinct in the two youngest and they untangled from the sister knot to weave their little arms around Vanessa. Unfortunately, Vanessa was still seated on the ground, so in less than a second she felt less like a mom and more like a forgotten statue in an overgrown garden.

"Philip." Vanessa used one hand to pull Zoe's arm off her mouth, and the other to push Audrey's hand from her eye. "You're scaring my kids."

Philip stepped closer and leaned in to stare at Zoe's hair. Vanessa snapped her fingers in front of his face, but she might as well have been snapping her fingers in front of King Tut's sarcophagus.

"A little help here," Vanessa called to Erica. But Erica was intent on the drawing in Philip's hand and seemed not to hear.

"*Erica!*" Vanessa poured all her frustration and worry into that one word, and it worked. Erica turned and blinked in surprise.

Audrey was on Vanessa's shoulders with her legs locked around her mother's neck. Becca and Maddie held tight to each other as they crammed their knees into their mother's back to maintain contact while simultaneously keeping their distance from Philip. Zoe had curled in Vanessa's lap in an attempt to hide.

And looming over this tableau was Philip. As Erica watched, he leaned in until his nose was a mere inch from Zoe's curls. Zoe whimpered in fright. Audrey balled up a little fist and punched him in the shoulder.

"Right." Erica nodded.

She put her mouth next to Philip's ear and yelled, "Philip!"

There was no response so she backed up a few steps and ran at him. The shove she delivered knocked him off his feet. As he reached out his hands to catch himself, he let go of the paper, which was caught by a puff of wind and transported to the top of a tree, where it stuck.

As Philip hit the ground, the girls jumped into action. Audrey scampered for the tree, closely followed by Becca. Zoe slowly climbed out of Vanessa's lap to stand beside Maddie, who smiled at her kindly and held her hand.

Vanessa, free of the arms and legs that had held her hostage, scurried to help Becca pull Audrey out of the tree.

While Vanessa worked to save her youngest

child from a possible broken bone, Erica grabbed Philip by the hand and pulled him to his feet.

"What's with the stares?" she asked. "Kids don't like to be stared at like that."

"Sorry." Philip shook his head and kept his eyes pointed to the ground. "It was that diagram."

"What about it?"

"Annabel drew diagrams that looked almost exactly like that."

"So. The girls probably saw one of her diagrams in the lab and liked the way it looked so copied it."

"Not likely. Annabel tore them up as soon as she drew them. Said they didn't meet DTA standards, but they helped her figure things out. It was how she understood time."

"What does that mean?"

"I think it means that one of those girls is Annabel's ancestor."

"That's a stretch!"

"Really? They have the gene. She has the gene. They share mannerisms—"

"You call drawing a diagram a mannerism?"

"Not just a diagram, Becca called it a time map. That's not something that's taught. It's innate, it has to be."

"Maybe, but—"

"Do you really believe that it's a coincidence that Annabel and those girls draw diagrams like that? You believe there's no connection?"

"Still—"

"Did you know that Annabel comes from a long line of time travelers? They called it the family business."

"I don't know—"

"She's descended from the Rossi sisters. You know, the ones that invented time travel in the first place."

"Oh, Philip!"

"I'm not crazy! There's a connection. Somewhere."

"Philip—"

"Maybe some distant relation or something. Those curls, they're just like Annabel's. And—"

"Philip!"

"No, listen. I think—"

"Philip! Those are the Rossi sisters!"

Philip froze.

"Becca is Rebecca. Maddie is Madeline. Then there's Zoe and Audrey."

"The Rossi sisters?" Philip slowly processed the information. "Are you sure? Why are they here?"

"They're here to fix the timeline."

"But they don't—"

"Don't try to figure it out. It's a long story."

"So one of those little girls is Annabel's ancestor! But which one?"

"Does it matter?"

"I'd like to know. I want to see if I can see Annabel."

"In that case, look at Vanessa."

"Why?"

"She's definitely Annabel's ancestor."

Philip in looked in awe at Vanessa. She stood at the bottom of the tree with Becca as the two of them tried to coax Audrey out of the tree. Maddie, who had advanced climbing skills herself, was about halfway up the tree and was seconds away from reaching her little sister.

"Let's keep this between the two of us, for now. They've got enough to think about."

Erica looked at the little family and nodded.

"You know," she added, "I love the way the older ones take care of the younger ones. There's a strong family bond there."

"Something they share with Annabel." Philip took out the photo of Annabel and looked at it lovingly. "She's all about family. We were about to start ours."

"Oh, Philip! I'm so sorry. Maybe we can put it right."

"Maybe."

"Look, we've been up all night and will need rest. Have you ever built a shelter?"

"No, but I'm willing to give it a try."

Erica scanned the surrounding woods.

"There, that looks like a good spot." Erica headed toward a particularly dense part of the woods that had several downed trees.

"Love you," Philip whispered. He gently kissed the photo, put it away, and followed Erica.

Zoe, who had been behind the column searching for four leaf clovers, popped her head around to stare in his direction. She had not meant to eavesdrop on Erica and Philip, but that didn't matter. She had heard every word.

Chapter 21

PHILIP HESITATED AT THE door of Suzzallo Library. The library had only been open ten minutes but was already humming with academic activity. The few students who noticed his tunic gave him odd looks before going about their business, but mostly he was ignored. College students were by necessity a self-absorbed group.

Everything was exactly as he had imagined a university library from this time period would be. He had never seen Gothic architecture in person before, only in books, so he was surprised at how small and unimportant it made him feel. But he would not let that bother him. He had research to do.

Thankfully, he could breathe easy about the rest of the group.

He had helped them build a rudimentary hut by gathering branches and stacking them against a fallen tree. That had been easy.

The hard part had come when everyone settled down to rest. He knew Vanessa and Erica would not close their eyes until he was settled, so he pretended to sleep. But every second his eyes were closed was torture. He had not taken a real breath until the small lean-to was finally filled with gentle snores.

Philip could not risk sleep. If he let himself drift off, he would lose every memory of his beloved Annabel. Without the gene or the sleep machine, his brain would take the first opportunity to reset itself to match the current timeline.

Annabel would be lost to him. Forever.

A tug on his jacket caused him to look down and there was Zoe, her hand held up to him.

Philip stared at the little hand, unsure what to do. So Zoe gave him a shy smile and grabbed his hand firmly in her own.

Philip looked nervously around the library. Zoe, though dressed as a boy, had lost her cap. With her golden curls exposed, she was undoubtedly a girl and totally out of place in this all-male university.

Philip pulled her out of the doorway and into a corner.

"What are you doing here?" He kept his voice low as he scanned the room to see if anyone had noticed Zoe.

They had. Several students whispered as they pointed at Zoe.

"We're family." Zoe's curls bounced merrily as she nodded.

"What—?"

"I'll keep you safe. Don't worry."

"Keep me safe?" Philip was flabbergasted that Zoe believed she could protect him. Did she think he was going to be attacked by an army of ten ants? Because stomping on a few ants was all the protection a child her size could provide.

"It's what family does." Zoe pulled her shoulders back to an unnatural angle. "I'll protect you."

"I don't need your protection."

"Yes, you do."

"You are a child. I am a grown man. A child can't protect—"

"I'm older than you."

Philip was silent for a moment. He had very little experience with small children, but he had heard that they responded to logic.

"Zoe. It's Zoe, right?"

Zoe nodded.

"Okay Zoe. How old are you?"

"Twenty-eight."

"Come on, now Zoe. Don't you mean"—Philip quickly scanned Zoe head to toe— "more like eight?"

Zoe put her hands on her hips as she stubbornly shook her head.

"Okay, but even if you're twenty-eight, I'm thirty-five, so—"

Zoe shook her head so hard that several golden hairs detached and floated gently to the ground.

"I'm thirty-five—"

"No. You're not even zero. You're minus zero."

"Nobody is minus zero."

"You are. You're not born."

"Look at me. I'm a grown man."

"No, you're minus zero. You're parents aren't even born yet."

Philip blinked several times as this logic sunk in.

The adult part of his brain thought it was nonsense, but there was a tiny part, the part that was still connected to his child-self and hidden way in the back, that applauded the logic.

"No, Zoe, I don't think you understand—"

"I'm older than you."

He shook his head.

"It doesn't work like that—"

"Yes, it does. Whoever was born first is older. I was born first, so I'm older."

"Wait—"

"I heard you and Erica. Talking about Annabel. She's your wife, right?"

Philip nodded.

"Erica said my mom was Annabel's answer-sister. Which means we're family."

"I agree with that part, but—"

"I'm kinda confused. Annabel is my mom's answer-sister, which would make her my answer-aunt. But she's like you, not born yet."

"It's not really answer—"

"I don't know what to call you—"

"Philip. Just call me Philip."

"Not your name. I mean like uncle or something."

"How about—"

Philip stopped speaking as a radiant smile spread across Zoe's face.

"You'll be my little brother. I've never had one of those. And I'll protect you, like my big sisters protect me."

"That's very sweet, Zoe, but—"

"Philip." Zoe grabbed a nearby chair, dragged it into the corner, and climbed up so she could look down her nose at her 'little brother.' "Little brothers listen to their big sisters. So you"—she poked Philip in the chest—"need to listen to me."

"I will, Zoe, I promise." Philip looked around nervously, but no one was in sight. "Right now I've got things to do. Alone."

Quicker than Philip thought possible, Zoe's smile turned into a scowl. She stomped her foot and shook her head stubbornly.

"Zoe, you have to go back."

Zoe crossed her arms and glared.

"Look, Zoe, your mom is going to be very worried about you."

"I left a note." At the mention of her mother, Zoe's mood brightened considerably.

"A note?"

"A note." Zoe nodded. "So it's okay. Mom won't worry. I can stay."

"What did you say in the note?"

"That I was coming here to protect you."

"But you couldn't have known I was coming here. Where exactly did you say you were going?"

"The liberry. Or at least, I drew some books. Every time I try to spell liberry, Becca says it's wrong. I didn't want to write it wrong so I drew a picture instead."

"But how did you know I'd go to the library?"

Zoe rolled her eyes. "Where else would you go?"

"Where else, indeed. But Zoe—"

"Just what do you think you're doing?"

Philip was so intent on his conversation with Zoe he had neglected to keep watch for nosey students. He twirled to face the owner of the gruff voice and found himself face-to-face not with a student, but with a librarian. A big, burly, mean-looking librarian with flowing red-orange hair that fell just below his shoulders.

"I cannot allow you to bring that girl-child in here." The librarian's face was suffused with a burgundy color that clashed badly with his hair.

"I wasn't—"

"Don't tell me you weren't when you're standing right in front of me. I caught you red-handed."

"I mean, I'm here, but—"

"Oh, I know why you're here. You're not the first of your kind to come in here, you know."

"I—"

"I, I, I. That's all you guys ever care about. Never a thought about the consequences to anyone else. Are you one of those crazies who don't believe the science, or do you just not care if this little one is stunted for life?"

"I—"

"I'm sick of you guys. Just because females have a lesser capacity, it doesn't mean they don't feel."

"No, I—"

"Didn't you have a mother? What's wrong with you? Why would you endanger this child by bringing her here?"

"I'm a scientist. I just—"

"Ah, so that's it. She's part of an experiment. What's being tested? Brainwaves? Growth pattern? What?"

"No—" Philip stopped short when the librarian gave him a quick once-over and leaned in until they were nose to nose.

"You're not connected to this university, are you?"

"Well, I—"

"Thought not. Get out of here, you weirdo. I bet you're not even a real scientist."

"My credentials—"

"Not that it matters. You're not using my library for your experiments. So leave now."

"No, I—"

"Don't say no to me! Now go!" The librarian pointed to the door and used his considerable bulk to loom over Philip.

Philip opened his mouth to argue that he would never hurt any child, but he caught sight of Zoe's terrified face and realized he had to get her out of there fast. So he tamped down his pride, grabbed her hand, and pulled her to the door so fast her feet barely touched the floor.

"Take her somewhere safe, way from academia," the librarian yelled. "If I see you in here again I'll call the police."

The librarian watched as Philip threw open the heavy library door dragged the child outside.

"Someone should do something about loons like

that," the librarian grumbled.

He continued to watch as the door slowly closed. It was an extremely heavy door, so the library had installed a special hinge that kept it from slamming closed. Fewer students got hurt that way.

"One of these days, one of those kooks is going to hurt someone."

With only a two-inch gap left until the door was fully closed, Philip turned to look back at the library.

"Think you'll sneak back in, do you?" The irate librarian's scowl was intense. So much so that an approaching student swerved back into the stacks to find books on snail morphology without help.

"I'm calling the cops now. No underground experiments on my watch."

He picked up a phone and dialed a number.

"Campus police," he barked into the receiver. As he waited the few seconds it took to be connected, his fingers never stopped their *TAP, TAP, TAP* on the counter.

"We've got a problem in Suzzallo," his growled when he finally heard the *CLICK* that let him know someone was on the line. "I'm going to need all the manpower you have."

He slammed his fist on the countertop
with a *BANG* that echoed throughout the library.
But he didn't care. He had a mission. He would
make an example of that man and put an end to
these experiments once and for all.

Chapter 22

PHILIP HELD TIGHT TO Zoe's hand as they darted away from the car they had been hiding behind and ran full tilt for the thicket of trees. There was a yell in the distance followed by a *CRASH*, which prompted Philip to dive behind a fallen log and pull Zoe down with him.

"Did they see us?" Philip was panting so hard he barely had the air to whisper. So he took the first full breath since he and Zoe had begun their mad scramble to safety, motioned for Zoe to stay down, and he peeked his head around the edge of the log. The focus of the search was still in the buildings. No one seemed to have noticed the trees at all.

"Why are they chasing us?" Zoe whispered, her eyes wide with worry. "I don't like being chased."

Zoe enjoyed running and relished every chance she got to zip along with the wind blowing through her hair. Running was easy for her and she excelled at it the same way Audrey excelled at climbing. It was her favorite form of play.

But being chased was scary. All those men with guns! That was not play, and it was no fun at all.

"I think it was that librarian. He seemed to be very upset about something."

"Why?"

"Don't know. We need to get back to the others."

Taking Zoe by the hand, Philip headed for the trees. But before they could take more than a couple of steps, Vanessa crashed through the trees toward them, eyes wild with fright.

"Oh Zoe, I thought I'd lost you." She grabbed her daughter in her arms and hugged her tight. "Don't ever, ever do that again. Ever."

"I won't, Mommy."

"Are you hurt?" Vanessa set Zoe on the ground and inspected her for injuries. She twirled Zoe around, tested her arms, and looked at her hair. When she found several twigs entwined in Zoe's curls she turned on Philip like a mother bear protecting her cub. "What are you, some kind of monster?"

"No, you misunderstand—"

"She's eight, you pervert!"

"It wasn't like that. I tried—"

"Whatever you have to say, I don't want to hear. I'll be having a long talk to my daughter."

"Good. Then she can tell you—"

"Shut up, you pervert! And if you ever try to get within ten feet of any of my daughters again I'll…I'll…I'll—"

Vanessa's imagination failed her. There was no threat great enough to make her feel her children would stay safe. He was a child predator, the lowest type of human being that existed. Nothing could wash away the fear, loathing, and disgust she felt toward this man.

She would find a way to protect her child, her children. The first step was to get, and stay, as far away from the creep as possible. She grabbed Zoe's hand and headed for the trees.

"Wait, Mommy, we can't leave my little brother." Zoe dug in her heels and put a brake on Vanessa's plan for a quick escape.

"Little brother?"

"Philip. He's my little brother."

"You're sick," Vanessa mouthed at Philip.

"I didn't do anything wrong," Philip mouthed back, which made Vanessa shake her head in disgust.

"Sweetie." Vanessa knelt down until she was eye level with her child and took her by the shoulders. "It's not your fault. You didn't do anything wrong."

"So you're not mad, Mommy?"

"Not at you! I love you, and will always love you! No matter what."

"But you're mad at Philip?"

"Yes, sweetie. Mommy is very mad at Philip."

"Why?"

Vanessa glanced at Philip. He had taken out the photo of his wife and was staring at it as if he could will her into being. He was a sad and a broken man, by all appearances as far from dangerous as a person could get. Vanessa pulled her attention back to her daughter.

"Well, sweetie, first of all he took you away and I didn't know where you were."

"No he didn't."

"He didn't?"

"I followed him. He didn't see me because I was very quiet. I told you."

"No you did not! I'd never—"

"It was a note."

"A note?"

"By your head. So you'd see it when you woke up."

"You mean that drawing of boxes?"

"Those weren't boxes, Mommy, they were books. So you'd know I was going to the liberry. I'm not very good at spelling liberry."

"Zoe, sweetie, why would you go to the library? And why would you go by yourself?"

"I wasn't alone. I was following Philip."

"But Zoe, you don't go off with strangers! You know that."

"Philip isn't a stranger, Mommy. He's family."

"Sweetie…" Vanessa shook her head gently. "Philip isn't family—"

"Look, I know you don't trust me," Philip interrupted, "but we need to get out of here."

Philip pointed toward a large group of armed men who had gathered between two buildings. Fortunately, they still had not looked toward the grove of trees.

"What are they doing?" Vanessa asked.

"Looking for us."

"What? Why?"

One of the men's heads turned in their direction and Philip threw himself down to the ground and pulled Vanessa and Zoe down with him.

"Look, I'll tell you everything I know. After we're somewhere safe."

Vanessa studied Philip for several seconds before she nodded. She grabbed Zoe's hand and crawled toward the trees. Philip followed. They didn't say another word until they stood in the clearing, safely away from the searching men.

∞

Thirty minutes later—after Zoe gave a rousing rendition of her adventures complete with swordfights and a red-haired giant—all was well with the little group. It was decided that the time had come to move on, and that all evidence of their makeshift camp needed to be hidden. Just in case.

So as everyone began the task of restoring everything back to its natural state, Vanessa pulled Zoe to the side.

"Zo-Zo, I like the way you shared your adventures with us," Vanessa smiled. "But I'm confused. Why do you call Philip your little brother?"

"Because he is my little brother."

"Zoe, sweetie, you don't have a little brother."

"I know, Mommy."

348

"Then how can Philip be your little brother?"

"He's my answer-brother."

"Answer-brother?"

"Yes, Mommy. But he's not borned yet, and I am borned, so he's my little brother."

Vanessa did her best to work through the logic before she spoke again.

"Zoe, darling, what's an answer-brother?"

"I don't know." Zoe shrugged.

"Where did you hear the term, 'answer-brother'? Who said it?"

"Erica and Philip. They were talking over there"—she pointed to a column—"and I was picking flowers."

"They said Philip was your answer-brother?"

"Kind of."

"They said Philip was kind of your answer-brother?"

"No, Mommy. They said you and Philip's wife were answer-sisters. Which makes Philip your answer-brother. I figured that out by myself."

"Answer…sister, answer-sister, answersister…" Vanessa repeated the phrase several times, and each time she changed how she said it until it all finally clicked into place.

"Ah, ancestor. Now I understand. But Zoe, wouldn't my brother be your uncle, not your brother?"

"Mommy?"

"Yes, Zo-Zo."

"I'm hungry. Can we eat?"

It turned out that it wasn't just Zoe who was hungry. As soon as food was mentioned, it became the most important thing on almost everyone's mind.

Fortunately, Philip had come prepared with rations for a several days. Unfortunately, the rations were for one, so as soon as everyone ate, most of the food was gone.

That got the adults into a long, heated discussion about the ethics of stealing, followed by a second long, heated argument about who would make the best thief.

"This is my mess, I'll get the food." Philip had said the same sentence at least ten times already, and was prepared to say it ten times more. He had to keep Annabel's ancestors out of danger. The worst thing that could possibly happen would be for one of them to get hurt while trying to—

Becca and Maddie tossed two cardboard boxes, one full of food and the other clothing, on the ground in front of the arguing adults.

"Oh, God," Vanessa moaned as she stared at boxes, "I've raised thieves!"

"Look, Mom, we got food, clothes, and even..." Becca dug around in the box and pulled out a pair of sneakers and handed them to Erica. "Those heels must be killing your feet."

"Becca, Maddie." Vanessa's eyes still hadn't left the box. "What have you done?"

Maddie looked at Becca. Becca winked and nodded. Then the two girls began to speak, tag team style.

"It was so easy..." Becca pulled out a man's shirt out of the box and handed it to Philip.

"Even easier than before..." Maddie put a baseball cap on Audrey's head. "That looks great on you."

"You know, when we stole those clothes from our neighbors." Becca pulled out knitted hat, put it on Zoe's head, and stuffed the curls inside. "There, now you can pass for a boy."

"I wasn't even worried about getting caught this

time." Maddie pulled a candy bar from the food box and handed it to Audrey. "Here, Audrey, put this in your pocket for later."

"Not even a little." Becca grabbed another candy bar from the box and gave it to Zoe. "Don't worry, Zoe. We got one for you too. Pocket."

"We got a lot of good stuff." Maddie pulled out a loaf of bread, a jar of peanut butter, and a bag of apples. "See. We've got lunch!"

"And Mom…" Becca searched the box of clothes and pulled out a silver heart necklace, which she put around her mother's neck. "This is for you."

Vanessa touched the necklace. She had failed as a parent. She sank to the ground and put her head between her knees.

"Are you sick, Mommy?" Audrey put her little hands on her mother's arm.

Vanessa opened one eye. "Just a little, sweetie."

"Coffee makes you peel better. Should we pind coffee?"

"I'll be fine, darling. This is a different kind of sick. I'm afraid coffee won't help."

Becca and Maddie burst out laughing. They dropped what they had in their hands and wrapped their arms around their mother.

"It's okay, Mom, we're just giving you a hard time." Becca giggled.

"We didn't steal anything," Maddie added.

"What do you mean?" Vanessa sat upright so quickly her head swirled. She put a hand to her forehead. "You brought back two whole boxes of stuff."

"Mom..." Becca rolled her eyes. "How many burglars walk around with their loot in boxes?"

"Okay," Vanessa conceded, "so how did you get the stuff?"

"You guys kept arguing and arguing," Becca began, shaking her head, "so Maddie and I decided it would be quicker—"

"And better—"

"—If we did it ourselves."

"We went to the dorms." Maddie nodded.

"You should have seen us." Becca swaggered several steps. "We strutted like crazy. Nobody even thought to suspect we were girls."

"We were pretty good, weren't we?"

Becca nodded happily, and did a complicated congratulatory fist-elbow-knee bump with Maddie.

"Girls!"

"Right. So when we got there, the lounge of the

dorm was full of guys."

"All ages. Old ones, kids, ones that looked like they were in college."

"They were having a clothing and food drive."

"We told them we knew of a family that really needed help—"

"So they handed us a couple of boxes and sent us on our way."

"So you don't have to feel guilty, Mom."

"You didn't send us scampering down the road to a life of crime."

"They gave us the stuff. We didn't steal it."

"That *does* make me feel a little better," Vanessa admitted. "Except you still got the food and clothing under false pretenses. We—"

"We *are* a family in need, Mom." Becca's jaw jutted out stubbornly.

"Please, Mom?" Maddie grabbed an apple and handed it to Vanessa. She looked for a second at the shiny redness.

"But they thought—"

"We told the truth and they gave us what we needed." Becca put her hands on her hips. "Nothing wrong with that!"

"Besides, we can't save the world unless we

blend in!" Maddie gently guided Vanessa's hand until the red apple touched her lips. Vanessa felt a little like Snow White. "Eat it, Mom."

"Fine." Vanessa took a big bite of the apple. It was a good one. As juice trickled off her chin she closed her eyes to fully enjoy the crunchy sweetness, and a memory of apple picking with Tony popped into her head.

Vanessa's eyes popped open. This was not the time to allow grief to cloud her thoughts. It might get in the way of putting right what was wrong.

She looked around. Everyone was either eating an apple or a sandwich.

Or both. Vanessa watched as Audrey bit into an apple, and without chewing, bit into a sandwich. It seemed to be a successful combination because she smiled happily.

When both apple and sandwich were nearly gone, Audrey handed the remains to Vanessa.

"Can I go play, Mommy?"

"If you stay where I can see you."

"Thank you, Mommy." She tugged Zoe's shirt. "I'll race you to the top!"

Zoe sprinted for the other side of the clearing.

Audrey giggled and would have followed, but

Vanessa snatched her up.

"No climbing, Audrey." Vanessa looked her straight in the eyes. "I mean it. Keep your feet on the ground."

Audrey blinked, but didn't answer.

"Audrey, promise me. No climbing. Mommy has other things to worry about right now."

"Okay, Mommy." Audrey wove her little arms around her mother's neck and hugged tight. "I promise."

Vanessa kissed the munchkin on the cheek and sent her to play with Zoe.

Without a word, almost as if it were part of a plan, the two little girls gathered sticks. In another minute Becca and Maddie joined them and the four used those sticks to build a miniature structure.

"Now," Vanessa said as she turned to Erica and Philip, who had each just taken a final bite of gooey black bread, "we need to research. Find out what exactly has been changed, and when."

"We did that already."

Vanessa turned at the sound of Becca's voice.

"Before we went to the dorm—" Becca seemed to have magically appeared next to Vanessa, her body turned so Vanessa couldn't see what she had behind her back.

"We got to talking—" Maddie also had her hands behind her back.

"About how Dad always said—"

"We could accomplish anything—"

"As long as we thought it through—"

"Wait, girls." Vanessa turned to face her daughters. "What did you do?"

"We did"—out jutted Becca's chin—"what Dad would have wanted us to do."

"What he believed we could do." Maddie nodded.

"Which is what?" Vanessa wasn't sure if she should be confused or concerned.

"This." Maddie pulled a stack of papers from behind her back and handed them to Vanessa. Becca slammed her papers on top.

Vanessa blanched when she realized what those papers meant.

"Girls! Someone might have—"

"Maddie and I are practically adults." Becca held her head high. "We can do a lot more than you give us credit for."

"We're not children, like Zoe and Audrey." Maddie pointed to the two younger children.

"Playing with sticks."

"Dad would have wanted us to do the research."

"He would have believed we could do it."

"So we did."

"When?" Vanessa swayed with a wave of dizziness that threatened to engulf her. Erica grabbed her elbow to provide support.

"Before we went to the dorms. It didn't even take that long."

"But how did you know where to look? Whatever he did, he could have done it anywhere—"

Philip stopped talking only when Maddie pulled a diagram from the back of her shirt and stuck it in front of his face. One look was all it took for him to realize it was much more complicated than before.

"I don't understand."

He grabbed the diagram, turned it, turned it again. "It looks different. What did you add to it?"

"This is a new one." Becca took the paper out of Philip's hand, flipped it 180, and handed it back. "Maddie drew the first one by herself. We got together to draw this one. We didn't want to leave anything out, so even Audrey contributed to it."

"Can I see it?" Erica held out her hand and kept it out until Philip begrudgingly handed her the diagram.

It was amazingly complicated. The tree-shaped combination of lines, squiggles, letters and numbers held center stage, just like the first diagram. But where the earlier tree shape had a background of whitespace, there was no whitespace on this page. Instead, what served as the background had been filled in with dots and symbols that looked suspiciously like a star chart. She looked it over and handed it back to Becca.

"What does this tell you?" she asked.

"That a huge change was made in the early 1940s, here." Becca pointed to a spot on the trunk of the tree where there were more squiggles than straight lines.

"So we focused our research on that time period, and of course on women," Maddie said.

"Because we already knew that whatever was changed, it deeply affected how people thought about women."

"You know…" Maddie smiled happily. "Some of those librarians are nice."

"Very helpful." Becca nodded in agreement.

"They didn't ask why we wanted to know this stuff."

"And they even gave us paper and pens."

"We stayed away from one of them, though."

"He was a Grumpy Gus. He had kind of a sour face." Becca grimaced.

"Like he hates the world or something."

"Was he a big guy?" Philip asked. "Red hair?"

"Um huh." Maddie nodded.

"Can't be that many huge, red-headed librarians on campus. Probably the same one who sent the soldiers after us."

"Like I said," Maddie agreed, "he hates the world."

"Anyway," Becca continued, "Maddie and I have a plan."

"You have a what?" Vanessa had thought it best to remain silent while her head twirled. But the world was no longer spinning past her eyes at ninety miles an hour. It was time to step up assume her motherly duties.

"A plan, Mom. We know what we need to do to put things right."

"Becca, wait a minute." A few days ago Becca was afraid to walk down the street by herself. Now she seemed to think it was her responsibility to save

the world. Vanessa needed to stop this
before the child had a nervous breakdown. "You're
a child. Let the adults worry about—"

"Read it, Mom." Becca pointed to the papers in
Vanessa's arms. "Read the research, then we'll
talk."

Vanessa looked her oldest daughter straight in
the eyes and saw only confidence there. So she
nodded and distributed the papers between the
three adults.

But before she had time to start on the first page,
Maddie whispered in her ear.

"Mom, do you mind if we go play with Zo-Zo
and Audrey? You don't need us here, do you?"

Vanessa smiled at her daughters and motioned
for the girls run play with their sisters.

She examined the research her daughters had
gathered. The more she read, the more horrified she
became.

"This doctor is an absolute monster," Vanessa
whispered. "Have you gotten to the part about the
experiments that he did?"

"On orphans, no less." Erica continued to read.
"Those poor, poor little girls."

"With what they were put through, it's little

wonder some of them died and others went crazy." Vanessa shook her head.

"Torture like that could drive anyone crazy." Philip added.

"And this"—Vanessa flicked the paper in her hand—"was what was used to prove women are weak creatures."

"Awful!"

"I don't get how this could have happened." Vanessa looked away from the atrocities on the paper to watch her children at play. "Shouldn't someone have protected those children?"

"Could this be what changed?" Erica sighed. "I certainly don't remember hearing about this before. I think I'd remember."

"Based on this"—Philip held up a paper—"your job would give you brain fever and make you sterile."

"Do you have the name of that doctor?"

"Dr. Joseph Smith."

"We've got to stop this." Philip slammed his fist into his palm. "We should—"

Vanessa grabbed his arm. "We should listen to the girls' plan. They deserve that."

Erica and Philip looked at the piles of papers in

their hands. Vanessa held up the diagram.

"Agreed?" Vanessa asked. Philip and Erica nodded.

"Hey girls," Vanessa called, "what are you working on?"

"Just something."

"Let me see."

As Vanessa strode across the clearing, Zoe lifted up a strange object made of sticks. It was cone-shaped on the lower portion, with sticks radiating out of the top like an array of antennas.

Philip grabbed Erica's arm.

"What does that look like to you?"

Philip pointed at the stick object. Erica looked and did a double take.

"It looks like our future built of sticks," Erica sighed. "Why can't this be easy? How can they—?"

Philip shrugged.

"What does that mean for the timeline?"

"No clue. This is not something I've studied. I don't think anyone has studied it."

"The force is strong in those little ones."

"The what?" Philip asked.

"Never mind," Erica had momentarily forgotten that to Philip, movies were an antiquated form of entertainment from the long-distant past.

He had never seen a *Star Wars* movie and probably wouldn't want to watch one if given the chance. "It's a joke for another time. Let's go see what those little monkeys have planned."

Chapter 23

IT WAS A DOOZY of a plan. Philip was to show himself to the soldiers as a diversion. After he led them to the other side of campus, he was to double back and meet Erica at the portal. They were to stand guard until Vanessa and the girls got back.

"That doesn't work for me." Philip grimaced and crossed his arms. "If the soldiers catch me, I won't make it back at all."

"And all you want me to do is stand outside a door? Why do I get left out of all the fun?"

"It's our plan." Becca's chin jutted out stubbornly.

"Your plan. I see." Erica shook her head. "What exactly am I supposed to do at that door?"

"Make sure that creep, Douglas, doesn't sneak through the portal into the DTA."

"Ah ha!" Philip shouted. "You forgot that he doesn't have to go through the DTA's portal. He has his own time machine."

"That"—Maddie's chin shot up into the air and her eyes gleamed—"is the other part of our plan."

"The other part—?"

"We plan to destroy Douglas Whitfield's time machine." Becca leaned in conspiratorially.

"Then grab the brochure," Maddie added. Her eyes twinkled at the thought of the coming adventure.

"And get rid of anything he could use to build another time machine," Becca finished with a crisp nod.

"And what will I be doing in this plan of yours?" Vanessa asked with a raised brow.

"You're with us. We need you to drive. None of us know how, yet."

"You forget." Erica shook her head and scowled. "In this timeline, women aren't allowed to drive."

"Only if they look like women," Maddie answered smugly. "Mom can look very manly, when she wants to."

"Thanks, I think." Vanessa scrunched up her nose. She was a petite woman and therefore made a very small man, but she appreciated the vote of confidence from her children. "Where, exactly, do you want me to drive?"

"The creep's time machine won't be on campus. So we'll have to find him and follow him until he leads us to his time machine. Then we'll use it to go back to the 1940s—"

"Maybe the only jump he's made. I doubt he's got the gene, so he can't have made very many. Not without forgetting everything."

"Right. So the machine will be set to the right time. We'll go back to that doctor—"

"The maniac that did all those experiments," Maddie clarified.

"Who," Vanessa interrupted.

"What?" Maddie asked.

"The maniac *who* did all the experiments," Vanessa explained. "'Maniac' refers to a person, so you use who, not that."

"Vanessa, do you really think an English lesson is appropriate right now?" Erica asked with a raise of the brow. "Don't you think we've got more important things to focus on?"

"Old habits," Vanessa chortled. "Sorry. Go on."

"Well, we need to make the maniac, *who*"—she nodded to her mother—"is doing the experiments, stop. Somehow. Convince him that what he is doing is wrong."

"Morally," Maddie added, "but if that doesn't work, we'll convince him that his data is wrong."

"How do you propose to do that?"

"The moral issue *should* be easy." Maddie bit her lip and cut her eyes toward her sister.

"But if he's not an ethical person—"

Becca turned to Maddie. Maddie nodded, so Becca continued.

"Remember that research we brought back? It included copies of the data, and we noticed—"

There was a loud *SNAP* somewhere in the forest, followed by the rustling of a large animal making its way through the dense brush.

"What was that?" Audrey whispered. She jumped into her Vanessa's arms and attached herself.

"Is it the dragons, Mommy?" Audrey whimpered, her chin trembling like Jell-O on a train.

Vanessa shook her head and put her finger to her lips.

"I think—" Zoe began, but was shushed by her two older sisters.

The rustling continued to get closer. Vanessa

spotted a huge tree about twenty feet away and led the others to hide behind it.

Just then a soldier stepped into the clearing a mere ten feet from the makeshift shelter. And he was not alone. Vanessa craned her neck and could see that there were more soldiers directly behind the first one, perhaps as many as twenty.

"Let's go," she mouthed and pointed away from the soldiers.

"Where?" Erica mouthed back.

"Maybe to—"

"I found something!" a male voice yelled.

Rustles turned into crashes as every soldier raced to be the second to the campsite. One man spotted the boxes of food and clothing and rummaged through them until he came across Philip's tunic, which he waved high in the air.

"Just like the librarian described," the soldier crowed. "This must be his camp."

"Spread out and keep searching. He can't be far," another soldier growled. "We'll get him. Make an example."

Philip broke out in a cold sweat and licked his lips as the pure menace in the man's voice sunk in. That man was out to get him, and he meant business.

He would have to make a run for it. There was no other way. It would have to be every man for himself—

Philip felt a warm, soft hand sneak into his. He looked down to find Zoe smiling encouragingly up at him. Gone was the overwhelming fear.

Vanessa flapped her hands several times. When she got everyone's attention she scrunched up her shoulders as if she were making herself shorter, and walked two fingers across her palm. Her obvious message was that they should crawl away.

She just happened to be looking at Philip when his eyes grew very wide. She twirled around to find one of the soldiers just behind her, reaching as if to grab Audrey from her back.

"Run!" Vanessa yelled as she gave the soldier an elbow to the nose and took off. Judging by the loud crashes in her wake, everyone had followed her lead and dashed through the woods like deer from wolves.

She could only hope that the wolves, also known as the soldiers, hadn't also followed.

Vanessa broke through the bushes and paused just long enough to check if there were armed men patrolling the columns. There was no one in sight.

Which was fortunate. That mad scramble through the woods had created enough noise to warn a deaf man that she was on the way.

She stood panting while she waited for the rest of the group to make it out of the woods.

"You okay, Audrey?" Vanessa asked her daughter. Not that she was worried. This was right up Audrey's alley. The little monkey probably enjoyed every minute of the wild run.

"That was pun, Mommy! Can we do it again?"

Philip broke through the bushes with Zoe under his arm like a football, followed closely by Maddie and Becca.

"I didn't know," Becca said, sucking in a lungful of much needed air, "that you could run like that!"

"Where's Erica?" Vanessa scanned the forest.

"Here!" Erica said as she stepped through the brush. "I hung back, to see if we were being followed."

"And?"

"The soldier you elbowed laughed it off and said that it was just a bunch of crazy women. They decided to look elsewhere."

"What about my tunic?" Philip asked. "Did they just ignore that?"

"The soldier's nose started bleeding so he used it as a rag. Said it couldn't from the guy they were looking for. It was too soft and girlie for a guy to wear."

"Of all the sexist—" Philip bristled with anger. "That was my favorite tunic!"

"Thank goodness for sexism. This time, at least. Without it we'd still be running. At least now we've got a little breathing room."

"You think we're good?"

"Looks that way."

"Mommy, I want to play horsey again." Audrey kicked her feet into Vanessa's sides. "Giddyup!"

"Ouch! That hurts Mommy, munchkin." Vanessa cringed in pain. She twisted around to encourage Audrey to slide off her back. "Besides, horsey is tired."

As Audrey's feet touched the grass, she shrugged and skipped happily to join Zoe, who had gathered a pile of sticks in front of her. Soon both little girls were happily building and destroying structures.

"Now," Becca said as she pushed up her sleeves,

"back to the plan."

"Wait a minute." Philip stepped forward. "I found a couple of holes in the plan."

"Umm, I don't think so." Becca scrunched up her nose and shook her head. "What we need—"

"Becca!" Now Vanessa stepped forward. "Don't you want to hear what Philip has to say?"

"Not really." Becca shrugged.

"Becca!"

"Our plan is solid." Becca pursed her lips.

"It won't hurt to listen." Vanessa raised her brow and tilted her head, which elicited a sigh from Becca.

"Fine." Becca turned to Philip. "What are the holes?"

"Your plan is to send me racing around campus to call off the guards, right?"

"Right."

"But the guards don't care about you. You're just a bunch of crazy women who couldn't hurt a fly."

"Hey!"

"That's what the guards think, not me. All you have to do is leave campus, and you're safe."

"I guess so." Becca shrugged. She looked around for Maddie and spotted her building a boat out of sticks.

"Maddie! We need you!" Becca called. When Maddie looked up, Becca motioned for her to come. But it wasn't a why-don't-you-join-me kind of motion, but a get-over-here-now one.

"Yes?" Maddie asked as she joined the group.

"We're discussing the plan. Philip has found holes in it," Vanessa said bluntly.

"Not likely," Maddie muttered.

"What did you say?" Vanessa wasn't sure if she had heard her usually polite daughter correctly.

"Nothing, Mom."

"Okay, Philip." Vanessa pulled her eyes away from her daughters long enough to give Philip a nod. "We're listening."

"Right," Philip continued. "So I don't need to draw the guards off."

"In that case," Becca said, shrugging, "you can go straight to the portal and stand guard with Erica."

"Umm, no."

"What do you mean?"

"That brings me to the other hole in the plan."

All eyes were on Philip, except for those that belonged to Zoe and Audrey. A stick tower tottered dangerously as the finishing touches were added. The two builders were much too busy to care about any old plan.

"I"—Philip tapped his chest—"am the only one who knows anything at all about Douglas Whitfield. How are you going to find him when you don't even know what he looks like?"

Maddie and Becca looked at each other for a full ten seconds before Maddie nodded and turned to her mother.

"Sorry, Mom, but we kind of didn't tell the whole truth." Maddie turned away so she wouldn't have to see her mother's face. "We already know where the other time machine is."

"What? You lied to me?"

"Wrong focus," Erica said to Vanessa. She turned Maddie back toward the group.

"You know where to find the time machine?"

Maddie nodded, then shot a quick look at her mother, who was listening but didn't appear angry.

"How?" Erica asked.

"The diagram." Maddie's eyes brightened. "It's very accurate."

"So you think." Philip grumbled.

"So we *know*." Becca threw her shoulders back

and stood tall.

"Oh," Philip could barely hold back a sneer. "How do you know? You're kids."

"We may be kids, but we know how to read a time map." Maddie dangled the diagram in Philip's face. "Look at it. Can the grown man read it?"

"Maddie! That's rude," Vanessa admonished.

"Sorry, Mom."

Vanessa lifted her brow.

"Sorry, Philip."

Philip pulled the diagram down from in front of his face and studied it carefully. He crossed his eyes, squinted, and looked at the diagram from every angle imaginable. Finally he sighed in defeat.

"No, the grown man cannot read it. Are you sure you can?" he asked.

"Positive," Maddie replied with a firm nod.

"Then I give up. I'm in. I never understood Annabel's diagrams either," Philip admitted.

"Okay." Erica rolled her eyes. "Now that that's done, let's figure out how to destroy the extra time machine, shall we?"

"And everything he might use to rebuild it," Vanessa added. "That could take a lot of searching to find—"

Becca and Maddie gave each other another one of those looks that meant they knew more than they had admitted.

"What?" Vanessa asked suspiciously.

"We have another plan," Maddie confessed.

"One that would handle everything," Becca continued. "The extra portal, making sure he'd never get to build a new one, everything."

"Do we have to split up for this new plan?"

"No."

"Then why even mention the first plan? I never liked the thought of splitting up. I would much rather—"

"There's a tricky part." Maddie bit her lip and looked at her sister.

"What kind of tricky?" Vanessa asked.

"The whole plan," Becca grimaced, "relies on Philip."

"I told you I'm in!" Philip's brows furrowed. "You know I'd do anything to put things right. I—"

"Now," Becca interrupted. "But you won't feel like that later."

"What do you mean, later?"

"Philip," Maddie sighed. She opened her mouth as if to say something, but snapped it shut and shook her head instead.

"What Maddie is trying to say," Becca began, "is that you're barely hanging on. Soon you won't remember us. Not Mom, not Erica, not even Annabel."

"But—"

"You won't have a reason to want to help."

Philip pinched his lips together and stared off into the distance. Then he slammed his fist into his palm.

"I'm not ready to give up yet." Philip's jaw jutted out stubbornly. "There's got to be a way."

Chapter 24

ONE AFTER ANOTHER, PHILIP, Vanessa, Erica, and the girls crept around the corner of a very ugly, utilitarian university building. Vanessa pulled away from the gray concrete blocks of the building and looked toward the roof.

"What building is this?" she asked. "I don't recognize it."

Philip and Erica shrugged as they edged to the corner and peeked around it. Becca spotted a placard attached to the side of the building and pointed.

"Military Arts," Becca read. "I don't remember it either."

"Me neither, and I think I'd remember something this ugly," Maddie added.

"I do," Audrey shouted as she jumped around like a demented kangaroo. "I memember the building."

"Do you really, Audrey? 'Cause I don't," Zoe chided.

"Not really." Audrey paused and gave a quick shrug before she continued her kangaroo impression. "But I like it. It looks really, really, really, really, really strong."

"Alternate timeline," Erica called from her spot at the corner. "Half a century for World War II. Things have to be different."

"Poor ugly thing." Vanessa patted the concrete blocks of the building much as she would a dying horse. "You should never have been built. Let's see if we can put you out of your misery."

"Admiring the architecture is all well and good," Philip whispered. He grabbed Erica's arm and pulled her away from the corner. "But company's coming. Led by our old friend, the librarian. Looks like he's on a mission."

Vanessa motioned her kids to stay put before she tiptoed to carefully peek around the corner. Several buildings away, a troop of men combed the area, led by a big man with red hair. She watched as he ordered one group to poke bushes with long sticks and another to climb the trees. No possible hiding place was to be overlooked.

After one soldier jabbed deep into a rhododendron of massive proportions, a yelp signaled the discovery of an interloper.

The soldier dove into the bush, grabbed the man who was trying to scramble away, and marched him to the redheaded librarian. The librarian glared at the man's clothes, which were frayed with age, then lifted the raggedy man by the collar and looked him closely in the face.

"Not him, keep looking," the librarian tossed the man away so hard the poor man hit the ground with a *THUMP* that was clearly heard by Vanessa, two buildings away.

"Look what I found!" yelled a soldier peering over the top of a bush. He disappeared behind it and immediately reappeared holding the arms of a squirming woman and child of five, each as tattered as the man.

"What do you want us to do with these two?" the soldier asked.

"Can't have riffraff like that on campus," the librarian sneered and flapped his hand dismissively. "Send them to the mines."

"Wait!" the tattered man yelled as he struggled to regain his feet. "That's my wife and daughter. Please don't hurt them."

"You've already hurt them." The librarian's lip

curled in disgust. "You brought them on campus, probably the most dangerous place for their kind. You broke the law. Don't you know that when a female goes crazy, it puts everyone in danger?"

"We needed a place to live. This was—"

"Quiet," the librarian yelled at the quaking man. He turned to two nearby soldiers. "Take him, too. Anyone stupid enough to bring females to a place of learning deserves a few years in the mines."

He watched coldly as the soldiers pulled the family toward a waiting car. At one point the child tripped and began to cry. The woman reached for her daughter, only to have a soldier jerk her away from the child.

"March," the soldier growled as he pointed to the car.

The man broke away from his captors and scooped up the sobbing child. The soldiers quickly followed, but when they gripped his arms he gave them a look that belied his tattered clothing and contained so much dignity that they released his arms immediately. He walked to his wife and put his free arm around her shoulders. Together they walked the rest of the way to the car, escorted, but untouched, by the soldiers.

"Well that was interesting," the librarian muttered. He turned to the soldiers waiting for orders. "The rest of you, I want every inch of this campus searched. Who knows how many other squatters we have. I want them all found and out of here."

"He's mean," Zoe whispered.

Vanessa looked down to find all four of her daughters crowded near her feet.

"What a psycho," Erica agreed in Vanessa's ear, making her jump.

Vanessa turned her head to find Erica in her personal bubble, and Philip not far behind.

"Sheesh!" Vanessa elbowed Erica, causing her to move back a step. "What're you trying to do, scare me to death?"

"It was the shouting." Maddie crawled backward until she was clear of her sisters and could stand.

"We wanted to see, too," Becca seconded as she joined Maddie.

Vanessa opened her mouth to respond, but a cold breeze across her feet made her realize that her two youngest daughters were missing.

"Where are Zoe and Audrey?"

She frantically searched everywhere, including bushes that were all too small to hide anything bigger than a cat.

"Vanessa," Erica hissed, "they're heading our way."

"I can't find Audrey or Zoe!"

"We have to hide!"

"Mom!" Becca tugged on her mother's shirt.

"In a minute, Becca." Vanessa turned a grim face to Erica. "What do you want me to do, leave my children to be found by that monster?"

"No." Erica's face turned redder than a ladybug's wings. "But we can't stay out in the open like this—"

"Mom!" Becca tugged so hard on Vanessa's shirt it ripped.

Vanessa turned to reprimand Becca, but Becca pointed at two pairs of little kid shoes disappearing through an open window on the second floor.

"What are they doing up there?" She ran to the sheltered door located midway along the building and frantically tried to open it. It didn't budge.

"Help me," she whispered. "I have to get them out of there!"

But before Philip and Erica could move
so much as a single step there was a *CLICK* and the
door swung open to reveal Audrey and Zoe,
smiling happily.

Vanessa shoved through the doorway to grab
the two little girls and hug them tight. Becca and
Maddie followed.

"You scared Mama," Becca said in her most
disapproving voice.

"Yeah," Maddie agreed, "you shouldn't do
that."

Then they wrapped their arms around their
mom and little sisters and squeezed tight.

Erica and Philip took one final look around the
corner and joined the family inside. Philip guided
the door so it would close quietly. Then he locked it
tight.

"Sorry, Mommy." Audrey's voice could barely
be heard through all the arms. So Vanessa broke the
hug and everyone took a step back.

"The mad man was coming," Zoe piped up.

"Mad man?" Vanessa asked.

"The big bossy man with red hair and a grumpy
face," she explained. "He's mad at everyone."

"We don't like him," Audrey said.

"We knew we needed to hide, so he couldn't find us."

"A window was open. It was easy."

"I went with her because it was dark inside," Zoe chimed in. "Audrey doesn't like being alone in the dark."

"Sweeties! You didn't need—"

Erica's sharp elbow connected with Vanessa's ribs and got her immediate attention.

Vanessa turned to find Erica with one finger to her lips and the other pointed at a low window nearby.

"They're here," Erica mouthed.

Philip had been exploring the room, which was a storeroom, and motioned everyone to scramble behind a large pile of boxes. As soon as everyone was safely hidden from view, shadow after shadow danced across the walls as an army of men marched past the only source of light. Every so often a shadow would loom large and menacing, proof positive that this room was only a temporary sanctuary.

Finally the dance of the shadows stopped and everyone could breathe normally—for a bit, at least.

"That's the closest they've gotten all day," Philip

whispered. "We need to get off campus, and soon."

While the adults argued in whispers about the best route to the time machine, Maddie tiptoed to the window to look outside. Becca instantly knew by the look on her face that there was trouble.

"What?" Becca asked as Maddie had returned to the relative safety of the boxes.

"They're pitching tents outside." Maddie's voice wavered and she had to clear her throat before she continued. "We're trapped."

Chapter 25

"Hey, Becca," Maddie whispered.

"Hey, Maddie," Becca answered in a mocking tone.

It had been two hours since they had become trapped in the storeroom. Two hours in a confined space that would be reasonably comfortable for one person, but was entirely too snug for seven.

Becca and Maddie did their part to alleviate the overcrowding by carving out a sitting area where they could draw on boxes with pencils they found on the floor. It was not the most exciting thing in the world to do, but it beat the next best option, which was to do nothing.

Still, there was no reason for Becca to be so hateful. She wasn't the only one who was bored to tears.

"Becca!" Maddie tried again.

"Maddie!" Becca replied, every bit as mocking as the first time.

"Listen," Maddie pleaded. "This is important."

Becca looked at her sister and realized that whatever Maddie had to say, it was indeed something she felt was important. Becca put down her pencil.

"I'm listening," Becca said.

"Remember what Dad showed us?"

"Dad showed us lots of things. And which timeline are you talking about?"

"The real one. The one where Dad would bring us with him to campus while Zoe took a nap."

"I remember the library, and playing on the bike racks."

"No, I'm talking about those tunnels—"

"The tunnels!" Excitement caused Becca to whisper louder than planned.

Vanessa, good mom that she was, always kept part of her brain tuned in to her children. So even though she was deep in conversation with Philip and Erica, the word "tunnels" coming from Becca's mouth immediately caught her attention.

"Girls." Vanessa crawled to the preteens to sit cross-legged beside them. "Did I hear something about a tunnel?

Becca and Maddie fidgeted uncomfortably and looked away from their mother.

"Maddie?" Vanessa took Maddie by the chin and gently turned her face until their eyes met. "Tunnel?"

Maddie shifted her eyes down, away from her mother. Vanessa dropped her hands and assumed a carefree tone.

"You know, your dad mentioned the tunnels to me, too."

That got the attention of both girls.

"He did?" Becca asked.

"Yep. But I had just had Zoe so I was a little busy. I didn't listen very well."

"Dad told you?" Maddie asked.

"Your dad and I tell each other almost everything, you know."

"You know about the tunnels?" Becca tilted her head to the side.

"*Know* might be too strong a word." Vanessa bit her lip. "Let's just say I was vaguely aware they existed."

"But Daddy said…" Maddie's voice trailed off and she turned to her sister.

"Daddy made us promise not to tell you," Becca

blurted.

"Because you would think they're dangerous," Maddie added.

"He's right," Vanessa agreed. "I would normally think they're dangerous. But—"

"Daddy didn't think they were dangerous." Becca shook her head.

"Just a little scary for people who don't like small spaces," Maddie said.

"You wouldn't like it." Becca wrinkled her nose.

"It was going to be our secret."

"They go all over the campus, but underground."

"Like secret passages."

"They're called steam tunnels."

"'Cause they carry steam to heat the buildings."

"Dad wanted to take us."

"But he said we needed to be older."

"...Than we were then, of course. We're old enough now."

"But we'd have to get permission."

"Because otherwise, he could be sent to jail."

"For endangering children."

"Not that we're really children."

"Or that he would ever put us in danger."

"He'd never do that. He loves us."

"But if he could convince someone to give us a tour."

"He said it would be okay."

"He said one day—"

"He said—"

"He—"

Becca and Maddie locked eyes, and in perfect unison their chins shook and eyes filled with tears. Vanessa grabbed them both and pulled them tight.

"Hush, sweeties. It'll be okay," she whispered.

"Oh, Mom!" Becca wrapped her arms around Vanessa and squeezed. "What if it's not okay? What if we don't get him back?"

"I want Daddy," Maddie whimpered.

"Me too!" Audrey wailed. She climbed on Vanessa's back and attached herself, monkey style.

Vanessa felt a tap on her shoulder. She turned to find Zoe, tears streaming down her face, beside her.

"Daddy," the heartbroken child sobbed.

Vanessa desperately wanted to hug Zoe. The child looked so lonely and forlorn, standing by herself. But Audrey's arms had Vanessa's trapped.

She wiggled her shoulders in an attempt to free an arm, but before she could make any headway,

Becca snaked out a hand and pulled Zoe into the fold.

The crying session lasted a full twenty minutes.

Vanessa was proud of the restraint shown by her daughters. They knew they needed to remain quiet, so wails were tamped down to whimpers, and shouts to sobs.

Becca was the first to regain her composure. She backed out of the sad pile of humanity wallowing in self-pity and cleared her throat loudly.

"Enough," she admonished sternly. "Less crying, more doing."

It was as if she'd slapped a big red *STOP* button on the tear machine. Her sisters immediately sat back and wiped their faces.

Vanessa was familiar with the quick-changing emotions of her daughters, but this was something she'd never seen. Before she could uncross her legs and stand, they were conducting a full-blown search for the tunnels, all while staying out of the line-of-sight of the window.

It was Vanessa who found the entrance to the tunnels, and quite by accident.

She had been standing next to another boring pile of boxes, lost in memories of her husband, when Audrey scrambled toward a high shelf. Vanessa automatically grabbed her daughter's leg as it rose in the air, but lost her balance. She reached out a hand, knocked over a box, which crashed into another box, which crashed into still another box, until the domino effect took hold and a series of boxes crashed to the floor…revealing a door with a sign on it that read *UTILITY TUNNEL – AUTHORIZED PERSONNEL ONLY.*

"Duck!" Becca hissed as she pointed toward the window. A form rose up to block the light as everyone quickly dived out of sight.

"I think they heard that," Erica whispered.

"They'd have to be deaf not to," Vanessa responded.

Philip crawled to the door and reached up to try the knob.

"Locked," he said sadly.

Just then shouts at the entrance door signaled that they had been found.

The shouts soon turned to loud *BANGS* that reverberated through the room. Erica jumped to her feet and ran to the tunnel door.

"Erica, get down!" Vanessa hissed.

"Why?" Erica shrugged. "They know we're here."

Vanessa thought for a moment before she climbed to her feet. She watched as Erica opened a box and dumped its contents on the floor. She rummaged around for a moment and moved on to repeat the process with the next box.

"What are you looking for?" Vanessa asked.

"Something wire-like. Maybe a paperclip."

Vanessa motioned her daughters to help, and soon everyone was ripping open boxes and searching through them.

"Why are we looking for something wire-like?" Vanessa asked.

"I loved mysteries as a kid." Erica continued her search through box after box. "One of these boxes has to contain office supplies."

"I found something wire-like!" Maddie had to yell to be heard over the pounding at the door. She held up a notebook she had just pulled from a box.

"Perfect!" Erica rushed to grab the notebook. She quickly unwound enough of the spiral that she could straighten it out.

"What are you going to do with that?" Vanessa asked.

"Get us out of here," Erica answered
with a definitive nod. "Every good detective should
know how to pick a lock."

As Erica worked on the lock, Vanessa gathered
her children and Philip watched as the threshold of
the entrance door began to splinter.

"Hurry, I don't think that door's going to hold
much longer," Philip shouted.

"I'm doing the best I can," Erica said so quietly
everyone had to struggle to hear. "The last time I
tried this I was fourteen years old."

All eyes were on Erica as she knelt beside the
door and twisted the notebook around at different
angles. She closed her eyes and pursed her lips as
she concentrated.

Suddenly she tossed the notebook across the
room and sighed.

"You're not giving up, are you?" Vanessa asked
in a panicked voice.

Erica shook her head, smiled, and opened the
door.

"You're a genius!" Vanessa yelled as she gave
Erica a hug.

Then, as a loud splitting sound indicated they were about to have company, Vanessa, Erica, Philip, and the girls rushed into the tunnel and locked the solid steel utility door behind them.

Chapter 26

IT WAS A LONG, dark, scary trek. Scary because it was dark, dark because time travelers rarely remember to bring flashlights, and long because no one had any idea where they were heading or which way to go.

For a utility tunnel it was relatively spacious and uncluttered, even though it did contain more than a reasonable number of spiders and other creepy-crawlies.

Squeals and squeaks peppered the trip, some by the trekkers, some by rats that didn't appreciate all those feet tromping through their cozy hideout.

But not one person wavered in their resolve to trudge on until they found a way to get off campus. Not even Audrey, who hated the dark.

The lack of a map was a huge drawback. The tunnels twisted, turned, split off into multiple tunnels, and sometimes stopped abruptly. They repeatedly opened doors they were sure would lead them off campus, only to find themselves still in the danger zone.

It was worse than the time Tony and Vanessa had taken the girls to a nighttime trek through a corn maze. They had spent two hours lost in the dark with four kids, but at least the moon and the stars had given some clue as to which direction they needed to go.

After about the forty-seventh time a door opened to yet another building still on campus, Maddie took the point and led the group down a narrow, dank tunnel that dead ended into a little square room with a manhole cover for a roof. Philip climbed the ladder attached to the wall, peeked his head out, and smiled down at the bedraggled little group.

"This is definitely off campus," he said as he climbed to the surface and motioned everyone to follow.

"Now what?" Erica asked as she maneuvered the manhole cover in place and took in their surroundings.

They were less than ideal. The manhole was located in the middle of a cracked and broken cement slab that provided no shelter from the cool breeze coming off the nearby lake. Weeds were varied and rampant. Vanessa, Audrey asleep on her back, did a quick head count and then pulled Zoe away from a plant that looked suspiciously like poison ivy.

"Where are we?" Vanessa asked as she walked over to inspect a dilapidated rowboat rotting away under a bush.

"Shouldn't this be the waterfront activities center?" Erica looked at the rundown shacks a few feet from a pier. "I remember a nice building here."

"My guess is it was never built. Nobody seems to use this place very often." Vanessa kicked at the boat and her foot went right through and became stuck.

"Girls, a little help please," she called.

Becca and Maddie were busy exploring one of the abandoned shacks, but they stopped what they were doing and immediately ran to help. Becca slid Audrey off her mother's back, while Maddie freed the trapped foot.

"Wake up, sleepy head." Becca softly tickled her baby sister under her chin.

Audrey slowly opened her eyes and looked at her sister. Then she wiggled until Becca was forced to set her on the ground.

"Are we there yet?" Audrey rubbed her eyes.

"Where?" Becca knelt down until she was eye level with Audrey.

"I don't know." Audrey shrugged. "Wherever we're going."

"Yep." Becca nodded. "We're here."

"Where's here?"

"Where we're going."

"Good. Cause I'm tired."

"You just woke up." Becca mussed Audrey's already messy hair.

"That's why I'm tired. My dream wants me back."

"Wants you back?"

"Yeah, we were just about to—"

"Girls, come here," Vanessa called. Becca stood, kissed Audrey's forehead, and grabbed her by the hand. Together they joined Vanessa, who leaned against the old boat and massaged her bruised foot.

"We have a plan, of sorts. Becca, Maddie, are you

up for putting on the boy act again?"

The girls transformed before their eyes. A slouch here, a readjustment of the elbows there, a shift of the legs, and suddenly the girls had swagger even while they stood still.

"Guess so." Philip nodded. "How'd you girls learn to do that?"

"Watching."

"Mainly Dad, but sometimes other boys."

"The main thing is to look tough."

"And take up the most space possible."

"Boys take up a lot of space, even skinny ones."

"Daddy always—"

"Okay girls, we don't have time," Vanessa interrupted. "You've got work to do. You're going to the library."

"Yay!" Maddie clapped. "I love the library. I'm going to get a funny book—"

"Maddie," Vanessa interrupted with a raise of an eyebrow, "you're not going to read, you're going to research."

"How can I research if I can't read?"

Vanessa closed her eyes for a second as she reminded herself that the girl was only eleven, "I mean you're not going to read for pleasure. This is a fact-finding mission."

"What are we looking for?" Becca asked.

"Something that Douglas Whitfield changed in the past that made the world like it is. Something woman-unfriendly."

"I would do it myself," Philip explained to the girls, "but I'm not very good at history. No interest in it."

"But you're a time traveler!"

"A theorist. The professionals did the time traveling. I focused on the mechanics. The way the timeline works."

"That's boring," Zoe blurted.

"Zoe! Don't be rude!" Vanessa's cheeks burned. "Apologize."

"Sorry, Mr. Philip. I shouldn't have said you were boring."

"I thought you said my job was boring?"

Zoe shrugged.

Philip cut his eyes at Zoe and frowned. It was not pleasant to be thought of as boring. Especially not by a child of seven, who should be easy to impress.

But now was not the time. There was work to do. He shook off his feeling of inadequacy and turned his attention back to the upcoming mission.

"Women won't be allowed in the library—"

"I'm not going back!" Becca, feet shoulder width apart and hands on hips, shook her head firmly. "I'm not going back through those smelly tunnels."

"Or near that crazy librarian." Maddie assumed the stance and joined her sister.

"That would be crazy!"

"We'd get caught. We'd—"

"Wait a minute!" Philip put a hand on each girl's shoulder, but when the gesture was met by glares he dropped his hands and took a step back. "We're not going back on campus. We're going to the public library."

"Public library?" Maddie tilted her head as she made the words into a question.

"Public library." Vanessa nodded.

"But I thought," Maddie said, frowning, "they only had fun to read books."

"What made you think that?"

"You and dad." Becca nodded. "You always went on campus to do research."

"We had easy access as students. But anyone can go to public libraries and they have all kinds of books. Including ones about history."

"So…" Philip rubbed his palms together. "What do we look for?"

"He wouldn't have gone too far back in time," Erica suggested. "The further back you go, the harder it is to blend in. Clothing, money, speech patterns. He wouldn't have succeeded if he was too different."

"So not too far back." Philip nodded.

"Right," Vanessa continued, "and travel in the past was much harder. So he'd stay close."

"How close?"

"I'm not sure," Vanessa admitted. "But I doubt he could cross borders, so if we stick to the United States we should—"

"You're guessing, aren't you? Both of you. You don't have a clue." Philip slammed his fist into his palm. "We don't have time for guesses. We need to know. We need—"

"What, Philip?" Erica interrupted angrily. "Run a few scenarios through the computer? Consult with experts?"

Philip turned away. Vanessa saw the muscle of his jaw clench as he pulled out Annabel's picture.

"If you—" Vanessa put her hand on Erica's arm

to stop the flow of words.

"We've all lost someone," Vanessa said to Erica. She turned to Philip. "We can get them back."

"What if we can't?" Philip asked.

"We will," Vanessa assured him. "We've got the true inventors of time travel on our side."

Becca and Maddie, who had been quietly watching, engulfed their mother in a hug. Then, as if by magic, they assumed their boy personas.

"Yo, let's go!" Becca called to Philip.

"Yeah, dude," Maddie added.

"This is going to be fun." Philip shook his head and sighed. "Come on, tough guys. We've got work to do."

Off the three went. Vanessa waited anxiously for their return, but the wait was short. In less than an hour the three researchers returned, puffing like the big bad wolf's older and less fit brother.

"You found it?" Vanessa bit her lip. She knew they had not been gone long enough to do the type of in-depth research that was needed.

"Not"—Philip sucked in a breath—"yet."

"Then why—?"

Philip held up a hand as he struggled to get his breathing under control. After several minutes,

when the huffing and puffing had shrunk
to a more reasonable level, he pulled a dictionary-
sized book from inside his shirt. Maddie and Becca
followed suit.

"They let you check these out?" Vanessa asked
as she took the books and handed one to Erica. "I
thought you couldn't check out reference books."

Philip glanced at Becca and Maddie, who
quickly shook their heads.

"*Becca*!" Vanessa had intercepted the look. "Do
you mean to tell me you stole these?"

"No, Mama," Becca answered calmly. "You
weren't supposed to find out."

"Don't blame the girls; we had no choice," Philip
explained. "The library is only open two hours a
day."

"As soon as we got there," Maddie added, "they
told us they were about to close."

"We had ten minutes," Becca said. "I can't read
that fast."

"And we didn't want to have to go back
tomorrow," Philip explained, "in case campus
police expand their search."

"So," Maddie said with a shrug, "we said we
wanted to check out some books."

"But they looked at us like we're crazy."
Becca grimaced. "When they found out we wanted to take the books out of the library, they said they don't do that. You can only read them in the library."

"So I asked the librarian a hard question." Maddie grinned. "While Philip and Becca 'checked out' their books."

"And Philip asked another question while I helped Maddie 'check out' another one."

"More stealing." Vanessa groaned and plopped down on the ground. "What is your father going to say?"

"Mom." Becca put an arm around Vanessa's shoulders. "If we don't fix this, Dad won't be saying anything."

"About anything." Maddie added her arm to her mother's shoulders.

"Don't worry, Mom." Becca squeezed tight.

"We still know right from wrong." Maddie squeezed tight.

"As soon as the timeline is put back right—"

"—We won't have stolen anything."

"—All this will never have happened."

"We just need to find—"

"Got it!" Erica slammed a heavy book on the ground in front of Vanessa. "I knew those Women's Study courses would come in handy one day. Read this."

She had the book open to a page that detailed the suffrage movement. With her finger she pointed to the 19th Amendment, the one that gave women the right to vote.

"That doesn't help us." Vanessa frowned. She put a hand to her forehead and crinkled her brows. "I'm pretty sure I remember the 19th Amendment from both timelines. But—"

"But women couldn't vote in the second timeline, could they?"

Vanessa shook her head.

"That's because something happened to stop the 19th Amendment from being ratified. No ratification, no vote."

"Can I see that?" Erica handed Becca the book and she began to read.

"But how?" Vanessa sighed. "What could Douglas Whitfield possibly do—?"

"We've decided to call him Mr. Selfish," Maddie interjected.

"Douglas Whitfield makes him sound like a

normal person," Becca added as she continued to scan the book.

"Okay, so what could Mr. Selfish"—Vanessa nodded to her daughters—"possibly do to keep an amendment from being ratified?"

"I don't know. Maybe he found a way to bribe—" Erica was cut short by a loud squeal from Becca.

"I know! I know, I know, I know!" She shouted excitedly. She grabbed Maddie by the arm and pointed to a particular line on the page. As Maddie read, a smile spread across her face.

"Got to be." Maddie nodded happily.

"Would you two like to let us in on it?"

"He's not there," Becca explained.

"Who's not where?" Vanessa asked.

"The legislator—"

"Harry Burn," Maddie added.

"Harry Burn?" asked the confused mama.

"Yeah." Becca crinkled her nose. "I remember his name 'cause I kept imagining him with flaming red hair, like his hair was burning."

"And I remember him," Maddie said, "'cause I did a report on him. Last year."

"A report?" Vanessa turned to Maddie. "But you never—"

"No, Mama, before," Maddie explained. "When we were the real us. Before things got all messed up."

"Before Mr. Selfish messed things up, you mean," Becca corrected.

Maddie nodded her agreement.

"Okay." Vanessa kept her voice calm. "So why is this Harry Burn so important?"

"It was in my report," Maddie reminded her mother.

"But sweetie, I never read your report," Vanessa said very gently. "So can you tell me what was in it?"

"Oh, yeah. I remember." Maddie blinked about a million times as she fought to keep tears from forming. "I gave the report to Daddy to read instead of you because you had a big test."

"Thank you sweetie, that was very considerate."

"You're welcome, Mommy."

Maddie continued to blink madly.

"Sweetie," Vanessa encouraged. "Can you tell us now why he was important?"

Maddie was lost in thought behind her curtain of fluttering eyelids, so Becca elbowed her in the ribs.

"Oh, yeah." Maddie shook her head to clear it. "Harry Burn was going to vote against ratification. There was a whole big group of legislators who were against women getting the right to vote, and they all wore red flowers to show their unity. Including Harry Burn."

"Go on," Vanessa prompted.

"So at the last minute he surprised everyone by voting for ratification, instead of against. The red flower group was so mad he had to run and hide in the attic."

"He was afraid they were going to beat him up," Becca added.

"I drew a picture of him hiding behind a trunk in the attic for my report." Maddie smiled. "It was pretty funny."

"I bet. But that still doesn't explain—"

"Mr. Selfish must have stolen the letter." Maddie gave a definitive nod to Becca, who returned the nod.

"Letter?" Vanessa asked.

"Yes. The next day Harry Burn explained to everyone that he had gotten a letter from his mother asking him to support suffrage. So he decided that a good son should do what his mother says. So he voted for ratification, instead of against."

"Surely that wouldn't—"

"It was really close. That one vote made the difference, Mom."

"Read for yourself." Becca handed the book to her mother. "Harry Burn isn't mentioned anywhere in the history book, or the letter from his mom. That must be what happened."

The three adults looked through the pages in question. Erica turned to Philip, who had not had much input in the discussion.

"What does the theorist say?"

"The logic holds." Philip nodded. "Very small changes can have tremendous repercussions."

"But a letter?" Erica asked.

"If he could intercept the letter," Philip started, shrugging, "it would be the easy way to make a change."

The three adults sat quietly for several moments as they processed the information. Vanessa was the first to come to a decision.

"Maddie, sweetie…" Vanessa grabbed her daughter's hand. "Do you remember any more details?"

"Tennessee." Maddie nodded excitedly. "The

vote was August 18, 1920."

"That's a start. But how are we going to find out when he got his hands on that letter? There might be weeks—"

Maddie and Becca both shook their heads adamantly.

"No?"

"I saw a picture of the letter once," Maddie explained. "It was mailed the afternoon of the seventeenth, and since the vote was the next day—"

"We only have to hang out one day."

"What do you mean by 'hang out'?" Vanessa asked suspiciously.

"We have to make sure Harry Burn gets that letter."

"So we have to 'hang out' at the Tennessee legislature so Mr. Selfish can't steal it." Becca tilted her head at her mother. "You can understand that, can't you?"

"I understand you can't take that tone with your mother." Vanessa's eyes turned to slits and Becca immediately looked at her shoes.

"Sorry, Mommy."

Erica cleared her throat. When Vanessa looked

her way, she gestured to cut Becca some slack. Vanessa frowned, then nodded.

"Fine. So we—a group comprised mainly of women—need to plant ourselves smack dab in the middle of —"

Maddie and Becca shook their heads in unison.

"What do you mean, no? You don't even know what I was going to say."

"We have a plan."

"You have a plan. We just found out about this whole amendment and letter thing, and you have a plan?"

"It's a good one, Mommy." Becca's eyes glowed with budding confidence. "I promise it is."

Vanessa took one look at the hope on her daughters' faces and it was game over.

"Okay, little sweeties," Vanessa sighed. "Let's hear the plan."

"You won't like it, Mommy," Becca warned. "We have to split up."

"Three ways," Maddie added.

Vanessa gave a hard look at her two oldest children and growled, "Tell me. You want us to leave Erica all alone?"

"It's the only way." Maddie shrugged.

"She has to make sure Mr. Selfish doesn't do more damage." Becca nodded.

"We'll be busy cleaning up what he's already done," Maddie added.

"It could go on forever otherwise." Becca rolled her eyes. "It could turn into quite a mess."

"I understand why I need to stop him," Erica jumped in, "but not how." Erica had never gotten into a fight in her life and didn't have a smidge of confidence that she could keep Whitfield from using the portal. "Any ideas?"

"He won't expect you there," Becca reminded Erica.

"I realize that. But how—?"

"Bop him on the head," Maddie suggested. "That always works in movies."

Vanessa closed her eyes and pursed her lips at that little quip. Once the timeline was straightened out, she had a lot of work to do to straighten out the girls' moral compass. It seemed to have gone a little wonky lately.

"Right." Erica sighed. "Bop him on the head. But what if bopping him on the head doesn't work?"

"Bop him again," Maddie stated flatly. "And again. How ever many bops it takes."

"Like whack-a-mole!" Zoe yelled excitedly. "I love that game!"

"How about the rest of us?" Philip interjected. "What will we be doing while Erica guards the portal?"

"Mom, Zoe, and Audrey will guard the portal on the 1920s side." Becca stated the plan firmly, and when Vanessa opened her mouth to protest, Becca cut her off.

"We've thought it through, Mom. It has to be this way."

"And the three of us? What will we be doing while everyone else is doing all this guarding?"

"We have to make sure that letter gets to Harry Burn. So as soon as we get to the Tennessee Legislature—"

"Whoa there, little girl," Vanessa interrupted. "You're not traveling cross country without me! I forbid it! I won't—"

"Philip will be with us, Mom. He'll make sure we're safe."

"Philip is not your mother! He can stay and guard the portal."

"What about Zoe and Audrey?"

"What about them?"

"It's a long way from Washington to Tennessee. Do you really want to put them through that?"

"I'll let them stay here with Philip."

"Zoe will cry. You know how she sometimes gets. Philip won't know how to handle her."

"Then—"

"And Audrey will climb something, or get lost, or—"

"Stop! I get it." Every drop of blood drained from Vanessa's face and she broke out in a cold sweat. "Are you sure Philip can't do this by himself?"

"We can do this, Mom." Becca exuded pure confidence. "Trust us."

"We have a plan," Maddie put a hand on her mother's arm. "Trust us."

Vanessa grabbed Erica and pulled her to the side.

"What just happened here?" Vanessa whispered to Erica. "Did I just get demoted from mother?"

"I think you might have," Erica whispered back.

"What should I do?"

"What does your gut say? You always told me to listen to my gut."

As Vanessa studied her daughters, who appeared to be confident but normal, Philip joined her group.

"What are you whispering about?"

"I don't know what to do," Vanessa admitted. "I'm not comfortable letting them go all the way to Tennessee without me, but…"

As Vanessa's words trailed off, Philip nodded his understanding.

"Would it help if I told you about the cohesion principle?"

"The what?" Erica asked.

"It's a little known time travel principle, so little known I'd almost forgotten about it, that theorizes that certain things need to happen for the timeline to stay intact. So the timeline has the ability to self-correct."

"Self-correct? How?"

"I'm beginning to think," Philip started, pointing to Vanessa's daughters, "it uses time monkeys."

"So you think we should—?"

Philip nodded. Vanessa turned to Erica, who shrugged.

"Fine," Vanessa sighed. "Let's find Mr. Selfish's time machine and hope this cohesion principle is more than just theory."

Chapter 27

SEVERAL DAYS LATER VANESSA nearly fainted with relief when Becca walked into the warehouse that contained the 1920s version of Whitfield's portal, until she realized Maddie was nowhere in sight and the man with Becca had his arms tied tightly to his side and most certainly was not Philip.

"What happened? Where's your sister?" Vanessa squeaked. The high-pitched noise caught the attention of Zoe and Audrey, who had been busy building a dirt city across the room. The two girls immediately ran to hug their sister.

"No worries, Mom," Becca assured her mother as she returned the hugs. "She's coming. Philip had a problem with his shoe."

Vanessa scanned her daughter head to toe, saw she was okay, and turned her attention to the confused and disheveled-looking man being guided like a puppy dog. "Is this Whitfield?"

"Mr. Selfish himself. Oh, Mom, it was great!" Becca beamed as she guided Whitfield to a wall. He immediately slid to the ground and rested his head on his knees.

"First we hitchhiked to the train station," Becca didn't even pause when her mother cringed at the word "hitchhiked." "Then we jumped onto a cargo car while the train was moving—"

"You did what?" Vanessa grabbed her stomach, as if she'd been punched.

"It was going really slow." Becca bit her lip and changed to a matter-of-fact tone of voice. "The wheels had really just started turning. The train was barely moving at all."

"When I get my hands on Philip"—Vanessa glared at the door Philip should walk through at any moment—"I'm going to—"

"Philip won't remember it," Becca threw out before she turned to Zoe and asked, "Do we have anything to eat? I'm starving."

"What do you mean, Philip won't remember?" Vanessa twirled Becca around until they were nose-to-nose.

"He, um, kinda got knocked out. By Mr. Selfish here." Becca pointed to Whitfield.

Vanessa examined the man with his forehead on his knees, arms tied tightly at his sides and dirt smeared across his cheeks. No one could look less capable of physical violence.

Before Vanessa could form a response, Maddie rushed into the room dragging Philip behind her.

"Did you tell her?" Maddie's eyes glowed with excitement.

"I just got started," Becca whispered. "I think she's mad because we hitchhiked."

"Oh, but did you tell her about the Model T?" Maddie turned to her mother. "Did she tell you about the Model T?"

Vanessa shook her head.

"She should have started with that. It was so cool." Maddie threw her arms around her mother and squeezed tight. "You would have loved it, Mom. A woman and her daughter picked us up and drove us all the way to the train station."

Vanessa brushed Maddie's hair from her eyes but said nothing, which prompted Becca to join in the hug.

"Don't forget lunch." Becca smiled. "Philip was so cranky until the woman bought us lunch at that diner."

"I love that car!" Maddie's eyes shone.
"I want one. Can I get a Model T, Mom? Please? The woman said some people called it a 'Tin Lizzie.'"

"Maddie, I think—" Vanessa began as she put a little distance between her and her daughters.

"Tell her about the train," Becca interrupted.

"Oh yeah. Well, we got to the station just as a train was pulling out. Philip tossed me, then Becca, into an empty cargo car. We rode all the way to Idaho!"

"Mom, did you know there were cows out there?" Becca asked. "Lots of them. All over the place."

Vanessa nodded. "Cows were—"

"Then the excitement really started," Becca said. "We started slowing down. We were close to a station."

"And Philip"—Maddie pointed to Philip—"saw men with guns."

"—On the platform."

"They were searching all the cars."

"We were near the end of the train, pretty far from the platform."

"—So we jumped out the other side."

"—And ran for the trees."

"A whole bunch of other people jumped out too."

"A crazy lot of people."

"And that's when we saw him."

"Well, it was Philip who recognized him," Becca corrected. "We didn't know what he looked like."

"Saw who?" Vanessa asked.

"Mr. Selfish, of course," Becca explained. "Heading for the trees with all the other people."

"Philip didn't even hesitate. He tackled him." Maddie puffed out her chest like she had done the tackling.

"And they got into a big fight."

"Nobody from the train even stopped to watch. They just kept running."

"I guess they were afraid of getting caught by the men with guns."

"But Philip wasn't afraid of anything."

"He was winning."

"Until Mr. Selfish started fighting dirty."

"He picked up a big stick and hit Philip in the head. Knocked him out cold."

"So," Maddie said, shrugging, "I did it to him."

Vanessa blinked several times as she tried to untangle the mess of words that had flooded her brain. "Did what?"

"Maddie hit Mr. Selfish in the head with a big stick, of course."

"*Maddie!*"

"He was fighting dirty, Mama," Becca explained. "It gave him an advantage."

"It wasn't fair," Maddie added. "And he hit Philip."

"Now Philip doesn't know who we are. He's very confused."

"So I hit him. Mr. Selfish, I mean," Maddie said with finality.

"You should have seen her." Becca gazed at her sister with admiration. "She was good."

"*Whack!*" Maddie mimicked swinging a bat.

Words escaped Vanessa. All she could do was close her eyes, cringe, and hope her little girls wouldn't turn into homicidal maniacs.

"It's okay, Mama." Maddie wrapped her arms around her disheartened parent. "We haven't turned into bad people. I promise. Becca and I remember everything you taught us. Don't we, Becca?"

When there was no response from her sister Maddie hissed, "*Becca!*"

Becca looked up from Whitfield's head, which she was examining like it was an interesting art project, to find Maddie motioning for her.

"Oh, right." She patted the cringing Whitfield on the head and ran to her mother.

"You're the best mom ever!" Becca clearly misunderstood what Maddie wanted her to do. "No other mom would ever take her kids on such a great adventure!"

"Becca…" Maddie shook her head fiercely. "No!"

"Yes, she is!"

"Becca!" Maddie stomped. "Mom's worried we're hoodlums 'cause we hitchhiked and rode trains without paying."

"And beat a man up." Vanessa shrugged off the hug and glared at her daughters. "And stole. And pretended to be something you're not."

"Don't worry, Mom. We'll be normal again," Maddie promised.

"As soon as we get back home. We promise," Becca said.

Pinkie swear," Becca and Maddie said at the same time as they stuck out their pinkies.

Vanessa hooked pinkies with her daughters.

Pinkie swears were a sacred promise.

Which meant the world was going to right itself and her daughters would go back to being the sweet—

"Even if being a hoodlum *is* a lot more fun!" Becca giggled.

Maddie nodded and smiled her agreement.

Vanessa sighed and released her daughters' pinkies. "Let's get back to the others so we can get all this straightened out." She helped the two confused men to their feet.

Just before Becca stepped through the portal with Whitfield, she punched him in the stomach and he doubled over in pain.

"Becca!" Vanessa grabbed her daughter by the arm and pulled her back from the portal. "What are you doing?"

"He was holding his breath," the young girl whispered. "I saw him. I think he remembers more than he lets on."

Vanessa twirled Whitfield to face her and speared him with her eyes. What she saw made her take a firmer grasp of his arm.

"I'll take him, Becca," she said with that no-nonsense voice that Becca knew better than to argue with. "Help Maddie with Philip."

"Yes, Mama." Becca grabbed poor, confused Philip by one arm, Maddie grabbed the other, and they guided him to the door.

As soon as the three had stepped into the portal, Vanessa turned to Whitfield.

"Cut the act. Why aren't you confused, like Philip?"

Whitfield continued with the deer in the headlights routine, but every so often a glimmer of smugness would shine through.

"You're not fooling me. I know you know what's going on."

She looked from the portal to Whitfield.

"Philip forgot as soon as he lost consciousness, but not you."

She squinted as she studied Whitfield closely. "I'm pretty sure you don't have the gene, so that must mean—"

She again looked from the door to Whitfield. Her eyes turned to slits.

"You kept the best for yourself, didn't you. You gave them specs to an inferior portal? The original was better, wasn't it? Even people without the gene could travel. You built in a way to have the upper hand."

Whitfield smirked.

"You're a real piece of work, aren't you?"

"You can't stop me," Whitfield growled as his ego asserted itself. "Destroy my machine and I'll just build it again. Whatever you do, I'll undo it. You can't stop me."

"That's. Where. You're. Wrong." Vanessa punctuated each word with a progressively firm jab. Without meaning to, she balled up her fist and turned the last jab into a punch. The satisfaction she felt when the smirk on Whitfield's face was replaced by a grimace of pain was superb.

"Come on." Vanessa grabbed the man who had caused so much harm to so many by the front of his shirt and pulled him to the portal entrance. "It's time to fix time."

Chapter 28

"ARE YOU POSITIVE THIS will work?" Erica asked for the third time.

"No. I'm not," Vanessa replied, also for the third time. "But it ought to work."

"Maybe first we should—"

"Erica, stop. No more planning. No more talking. This is it. Just make sure you get back to the DTA before I destroy Mr. Selfish here's machine. *And* make sure Mr. Selfish loses consciousness—"

"Oh, he'll lose consciousness! I have no problem making sure of that."

"He should lose all his memory since he'll be traveling through the DTA's substandard portal."

"But if you destroy his machine you'll be stuck— "

Vanessa shook her head.

"Right, the time monkey gene. You'll use the DTA's portal."

"The only problem is Philip. We need him here until we can destroy Whitfield's portal. Then we'll send him back."

"Shouldn't be a problem."

"Except we have to send him back through the bad portal. Which will be fine as long as you don't somehow lose your memory. He'll need help."

"What kind of help?"

"He's going to have scrambled eggs for brains. He'll need help unscrambling them."

"Won't he just go to sleep and wake up—?"

"The girls drew another diagram." Vanessa grimaced. "There's a disturbance, right around the time Philip came from. They don't know exactly what it is, but if his brain remains this confused…"

"Don't worry." Erica winked. "Give me back my technology and Philip will be right as rain."

"You know, I never understood that saying. What's so right about rain?" Vanessa hugged Erica. "It's been so good to see you again! Good luck."

Erica nodded and stepped to the portal, but Vanessa grabbed her arm.

"Can you make sure Mr. Selfish here"—her chin jutted toward Whitfield—"never steps through a portal again?"

"Sure thing, boss." Erica saluted and clicked her heels together.

"You have changed," Vanessa said with a wide grin.

Erica gave a final nod, took a deep breath, and slammed her fist into Whitfield's stomach as she jerked him into the portal after her. The last thing Vanessa saw was Whitfield on a trajectory that would assure he woke up on the DTA floor in a puddle of his own drool.

Chapter 29

"THERE!" MADDIE POINTED TO the figure that had just slipped out of the basement door of Denny Hall and headed for the street.

"Philip, wait!" Vanessa called.

Philip looked in confusion from Vanessa to the building. But instead of waiting, he ran faster.

"It's about Annabel!" Vanessa bellowed.

Philip stumbled and halted. He turned halfway toward Vanessa, ready to escape at the slightest provocation.

"She's in danger," Vanessa continued. "I can help."

Philip hesitated. His feet shifted as he prepared to bolt.

"Philip!" Vanessa put every ounce of authority she could muster into that one word. If he left, the timeline was doomed.

Philip turned toward Vanessa and she stepped aside to reveal the docile and confused Philip her daughters led around like a puppy.

"We need to talk."

Philip stared at the pathetic version of himself. Then he gulped, nodded, and followed Vanessa through the door into the Denny Hall basement.

∞

Ten minutes later, Philip sighed at the story he had been told.

"Are you sure I caused all that?"

"Positive."

"What about him?" Philip pointed to the confused Philip. "What's going to happen to him?"

"He'll go back with you. It should all come out in the wash. Or the wormhole, as it were."

"Meaning…?"

"The two of you *should* reintegrate during the trip."

"Should. And if we don't?"

"You'll have a new twin brother."

Philip looked at the clueless Philip. He closed his eyes and imagined the sudden addition of a twin in his life. He grimaced.

435

"You're positive I did this?"

"Afraid so." Vanessa smiled gently.

"Has anyone ever done this before?"

Vanessa shrugged. Zoe brought a new diagram the girls had just drawn and showed it to her mother.

"It's time, Mom," Zoe whispered. "They need to go. Now."

Vanessa nodded. Becca and Maddie escorted the Philips to the portal door.

"Now what?" Philip asked. "Should I, uh, hold my hand?"

"Sure. It's best if you step through together."

Philip nodded. Vanessa opened the portal door. Philip took a deep breath, grabbed the other Philip's arm, and stepped forward. In perfect synchronization, Becca and Maddie punched both Philips in the stomach and shoved them through. Becca slammed the door closed.

"Girls! Why—?"

"If either is conscious they won't integrate," Becca explained.

"Besides," Maddie snickered, "did you see Philip? He was beside himself with worry."

Vanessa rolled her eyes at the corny joke as

Maddie and Becca giggled.

Maddie repeated the joke to Zoe and Audrey. Zoe immediately laughed in a very satisfactory manner, but Audrey didn't get it even after Becca explained.

So the tickle monster came out to play, and before long everyone was happy and relaxed.

"Time to go home," Vanessa declared with a smile. She was rewarded with a group hug of monumental proportions. Then off they went.

Chapter 30

THE URGE TO CURL up on the floor and sleep was nearly unbearable.

Erica had been waiting at the portal door for an hour, the longest hour in history. If it weren't for the fact that she had promised Vanessa that she would help Philip when he arrived back in his own time, she would…she would…she'd…

Erica slapped her cheeks as she realized she had been a millisecond from dozing off. She pried her eyes open with her fingers and stomped her feet several times. She would jump around if she needed to, as long as if kept her from sliding to the floor to enjoy blissful, relaxing, glorious—

The portal door opened and an unconscious Philip flew through the air and landed in a heap on the floor.

How comfortable he looked, lying there, sleeping so peacefully. Maybe now that he was back she could—

Erica shivered herself back to full consciousness and ran in place for several seconds. Then she pulled back Philip's eyelids to see if his pupils responded, pinched his arms when they didn't, and slapped his cheeks for good measure. Something was very wrong. Philip needed help, and fast.

So she did the only thing she could reasonably do. She pushed the emergency button located just outside the portal door and slid to the floor as a team of medics arrived.

She awoke in a hospital-style bed with her husband leaned worriedly over her.

"What happened?" Erica tried to sit up, but her head twirled in a very uncomfortable manner. It was only her husband's arms about her shoulders that kept her from toppling over. With his help, she managed to get into an upright position.

"Do you remember anything at all, darling?" Roderick asked gently. "We found you at the portal. But there weren't any jumps scheduled."

Erica struggled to remember, but was unsuccessful.

Just then a very pregnant Annabel stepped through the door dressed in a pristine white tunic.

She saw Erica was awake and waddled to her side.

"How are you doing?" She put a gentle hand on Erica's shoulder.

"Fine, boss, I guess." Erica grimaced. "Does anyone know what I was doing in the portal?"

"No. Or why my husband was with you."

Erica's eyes got very wide and her mouth fell open.

"Do you know?"

"I've never met the president." Erica's reverence was obvious. "Did either of us use the portal?"

"No idea. The cameras were down. But I do know you pressed the alarm."

"I'm sorry. I don't remember."

"Fair enough. Do you remember what you said to me?"

Erica's eyebrows danced around her forehead as she tried to remember, but she finally gave up and shook her head.

"You managed to say two things before you passed out. The first was 'We fixed the timeline.'"

"Oh," Erica said in surprise. "And the second?"

"You grabbed my arm, looked me in the eye and said, 'Philip did it for you.'"

"What does that mean?"

"I had hoped that you'd know."

Erica shook her head. "What about your husband?" she asked as a line of worry formed between her brows.

"He's still in the sleep chamber. The doctors say his brain has been through a lot of trauma. He needs time to heal."

"He'll be okay?"

"The doctors say he's going to be fine." Annabel smiled and placed a hand on her protruding belly. "Ready to pitch in well before this little munchkin is born."

Chapter 31

VANESSA HUSTLED HER TIRED children inside and the two youngest headed straight for the couch. Before she had time to reroute them to their room, they had curled up and fallen deep asleep. Vanessa looked at them and shrugged.

"Shall the three of us go check?"

Maddie and Becca both nodded, so together they tiptoed to the bedroom door. Vanessa paused a moment with her hand on the doorknob before she steeled herself and opened the door.

All three breathed a sigh of relief—the mound in the middle of the bed was Tony, snoring gently under the covers. Vanessa looked across the room and was relieved that her framed diploma was proudly displayed next to Tony's.

Vanessa softly closed the door and smiled.

"Looks like we did it, girls!" Her whisper turned into a yawn. "I'm exhausted."

"Us too, Mom," Becca stretched her back and winced. "Little Audrey isn't so little."

"See you in the morning, Mom." Maddie reached out her arms to hug her mother, but Vanessa pulled both girls in tight.

"I'm so proud of you girls," Vanessa whispered as she squeezed. She released them and nudged them toward their room. "See you in the morning."

∞

RING!

The phone next to her ear startled Vanessa awake. Her heart beat erratically until she remembered that everything was okay. She turned to her husband, only to find his side of the bed empty.

"Oh, no!" she gasped as she bolted up. "It's still happening!"

RING!

Vanessa stared at the cell phone on her bedside table for a full ten seconds before she reached out a trembling hand and answered with a shaky, "Hello."

"Vanessa?"

Relief flooded every cell of her body as she recognized Tony's voice.

"Sorry to wake you," Tony continued. "I need you to bring me the folder on the table. It has my homework in it."

"Tony! You're okay? Are you sure you're okay?"

"Of course I'm okay. So will you bring the folder?"

"Certainly. I'll—"

"And can you bring me a coffee too? I was running late this morning. I didn't have time to stop for one."

"Sure, sweetie." Vanessa smiled happily. "As soon as I get the girls ready we'll be right there."

As she hung up the phone, her four daughters raced into the room, breathless and excited.

"I plew, Mommy," Audrey squealed as she bounced around like a kangaroo on caffeine. "I plew, I plew, I plew."

"What?"

Becca and Maddie grabbed Vanessa's hands and pulled her into the living room. Once there, they swung her onto the couch.

"What," Vanessa asked as she realized every piece of furniture in the room except the couch was

in a pile against one wall, "have you girls
been doing in here?"

"Just watch, Mommy," Zoe called as the girls
built a human pyramid with Audrey on top.

"Very good," Vanessa said as she gave the clap
of a proud mama.

"Wait until you see the dismount," Becca said.

"Dismount?"

Without any further warning, Audrey dove
from the top of the pyramid, but instead of crashing
to the floor, she swooped upward and flew around
the room.

"Audrey," Vanessa gasped, "how are you doing
that?"

"With my dragon necklace, Mommy." Audrey
landed in front of her mother and pointed to the
green stone necklace around her neck.

"Mine works too," Zoe said. She took a little hop
and remained floating in the air.

"Oh, dear." Vanessa's brow furrowed in worry.
"Maybe we should—"

"Did we do something wrong, Mommy?"
Maddie cocked her head to the side and bit her lip.

"Not a thing," Vanessa assured her with a smile.
"Hurry and get dressed. We need to go on

campus."

"Can we look for that giant, red-headed librarian?" Becca asked. "I want to see if he's still mean."

"That answers that question," Vanessa muttered under her breath. Then louder she said, "Your dad forgot his homework, and his coffee. So get dressed!"

"Can we get muffins?" Zoe asked.

"Sure."

"Yay!" all four girls yelled. The three oldest ran to their rooms to get ready.

"Can I play there, Mommy?" Audrey asked, her hand on her necklace.

"I think we'd better keep that our little secret, Audrey. At least for now."

"Okay, Mommy. I understand." Audrey nodded and Vanessa gave her little monkey a big hug.

www.ingramcontent.com/pod-product-compliance
Lightning Source LLC
Chambersburg PA
CBHW050105120726
47904CB00004B/1221